Escape to Paradise

J. H. Ellison

DEDICATION

To my wife for her belief and encouragement.

CONTENTS

ACKNOWLEDGMENTS

Thanks to Mathis, Dima and Michele who made this book possible.

CHAPTER 1

In a rare moment of relaxation, Jake Moore took stock of his life. He had found success in the field of real estate by forming a partnership with a college friend, locating their office in Hollywood. Being a native of Oklahoma, this was quite a change. While in college, he had secretly married the daughter of a wealthy Tulsa oilman. The marriage was found out by her family and, with approval of their daughter, the marriage was annulled. They claimed he was after their money. This wasn't true.

Troubled by this, Jake was determined to prove them wrong—and that he could be highly successful. He was always a movie buff. The stars appeared to live a luxurious life, with big homes and driving expensive cars. He reasoned that the Hollywood crowd had plenty of money; that as their success increased they moved up into more expensive houses. To Jake this meant a steady supply of listings and sales.

He convinced his college friend and partner, Bret Owen, on his idea. They moved to California, studied real estate and passed their real estate broker exams. With the help of Bret's family, they formed Beverly Hills Realty and opened an office in Hollywood.

Jake and his partner worked hard to win the trust of the Hollywood elite. That translated into large commissions, usually after difficult negotiations between their clients' wants and what they could afford. A joke often told in Hollywood was, "A realtor called his actor client and told him he had good news and bad news. The actor asked, "What's the good news?" and was told that the price of the house he wanted had been reduced to $10 million. The actor agreed that was good news. Then the actor asked what the bad news was. He was told, "You have to put more than $1,000 down."

Jake drove a new Cadillac, but lived in a modest apartment on Venice Boulevard. Among his clientele were movie stars and moguls, corporate executives, recording stars and owners of major studios. He had developed a good and trusted connection with them, be they seller or buyer, and was often invited to their parties. Some had invited him on big game hunts in Africa and India.

His frugal lifestyle and his clients, who bought or sold their expensive homes through him, made it possible for him to build up a substantial financial nest egg of real estate holdings, stocks and limited partnerships. This enriched his bank account. He became part of the "swinging" Hollywood crowd. It was at a big Hollywood party that he met Rachel, a tall, willowy brown-eyed brunette beauty.

Rachel's parents, Michael and Gail Wilkinson, were top-rated movie stars, commanding large incomes. They had purchased a beautiful home that had a private projection room and swimming pool, in Coldwater Canyon.

Off of their pool was a large patio for dancing or just relaxing. It took a staff of five to keep the property in mint condition. The home itself was large and built in a Spanish hacienda style with a red tile roof. Professional landscaping and gardeners made their property grounds a showplace.

Even though Jake was accustomed to dealing with expensive homes and important people, the Wilkinson property and their daughter, Rachel, were intimidating. To marry into such a family was quite a step for a small town Oklahoma boy. He questioned whether or not he should get romantically involved with Rachel. Would history repeat itself?

Rachel was an aspiring young actress, hoping to follow in her parents' footsteps. She could be charming one moment and controlling the next. To say she was spoiled would be an understatement. Her parents had given her a bright red Jaguar sport coupe on her sixteenth birthday. On her twenty-first birthday they had given her an elaborate debutante ball, inviting other debutantes.

Jake's big problem was that he found her intriguing. Was this love? He reasoned that it must be. Trying to win over this beauty, Jake bought an expensive home in Brentwood with a swimming pool, and hired a housekeeper and gardener.

He learned to fly and purchased a used six-passenger Beechcraft which he wrote off as a business expense, showing customers from the air the neighborhood that interested them and pointing out the property he would be showing them. He would then take them on a tour of the property. This approach got him many sales.

He and Rachel became constant companions, often being asked by the Hollywood crowd, "When's the wedding?" To impress Rachel, he would fly her to Las Vegas to take in special performances by notable movie people or musical groups, or fly her to Santa Catalina Island and Yosemite. Their relationship opened many doors for Jake, increasing his business. Rachel and he were frequent visitors at Ciro's, Moulin Rouge, Trocadero, Coconut Grove and Brown Derby. His thoughts were so engrossed that his secretary had to buzz him several times.

"Yes?"

"Sir, Rachel is on line three."

"Thank you."

He picked up line three. "Hi, Rachel. What's up?"

"Am I interrupting anything?"

"No, I was just thinking about us and some of our dates. Speaking of that, let's have dinner tonight at the Trocadero."

"Okay, I want to give you some good news and invite you to a party at our house a week from now. I'll tell you about it tonight."

"That sounds good to me. I have some news also. Can I pick you up at six?"

"That's fine. I'll be ready."

Jake arrived on time at the Wilkinsons'. A maid let him in and escorted him into a spacious living room. He was greeted by Rachel's parents. Light conversation was shared.

Rachel, a vision of elegant beauty, entered wearing a form-fitting knee-length black sleeveless dress and long white gloves. A beautiful string of pearls graced her neck and she wore high-heeled black leather shoes. Covering her bare shoulders was a black mink cape. Jake never ceased to be amazed at so much beauty packed into such a small frame. She was breathtaking to look at.

"Ready!" she announced.

The two bid farewell to her parents and went to Jake's car. He opened the car door for her. Once seated, he closed her door and went around to the driver's seat.

On the way to the Trocadero, Jake commented, "You look mighty nice tonight."

Smiling, she quipped back, "Thank you, kind sir."

Making small talk, he asked, "How was acting class today?" It was a subject that he knew she enjoyed.

She described the various characters of the play, comments made by the director, her speech coach, the makeup artist skills and the scenes of the play. She cut her descriptions short as they pulled into the Trocadero. Turning their car over to a valet, the two went inside. Jake had called ahead and reserved a table in a secluded area, with a good view of the bandstand and dance floor. Rachel acted like a queen attending court. Escorted to their table by a waiter, she acknowledged people that she knew. Once seated, the waiter gave them a menu. After going over the menu, one they had seen many times before, they made their selections.

When the waiter left, Jake asked, "What is the good news you wanted to tell me?"

Rachel's face glowed with excitement, "I was given a part in a new movie."

"That is good news. Tell me about it."

"It's called *African Safari*. I play a supporting role. It'll be shot on location in Zambia, Africa. Isn't that exciting?"

Being a hunter since childhood, Jake's dream had always been to go on a safari. Now the girl he loved was going to the place of which he had dreamed. He felt a tinge of envy. He tried to conceal that by asking, "When is this to happen?"

"I was told in mid-September. Philip Zambrowski is the producer and the director is Wayne Ambrose. I'll introduce them to you at the party next week."

Whether on the dance floor or at their table, Rachel dominated the conversation, telling the storyline of the movie, the main actor and actress, their personalities and the costumes of the cast. Although he was interested in Rachel's good fortune, all this detail about the movie was getting on his nerves. Not once had she asked about his good news.

Jake finally interrupted her, "I also have some good news."

"What is it?"

"I got a call from a Sir Anthony Roberts in London. He's in banking, diamond mines in South Africa and shipping. He's listed in the *Who's Who* as a multi-billionaire. He's also a big game hunter. He and his wife Lady Jane want me to find them a house near movie stars in Hollywood and a ranch in Montana."

"An English knight planning to be a rancher?"

"He's a fan of the American West and movie stars. I've learned that he likes to have houses in various countries that he can visit and, for a short time, become part of that setting. He has caretakers who maintain the properties. One of his ancestors bought an interest in a ranch in Montana in the 1800s, in the Judith Basin, and lost it in a bad business deal. The stories about Montana, told by his ancestor, fired up his imagination about the Old West. Sir Roberts is bringing his business consultant with him to give advice."

"That is interesting. How do know him?"

"Remember Montana Bill Jackson, the new country-western singing sensation—the one I sold an estate to on Mulholland Drive?"

"Yes."

"He and his western band were on tour in England and Sir Roberts asked that Montana Bill join them at their table. He asked if he was from Montana. Sir Roberts stated they had a nice chat. He spoke of his interest in America and asked if Bill knew a good realtor he would recommend. Bill mentioned me."

"But, you don't know anything about Montana."

"I forgot to tell you that Oklahoma is my native state and I spent several years in Helena. So, you see I do know some about Montana. I'm also a lover of western history and books about the West written by Zane Grey."

Rachel had a shocked expression on her face. She was dating an "Okie"! She had read the book *Grapes of Wrath* and her opinion of Oklahomans was biased.

Jake sensed coolness the rest of their evening and little was spoken on the way to her house.

Next day he buried himself in work, making calls to Montana realtors. He learned that two ranches loosely matched what Sir Roberts described. Sir Roberts was looking for a "gentleman's ranch"—one that gave the feel of ranching, but not a huge working ranch that required on-site management and numerous ranch hands. It must have a stream, be close to a large city with a commercial airport and be located in an attractive setting. Jake found one in the Bitterroot Valley with a trout stream flowing through it and a beautiful mountain backdrop. The main house had over 4,000 square feet, a 1,400-square-foot guest house and a caretaker's cabin plus several outbuildings. It was a gentleman's ranch of 600 acres. It was listed at $8,900,000. He felt this was the closest match from Sir Roberts' description.

To be on the safe side, Jake added a large ranch to his carry-on list of properties to discuss with Sir Roberts. It was a true working ranch with 60,000 acres in the Big Hole area of southwestern Montana. It had a main house with 3,200 square feet and two guest houses of 1,100 square feet each and several outbuildings. It was more remote than the one in the Bitterroot Valley. Its asking price was $35 million.

Jake found one other gentleman's ranch. It was a 120-acre ranch with 2,000 acres of leased land. It was a spread near St. Ignatius, with the beautiful Mission Range as a backdrop. It has a 2,000-square-foot home and several outbuildings, and had poured concrete for a 5,000-square-foot timber frame house. Asking price is $1,100,000.

These ranches, accompanied by photos, were sent to Jake. Several other ranches were sent to Jake but he had a hunch these three would draw the most interest. What little he knew of the buyers, he guessed the Bitterroot or St. Ignatius ranches would be the choice. Both were in close proximity to the commercial airline terminal in Missoula. Both were small and easy to manage, had trout streams flowing through, and gave a feeling of ranching and the Old West, while being accessible to good shopping facilities in Missoula.

Next he searched his books for sales in the Hollywood Hills and Brentwood area. He found several in areas peppered with movie stars and movie moguls. They ranged from $4 million to $16 million. Now he was ready to call Sir Roberts.

Jake dialed the London office of Sir Roberts. He was put through to Sir Roberts. "Sir Roberts, this is Jake Moore. I have some properties to show you in Montana and in Hollywood."

"Good, let me check my schedule."

After a short pause, Sir Roberts said, "I have a couple of weeks free in early September. How about you?"

Jake looked at his calendar and replied, "That will work fine for me."

"Can you give me an idea of what we'll be looking at?"

Jake gave a brief description of the Montana ranches, each having trout streams, some with trophy-size elk, mountain goat and mule deer, with beautiful mountain backdrops. Then Jake told him of the Hollywood properties, stressing those in Beverly Park.

"Smashing! I'll look forward to seeing them. I'll let you know our arrival time at Los Angeles Airport."

"Good enough. See you in September."

That out of the way, he could think about the party that Rachel had mentioned. This was tomorrow evening. It had taken him most of the week to prepare for Sir Roberts.

When Jake arrived at Rachel's house, he was met by two attendants who directed him to a nearby restaurant parking lot. He was told that a valet there would drive him back. In the restaurant parking lot he was greeted by a valet who directed him where to park. Out of habit he noted the types of cars parked. It was clear that Rachel's guests were well-heeled. Among the many types of cars were Rolls Royce, BMW, Fiat, Lamborghini and Mercedes.

A valet drove Jake back to Rachel's home. He was greeted at the door by a party greeter who directed him towards a spacious living room, and a milling group of movie personnel. As if by magic, a caterer appeared with a tray of filled champagne glasses. Taking one, he was sipping on it when Rachel spotted him. Excusing herself from those surrounding her, she hurried over to Jake.

"Hi, I want you to meet the movie producer and director."

Taking Jake's hand she guided him over to a clustered group.

Interrupting the group she said, "Everyone, I want you to meet Jake Moore. Probably many of you already know him. Jake, I'd like you to meet Philip Zambrowski, producer of the movie *African Safari*, and Wayne Ambrose, the director."

Jake shook hands with the two, while sizing them up. Zambrowski was younger than he had thought, probably in his mid-to-late forties and a few inches shorter than Jake. Jake's quick guess was that his money to produce the movie was probably inherited. Ambrose, on the other hand, was probably in his late sixties, short and stout. Greetings were exchanged.

Philip Zambrowski spoke up, "Rachel tells me you spent some time in Montana. Do you do any big game hunting?"

"I have in the past, but now I prefer using a camera."

Philip said, "I picked up some nice trophies there. I'd like to get a good mountain sheep and grizzly trophy. Maybe after I return from Africa I might go on a Montana hunt and try to get those. After the movie is finished in Zambia, I plan to try for a Cape buffalo trophy."

"Good luck on your quest. I'm sure you're aware of the danger in hunting grizzlies. They have a mean disposition and are hard to kill."

"Have you hunted grizzlies?"

"No. A friend of mine who did get a grizzly told me that if I went after a grizzly I should shoot it in the hump on his back. It makes the animal's front legs useless. There are stories of grizzlies being shot in the heart living long enough to kill the hunter."

"I've heard such stories. It's exciting. But then Cape buffalos are also dangerous."

Before Philip could continue, he was called by a party member.

Philip said "Excuse me," and went to see what the person wanted.

Jake had the feeling the man was like an Old West false front—good-looking exterior but lacking on the inside. While Jake and Philip were talking, Rachel was like a butterfly flitting from one cluster to another of her guests.

Jake felt like the odd man at this party. The party guests were younger aspiring movie actors and actresses seeking to be noticed by those that had been in a movie or had directed one. To not be standing by himself, he moved over to the portable bar and refreshment table. He picked up a paper plate, putting some crepes and finger sandwiches on it. He asked the bartender for a Coke. With these he eased out the sliding glass door to the large patio. Finding an empty pool lounge chair distant from the door, he sat down and placed his Coke on the glass-top table beside his chair.

The evening air was cool and refreshing. From this hilltop location, lights of Hollywood could be seen, giving off a Christmas-like atmosphere. While taking in the beauty and enjoying his refreshments, a guy approached and said, "I'm Bruce Culp. Mind if I join you?"

"Not at all. Have a seat."

11

Bruce said, "I noticed that you weren't really part of this group. Neither am I. I'm cameraman for the upcoming movie being celebrated. It's sort of a command performance for me. If you don't mind my asking, what is your connection to the movie?"

"None. I'm a local realtor and a friend of Rachel."

Both men sat for a moment, enjoying their refreshments and savoring the relaxing setting. Bruce broke the silence, "I'll be glad when this movie is finished and I can go home."

"Where's that?"

"Wyoming. I have a small ranch near Chugwater. I miss the wide open spaces. Hollywood drives me nuts, too many people for me."

"I've been in that part of the county. I remember getting into a ground blizzard near Chugwater one winter. If it hadn't been for a kind trucker, I might have not have gotten out."

"Yep, Chugwater can get blistering cold at times. Are you a native of Montana?"

"No. I'm a native of Oklahoma, but I spent some time in Montana. Like you I enjoy the feeling of wide open spaces that Montana and Wyoming give. A person feels he has elbow room there."

"I know what you mean. After spending time in Montana, how are you able to handle all the crowds and traffic here?"

"I don't like the traffic and crowds. I was drawn by the business possibilities. I'm thinking one day I'll move back to Montana or my native state of Oklahoma, and a more laid-back lifestyle. Of the two, I prefer Montana. It's bigger with less number of people.

"My uncle has a realty business south of here in Torrance. When I was in Montana he would call and talk about how great business was in

California, but, he would also complain about the traffic problem. I'd kid him by replying that I was having traffic problems in Montana. I said I saw at least ten cars in the last eight miles. He'd tell me 'shut up'."

Bruce laughed out loud and said, "If you're ever up my way stop by. I'm well-known in Chugwater."

Glancing at the milling crowd going in and out of the door to the patio, he continued, "I think my command appearance here has been met and I can leave. Nice talking to you."

"Nice talking to you too."

Jake sat for a while longer before going inside. He didn't see Rachel. The party was still going strong when left. He really cared about Rachel, but a party animal he was not.

Next day Rachel called and asked what happened.

Jake said, "Yesterday was rather tiring for me. I had a nice conversation with your camera director, Bruce Culp, on the patio. I ran out of steam and decided to go home. I looked for you. Not seeing you, I left and went home to bed."

Jake could tell by her tone of voice that she wasn't pleased that he left without telling her goodbye. A thought that crossed his mind was, "Am I attracted to her by only her beauty or is it because we have things in common that we enjoy?" That thought triggered another: "What do we share in common?"

These thoughts troubled him. He tried to reason that he loved her very much. Trying to change the conversation, he said, "I talked to my British clients early this morning. They're coming in earlier than planned. They'll be staying at my place and we'll do some sightseeing before we leave for Montana."

"Oh. That means we'll not be seeing each other, since I'm leaving for Africa in a couple of weeks."

"That's about the size of it. I do wish you the best in your movie. Drop me a line or call me. Tell me what Africa is like."

"Okay." With that she was gone.

Jake organized a tour itinerary and his planned real estate showings. He arrived at Los Angeles Airport and entered the British Airlines terminal. He carried a sign that read "Roberts." When the flight from England arrived and began disembarking, he held up the sign. A middle-aged couple came to him.

"I'm Anthony Roberts and this is my wife, Jane. Are you Mr. Moore?"

"Yes sir. Come with me and we'll get your luggage." While walking to the luggage carousel, Jake asked, "Did I understand that you were bringing your business adviser?"

"Charles? Yes, he'll be arriving next week. He said if I found what I liked to place a minimum down payment to hold the property until his arrival. He will then go over the legal ramifications."

At the luggage carousel, Sir Roberts gave his luggage tags to an attendant. Jake let the couple know he'd get his car and meet them out front. The attendant loaded the Roberts' luggage into Jake's car.

With his guests seated, Jake headed for the freeway. He asked, "Sir Roberts, how was your trip?"

Sir Roberts smilingly said, "Long but fine. Can we drop the Sir bit? Just call me Tony."

Returning the smile, Jake said, "Providing you call me Jake."

Jake took an immediate liking to the couple. They hadn't let wealth and title go to their heads. A light conversation was carried on. Arriving at Jake's home, he introduced them to his housekeeper Marie, asking her to show the Roberts to the guest room.

Before they left for their room, Jake told them, "There's a heated pool out back if you'd like a swim. Or maybe you'd like to take a rest. I'm taking us to dinner tonight at the Coconut Grove, if that's alright with you."

"That sounds good to us. I've heard about it; that it's frequented by movie stars. I think we'll take you up on the swim and dinner."

"While you're changing, can I fix you a drink?"

"Martinis for us."

Jake placed a quick call to Rachel asking if she would like to join them for dinner this evening at seven at the Coconut Grove. She said she would. He said he'd pick her up at six.

Tony and Jane appeared in their swimsuits. Jake gave them directions to his pool and said, "I'll change, fix our drinks and join you. I've asked my girlfriend Rachel to join us tonight; she's the daughter of Walter and Gail Wilkinson."

Tony spoke up quickly, "I know the chap! He played the part of an English gentleman in the movie *Lord William*. It will be a real pleasure to meet him in person."

While Marie, Jake's housekeeper, guided the Roberts to the pool, Jake mixed up some martinis for the Roberts and a rum and Coke for himself. He was about to carry them out on a tray. Marie appeared and let him know she would bring them out when they were ready.

Jake and the Roberts enjoyed the warm refreshing water. Marie brought out some large towels and placed them on chairs that were placed around an umbrella table with a glass top.

With the enjoyable swim over, the three went to the chairs, dried off and sat down. Marie immediately appeared with their drinks.

"Tony, we should decide what you'd like to do first. What's your pleasure?"

"Since the ranch is more of a hobby, we'd like to see what's available in Hollywood first and get a better feel for Southern California."

"Okay, let me run some ideas by you, to see if you're interested. Knowing how much time you've allotted for your trip will help me put forth an itinerary. You indicated an interest in the movie industry and stars.

"I can show you the movie studios and homes of the stars from the air; I have an agreement with a local helicopter firm. Then we can follow up those that interest you on the ground.

"You also said you'd like to purchase a house in the Hollywood area, near movie stars. I assume you might be thinking of becoming a movie producer?

"From the air you can get a general feel for housing, and those belonging to those in the movie industry. After the short aerial tour I can then set up those houses that interest you for inspection the following day."

"That sounds exciting. I like the idea. Answering your comment about being a producer, I have given some thought to producing a movie."

Jake continued, "You also expressed an interest in the American Old West. California and Montana are rich with such history. In California there were twenty-one Spanish missions built. They stretch from San Diego to the San Francisco. They were built in the 1700s, along what's called El Camino Real—The Royal Highway.

"California has several old ghost towns. The ghost town of Calico, near Barstow, was restored by Walter Knott. He also built a 'ghost town' layout near his restaurant that he calls Knott's Berry Farm. It's an easy and short tour. It's like a movie set and gives one an insight into the Old West, including staged gunfights and train robberies."

Jake could see that he had given them exciting ideas. They were like any normal couple of their late forties or early fifties. Their faces glowed with excitement.

Continuing, Jake said, "To see ranches in Montana will take five days at a minimum. It will take one day to fly up and another to return. I can show you what I think you might like from the air and set up an inspection over the next day or so. Additional time can be allotted, if you wish."

Tony seemed amazed and remarked, "I can see why Montana Bill recommended you. I like your ideas. I can hardly wait. I had planned spending two or three weeks in America. From all that you're telling me, I may need to extend that time. Do we start the aerial tour tomorrow?"

"Yes. Lady Jane and you might like to take a short rest before we leave for the Coconut Grove."

"Right."

Before taking a brief rest, Jake called the charter helicopter service and made arrangements for a helicopter tour the next afternoon.

Lady Jane was dressed in a tailored dark cocktail dress and Tony wore a dark business suit. They made a handsome couple. Jake was also dressed in a dark business suit.

At the Wilkinsons' home, Jake introduced the Roberts. Tony and Walter really hit it off. Lady Jane and Gail carried on a light conversation. Jake was glad when Rachel appeared, wearing a stunning black-sequined cocktail dress. Jake introduced her to the Roberts. After brief acknowledgements, the foursome left for the Coconut Grove. The drive to the Grove seemed short, due to enjoyable light conversation between the foursome. Giving his keys to the valet, Jake and his guests entered. The maitre d' signaled to a waiter and they were escorted to a table.

During dinner and later dancing, Jake got a chance to relax. Rachel was a good hostess. She identified famous actors and their wives that were sitting at various tables, upcoming actors and actresses and movie gossip. The Roberts loved it. Title and wealth hadn't changed them. On the way to Rachel's house, they asked if she would come with them tomorrow for the fly-over. She said she couldn't, due to rehearsals for the movie *African Safari*.

CHAPTER 2

Jake was up early. He took his book of listings and sat at the glass table by the pool. Marie brought him a cup of coffee. While sipping his coffee he looked at the pages he had marked in his book of listings. He sat them aside when the Roberts joined him. Marie brought them coffee and took breakfast requests.

Tony said, "We had an enjoyable evening, thanks to you. Rachel was captivating. Even though we've been here but a short time, we love Southern California."

Lady Jane said, "Your weather is very pleasant. It's so nice being able to sit outside for breakfast. The sun is warm but not hot. Is it always like this?"

Jake replied, "Not always. We get rains in our winter months."

Their light morning conversation was interrupted by the appearance of Marie with their breakfast. Over breakfast the threesome talked about English and American lifestyles and customs. Completing their leisurely breakfast, Marie cleared the table.

Jake asked, "In our aerial tour of star homes, do you have any preferences?"

Tony and Lady Jane went through a litany of names.

Jake was both surprised and amused. He could tell that they were truly movie buffs. They had the enthusiastic excitement of an alcoholic going on a tour of distilleries.

Jake smiled and replied, "I'd best take along my map of the stars homes. I'll give you a map, also. You can then mark it up as a souvenir.

"Next I need to know what price range you are considering in a home, style, number of bedrooms and baths, and any other desires. I have my listing book that you can look through. Our tour will be after lunch."

Tony said, "Price isn't a problem, if we find what we like. We have three grown children, and we will possibly have guests dropping by. It would be nice if it has a behind-a-gate security system, pool and a place large enough for entertaining people."

"Okay, that gives me some ideas."

Next morning, on the way to Santa Monica Airport for the aerial tour, Jake went by way of Olympic Boulevard so that the Roberts could see the front entrance to 20th Century Fox Studios. This was exciting to them.

Jake said, "We'll see this and the other studios from the air. Many stars live in Beverly Hills; some also live in Brentwood. I'll point them out and show you the properties I've made appointments for you to see tomorrow. This will give you an idea of the proximity to those homes of stars."

"We appreciate your idea."

Pulling into Santa Monica Airport parking lot, Jake ushered Tony and Lady Jane to their awaiting helicopter and pilot. After brief introductions they boarded their helicopter. While the pilot was clearing takeoff with the control tower, Jake handed a map to the Roberts. It showed the location of movie star homes. The pilot flew the usual aerial tour route while Jake pointed out the homes.

"This is the home of Dorothy Lamour, Carol Lombard, Myrna Loy, William Powell, Ginger Rogers, Will Rogers, Dinah Shore, Frank Sinatra, Jimmy Stewart, Robert Taylor, Eddie Cantor, Charlie Chaplin, Errol Flynn, Jack Benny and Joe E. Brown.

"Next are the houses I'll take you through tomorrow. This is on Benedict Canyon Drive, next is Beverly Park and the last is on Mapleton Drive."

From the air it could be seen that these were all large estates, all had pools and were well-landscaped.

The Roberts had observed all that Jake had shown them. Tony commented, "I noticed that many of the houses you pointed out are of Spanish design. I did see a few Tudor styles and some Spanish Mediterranean. Are there any restrictive building codes?"

"Yes. Most developers insert building codes in their developments to keep potential builders from building homes that might diminish neighborhood values. Some go so far as to dictate style and paint colors."

"We're looking forward to what you'll show us. The one in Benedict Canyon and the one in Beverly Park looked very nice from the air. Are they on the list we'll see tomorrow?"

"Both are."

"That's great."

The rest of the flight was to give the Roberts an idea of the area and some house pricing. Returning to the airport they got in Jake's car, and on the way to his home went by MGM and Warner Brothers Studios, had a drive-in lunch and drove by some of the stars' homes.

"Jake, that was a most interesting tour. I found the drive-in lunch interesting. You Americans are very clever. That's the first time I've been served a sandwich by cute girls on roller skates. How do they manage to do that? Thank you so much for such an enjoyable day."

"You're welcome, Tony. As for the girls on skates, I can't answer that. I have a difficult time just trying to skate. I'd never be able to do that and balance a tray full of food."

Tony laughed and said, "Nor I."

Changing the subject, Jake said, "It's so nice out. It's a good day for relaxing around the pool. Do I have any takers?"

Both the Roberts agreed. Going to their rooms, each changed into bathing suits. Jake had just finished making some martinis when he was joined by the Roberts. The three took their martinis and went to the poolside table.

Jake asked, "For tonight would you like dinner at the Mocambo? It's a favorite place of the stars. Some of the stars that frequent Mocambo are Bogart, Henry Fonda, Errol Flynn and Jimmy Stewart, to mention a few."

"We'd love that. Perhaps Rachel could join us?"

"I'll see."

While the Roberts were sunning, Jake called Rachel. She agreed to join them for dinner at Mocambo. Like at the Coconut Grove, Rachel dominated the conversation. Jake was content to listen in, adding a few comments here and there. Rachel let everyone know she was leaving for Africa day after tomorrow, to do the movie shoot. This was a surprise to Jake. He was under the impression that she wouldn't leave for Africa for another week or so. He expressed this to her.

"Philip's going over with the camera crew and asked me along."

This was troubling to Jake, but he had learned that when Rachel had made up her mind it was next to impossible to change it. He would try to put this aside, enjoy the evening and get mentally prepared for tomorrow's property showing.

After a relaxing breakfast by the pool, Jake drove the Roberts to the first house, on South Mapleton Drive, for their tour. They were well pleased with the gated entry, exterior landscaping and traditional style. A maid let them in and returned to her work in the kitchen.

Going from room to room, Jake pointed out a spacious living room, family room, beautiful fireplaces that "burned" artificial wood, gym, staff suite, pool table room and wet bar, seven bedrooms and nine baths. He told the Roberts the house was built about 1933 and had been totally refurbished, had a second story guest house, spacious patio and BBQ. Lot size, 1.4 acres; asking price $20 million. The Roberts liked the house but Jake could tell by their remarks they had only a mild interest.

Next Jake took them to a house on Benedict Canyon Drive. The house was Spanish Mediterranean with a red tile roof. As they entered the adobe brick driveway, bordered with beautiful trees and shrubs, and parked on the huge adobe brick turnaround pad, Jake could hear excitement in the Roberts' voices. They were again let in by a maid.

Again he took the Roberts from room to room, pointing out fourteen bedrooms, fourteen baths, game room, gym, 2,000-square-foot guest house, pool room and gorgeous pool that looked like an

Arabian oasis with its pool lined by palm trees and a huge decking with poolside lounge chairs. He informed the Roberts that the house had 14,000-plus square feet and was located on 1.4 acres. Asking price was $18 million.

The Roberts seemed reluctant to leave. Based upon feedback from the Roberts, Jake felt that the house he now planned to show them on Beverly Park stood a good chance of being "the one."

Jake pulled up to the gate entry, identified himself and his purpose, and the gate swung open. He was getting positive vibes from the Roberts. The house reminded them of a French villa, and the landscaping was superb. A housekeeper let them in. The foyer was elegant with two statues mounted on each side of the passageway.

The housekeeper went about her work in the kitchen. Jake showed the Roberts through a formal living room and a formal dining room with French doors to a large exterior patio with views of city lights at night. Next came a grand kitchen with center serving bar and cook's catering dining area, cozy family room, spacious den with wet bar, a huge library/office with beautiful built-in cherry wood bookcases. The bookcases were full of rich leather-bound books. It would be a librarian's dream world.

Going upstairs he showed them five bedrooms. The master suite was huge with his and her walk-in closets and baths. There were two guest suites, ten bathrooms, and a quality home theater room with a state-of-the-art sound system and roomy soft seats for sixteen.

Going outside, he showed the Roberts a formal swimming pool, with fish statues spouting water, a gazebo, and a large pool decking with several pool chase lounges. The setting gave off a sense of peace and tranquility combined with grandeur.

Jake suggested they sit at the glass topped table by the pool.

Seated, he asked, "What are your thoughts on this?"

In unison they replied, "We love it! How large is the house and lot?"

"The house has 13,500 square feet and the lot size is four acres."

"What's the asking price?"

"$18 million. What most impressed you about this house?"

Tony quickly replied, "The theater room and library office." Lady Jane said, "The master bedroom suite, the cozy family room, the pool, and outside patio with its view. I thought those life-size statues in the garden area were superb. It was like being in a French or Italian villa."

Tony said, "I think Jane and I are in agreement that we'd like to own this house. What will it take to buy the house?"

"I think it might go for $17 million. I can try for a lower price."

"No, we don't want to take the chance that someone else might make an offer and get the property."

"Will your business manager need to see the property before making an offer?"

"No. If our offer is accepted, I can show him the property later."

Jake reached into his suit breast pocket and pulled out a blank real estate offer form that he always carried. Placing it on the table he began filling it out. When he filled in the offering price, he asked, "How much earnest money do you want to put down?"

"Would $340,000 USD do?"

"I think so."

With that, he turned the contract over for them to sign.

"When will we know if our offer is accepted?"

"I'll present your offer to the owner tonight."

Jake ushered the Roberts to his car, thanking the housekeeper on the way out. That night Jake met with the owner. He stressed that his clients were willing to put down $340,000 earnest money in escrow the next day if the price of $17 million was accepted. The Bank of England would provide financing for the balance. With some persuasion and reasoning, the owner accepted.

That evening he gave the Roberts the glad news that their offer was accepted and would be put in escrow the next day.

He then asked, "Since this went so quickly, what would you like to do tomorrow?"

"You mentioned Disneyland. We've heard about it in England. It sounded interesting."

"Then Disneyland it will be."

Next morning, after a quick breakfast, the threesome left for Disneyland. Traffic was light, since they were headed away from downtown Los Angeles. Arriving at the Disneyland parking lot, they caught the motorized tram to the entrance. Tony insisted that he buy the tickets. With Jake showing the way, Tony and Lady Jane became enthusiastic tourists.

They enjoyed visiting the shops on Main Street. They marveled at the animation that allowed the figure of Abraham Lincoln to stand up and deliver his speech. Frontier Land, depicting America in the early years, and Bear Country Jamboree was a favorite with Tony, the Steamboat Ride and Haunted House, with its photographic illusions, was favored by Lady Jane. Future Land was interesting to both. They went on several rides and had lunch at the Pirates of the Caribbean.

While having lunch, Tony commented, "Jake, I'm glad you suggested Disneyland. We're having a great time. Even though I realize its Hollywood's version of Americana I'm sure it's all based on some truths. The train rides were very interesting; the Grand Canyon section with lights flashing and the beautiful scenes was superb. I still can't figure out how they did the haunted house with all the ghosts dancing."

Jake replied, "It's amazing the visual and sound effects of which Hollywood is capable. Your new house and living among those artists with such skills may prove exciting. When we go on our ride of Pirates of the Caribbean you'll see more of their skills. Shall we go?"

The threesome went to their ride. Tony commented how realistically the tiny lights resembled fireflies, and on the animation seen on the ride. Afterwards they listened to some of the bands and observed the nightly parade along Main Street. Both Tony and Lady Jane carried on a lively talk about their day at Disneyland on the ride back to Jake's home. They thanked Jake several times for such an enjoyable day.

Arriving at Jake's house, Jake asked, "Are you ready for Knott's Berry Farm tomorrow?"

The Roberts answered in unison, "Yes!"

Before going to sleep, Jake refreshed his memory of Knott's Berry Farm from a pamphlet he received on his last visit. He wanted to make this was a pleasing tour for the Roberts, since they expressed interest in the American West.

Next morning during breakfast, Jake said, "Knott's Berry Farm is an American success story. Would you be interested in hearing about it?"

Both Roberts quickly said, "Yes!"

"Okay. In the early 1900s, Knott raised and sold berries from a small roadside stand on the state highway that ran by the family farm. To make ends meet they began serving travelers fried chicken.

From a nearby farm Walter Knott purchased newly cultivated plants. The new berry was a hybrid mix of red raspberry, blackberry and loganberry. The farmer who had developed the berry was Rudolph Boysen. When Walter Knott was asked the name of the berry, he told them boysenberry.

The Knotts then began serving chicken dinners and boysenberry pies in their newly built restaurant. Walt had a love of American history and early western pioneers. To give later generations a better understanding and a feel of the olden days, he built Ghost Town. Ghost Town is like a Hollywood Old West set. It has the Calico Saloon where a boysenberry drink or sarsaparilla can be bought."

Tony asked, "What's sarsaparilla? I've heard it mentioned in movies, but what's it like?"

"I really haven't tasted it. I'm told it tastes like root beer."

"All this sounds so interesting. We look forward to seeing this."

On the drive to Knott's Berry Farm, Tony and Lady Jane asked Jake about what they would be seeing.

Jake said, "As I stated at breakfast, we'll see the Calico Saloon and a fake gunfight staged by stunt men; old clapboard buildings such as a blacksmith shop that shows the tools of that trade; a Chinese laundry with an automated Chinese figure ironing as was done in the 1800s, singing western songs in Mandarin Chinese.

"We'll take a ride on the Calico Railroad. It's an old narrow gauge rail that Walter Knott brought in from Colorado. It pulls a passenger car which fake train robbers will attack; then a stagecoach ride, the jail with Sad Eye Joe behind bars, the volcano display, and trip to the Gold Mine where you can pan for gold. We can set in on a demonstration by a western fast-draw artist. By this time it should be time for dinner. After dinner we can attend the covered wagon show and visit the chapel, if you would care to."

Jake's audience was spellbound with what they were told was ahead of them. As Jake was going through what lay ahead, Tony managed to interject a few "smashing" and "bloody good" statements.

Pulling into a parking area, the threesome began experiencing what Jake had talked about. The Roberts were so engrossed in what they were seeing that they didn't think it unusual when Jake said, "I've seen the jail and Sad Eye Joe. I'll wait here while you see that display."

As the Roberts moved down the line of people peering into the cell to see Sad Eye Joe, a wooden statue with a hidden speaker, Jake wrote a short statement and handed it to a man that held a microphone. When the Roberts turn came to look into the cell that held Sad Eye Joe, they were shocked and surprised when Sad Eye Joe said, "Well howdy, Sir Roberts and Lady Jane! How's merry old England?"

Both were taken aback. They hurried to tell Jake what happened. When they saw Jake's smile, they understood the jest played on them and laughed. The day went quickly. They had a small snack for lunch and went to see the fastest gun exhibition.

Tony was amazed that the artist could draw a legal weight colt peacemaker .45 six shooter and hit a balloon target in $8/100^{th}$ of a second. He was even more amazed when the fast-gun artist drew and fired three shots, hitting three balloons at the same time—recorded on a crowd-visible time clock.

The three shots sounded as one. The artist then showed in slow motion how he did it. He showed his spectators that when his gun cleared the holster, he fired his first shot; then slid the gun's hammer across his holster to fire the next shot, and thumb-cocked the gun for his third shot.

All during dinner the Roberts excitedly talked to Jake about what they had seen so far. They talked at length about the saloon shoot-out, riding on a stagecoach, the train robbery, the fast gun exhibition, tools of the 1800s and panning for gold. With the aid of an assistant, Sir Roberts panned out a tiny fleck of gold. It was plain to Jake that this event would always be a focal point in telling others of their trip to California. Jake learned that with all of Sir Roberts' wealth, he was still a kid at heart. Jake liked that.

After dinner the threesome strolled around Ghost Town to kill time until the covered wagon entertainment began. When it opened at dark, the threesome entered an area that had covered wagons ringed in a circle. They took a seat on a bench in one of the wagons, lit by tiny subdued bulbs. In the center of the circled wagons was a fire pit that had a campfire going. A five-piece musical group entered and took positions around the fire, greeted the group and played and sang old western songs.

On the way back to Jake's house the talk was of Knott's Berry Farm and Disneyland.

Tony said, "The last two days have been interesting. Disneyland with its Frontier Town Riverboat and Keel Boat rides gives some insight into your nation's early beginnings in the 1700s. At Knott's Berry Farm, one gets a feel for your West in the 1800s. I can now understand why my grand uncle was taken by your American West and bought land in Montana.

"I used to sit and listen to him go on about Montana and your West. I caught his same zeal. Charlie should be here in a couple of days; then I can see Montana and see if it lives up to what I was told."

"One thing you'll see is why it's called the Big Sky State. When I fly us up, I'll give you an aerial look at Wyoming, a state with large ranches, and Montana. This will give you a feel of the vastness of these states, so thinly populated. Then we'll inspect the ranches I've lined up for you to see. Time permitting, I'll show you some things that might interest you.

Until Charlie arrives, do you prefer to rest and relax around the pool? Or would you like to visit Olvera Street in Los Angeles?"

"What's Olvera Street?"

"It was the beginning of what's now Los Angeles. You indicated an interest in our American West. Los Angeles was originally called El Pueblo de Los Angeles. It was settled by the Spanish in the late 1700s. Mexico took it over in the 1800s. Olvera Street still has standing some of the original buildings of that time. Also, it's a great place for shopping for Mexican-made goods, tasting Mexican foods, listening to

Mariachi music and watch performances by Aztec Indians and folkloric dancing."

"That sounds really exciting. Whenever we think you have surely shown us all, you come up with something else. Count us in."

"Okay. I'll try to think up some other things you might enjoy seeing on your trip."

"You've already shown us so much. You've found us a beautiful home that we really love, and you've shown us Disneyland and now Knott's Berry Farm. I can't imagine anything that can top that. We're very grateful. If you ever visit England, let me show you around."

Jake glanced over at the Roberts and with a big smile said, "That's a deal. I'll take you up on that offer one day."

Tony replied, "It'll be my pleasure."

Arriving at Jake's house, a tired but happy threesome called it a day.

CHAPTER 3

After a quick breakfast next morning, Jake drove the Roberts to Olvera Street. Jake parked and the threesome headed down Olvera Street. Jake purchased a pamphlet that gave the history of El Pueblo de Los Angeles and gave it to the Roberts.

Strolling by some of the shops, Lady Jane purchased a Mexican-style skirt and peasant blouse, saying it would make a good display in their gallery in England. Sir Roberts found a complete Mexican Grande's suit of black charro with short decorated jacket, ruffled shirt, sting tie, short boots and sombrero. Lady Jane was quick to find a matching charro for women. Purchases in hand, they went from shop to shop. Jake mused to himself, "I don't think they've missed a shop."

While touring the oldest buildings in Los Angeles and doing more shopping, they stopped to listen to strolling bolero musicians and watch the performances of the Aztec dancers and some of the folkloric dances.

At noon Jake asked, "Would you care to try some Mexican food?"

The Roberts replied, "We'd love to."

Jake led the way to Rosita's. The Roberts asked Jake to order for them.

He ordered a combination that had a pork enchilada verde, taco, refried beans, Spanish rice and a pitcher of dark beer. While their food was settling, each had a margarita.

Sir Roberts said, "I think I can speak for my wife and me. The meal was strange to us, but very tasty. We thank you."

"It's my pleasure."

With purchases in hand, the threesome headed for the car.

Lady Jane spotted a Mexican artist making small glass objects. She stopped to watch. Jake and Tony joined her. The artist used spaghetti-like strips of glass and a torch to make various types of animals, or whatever his customers requested. Lady Jane made a request and watched with satisfaction as the artist completed her request. Paying for the purchase, the threesome moved on. They almost reached the exit of Olvera Street when an artist making caricatures was spotted. They stopped to watch. Lady Jane got her husband to have a caricature made of them.

The drive back to Jake's place was full of lively chatter about the day's adventure. When they arrived at Jake's, Marie met the group, informing Jake that he had two phone messages.

Jake thanked Marie and addressing the Roberts said, "Tony, perhaps you and Lady Jane might enjoy a relaxing dip in the pool? I'll join you as soon as I check my calls."

Tony replied, "That sounds good."

While the Roberts went to change, Jake went over his phone messages. One was from his partner, Bret Owen, and the other was from Charlie, the Roberts consultant, stating he'd arrive at Los Angeles Airport at 9:00 a.m. on British Airways on Tuesday.

Dialing the office, he spoke with Bret. "Hi, Bret. I got your message to call you."

Bret asked, "How's it going with the Roberts? Better still, when will you be back in the office?"

"It might be a couple of weeks. Their business consultant is due in day after tomorrow. We'll give him a chance to rest and inspect their purchase in Beverly Hills; then we'll go to Montana to see the ranches I've selected. Have there been any calls for me at the office?"

"Yes, but none were pressing. I stalled them by telling them you were showing out-of-state properties and would be back soon. When did you say you'll be back in the office?"

"I would guess it'll be a couple of weeks, more or less. Thanks, Bret, for covering for me. I'll make it up to you."

Hanging up the phone, he quickly changed into his bathing suit and joined the Roberts in the pool.

He said, "One of those calls was from your consultant. He'll arrive the day after tomorrow."

Tony said, "Great! We'll then be ready to look at those ranches in Montana."

"Yep. I'll call and make arrangements to show them on this coming Thursday, three days from now. I thought Charlie might like a day of rest before we leave for Montana."

"Good idea. We want to thank you for such an enjoyable day on Olvera Street. In fact each day we've been here has been exciting and enjoyable. If we don't leave soon, we'll want to become permanent residents," Tony said with a chuckle.

In a more serious tone, Tony continued, "Jake, I don't know how you do it, but there seems to be no end to the adventures you've shown us. We'll never forget it."

"I appreciate that. How about tomorrow we go on an aerial tour?"

Before Tony could speak, Lady Jane said, "I'm for that. My feet are still aching from the tour of Olvera Street."

Both Tony and Jake laughed.

Next day Jake drove the Roberts to Santa Monica Airport. Jake had called ahead. They had his plane rolled out of its hangar and gassed up. Jake checked the oil level and did his walk-around check while the Roberts got aboard. Tony had taken the seat on Jake's right and Lady Jane sat behind Tony's seat.

With everyone in and buckled up, Jake started the engine and called the tower, "Santa Monica Tower, Beech Triple Nickel N requests taxi/takeoff instructions."

"Roger, Triple Nickel. You're clear to taxi to runway twenty-one and hold short."

"Roger Tower, Triple Nickel copies."

Jake added power and taxied to runway twenty-one run-up pad. There he checked his instruments, control surfaces and magneto readings while gunning up the engine.

That completed, he called the tower. "Tower, Triple Nickel ready for takeoff."

"Triple Nickel, you're clear to runway twenty-one, altimeter setting three-zero, wind NNE at three knots. Have a good flight."

Jake made his altimeter setting, taxied onto the runway, lined up with the center line and applied full power. Climbing out over the ocean and reaching minimum altitude, Jake turned his plane to fly along the coast.

Tony asked, "What's that island off to our right?"

"That's Catalina. It was originally owned by the Wrigleys, who produced the chewing gum. If you'd like to visit the island, I could fly you there tomorrow."

"I'd like that. I think Charlie might like to see it, also."

When they reached San Juan Capistrano Jake identified the old Spanish mission ruin. Circling a couple of times he told the Roberts what he knew of the mission. Turning the plane eastward he climbed higher to go over the Palomar Observatory, then dropped down as they flew over the Salton Sea. Both of the Roberts had watched the landscape below change from urban sprawl, to mountains and now desert.

Tony spoke up. "It's amazing that you can go from a heavily populated area to stark desert in such a short time."

"I noticed that also when I first moved to Los Angeles. One can enjoy all that the big city offers as well as vast openness of the desert a short drive away."

While telling this to Tony, Jake had changed direction, heading northward to fly over Indio and Palm Springs. Coming up on Indio, he said, "Tony, this is Indio. They hold an annual Date Festival each February. Date trees were imported from the Middle East and planted in this desert area. They did very well. The festival theme play is Arabian Nights, with a stage scene and dancing girls."

"That sounds interesting. When we get moved in we'd like to see the festival. Jake, you have shown us so many interesting sights.

Whenever we think that must be the end, you show us more. We never can guess what's next."

"Speaking of what's next, that up ahead is the Ghost Town of Calico. Remember what I told you about it when we were at Knott's Berry Farm and how Walter Knott bought and restored it?"

Tony and Lady Jane leaned forward in their seats to get a better view. To give them a better view, Jake slightly crabbed the plane. Reducing the plane's power, they descended to the minimum allowable elevation, and made several circling passes around Calico. He then went to a true north direction.

"What I'm about to show you is a bit of desert that requires respect, if one wishes to live. I'm going to show you Death Valley. It got its name from those that died trying to cross that valley. During the summer temperatures can reach 140°F. There are stories of lost gold and silver mines in or around Death Valley."

Tony remarked, "With all the modern technology, one would think that these could be found today, if they really existed."

"The two stories I remember about the area are the Lost Breyfogle Ledge and the Gunsight Silver Lode. As for ease to find, I'll let you be the judge. When we clear the next ridge you'll get a view of Death Valley."

When Jake's plane cleared the ridge, all viewed an almost unbelievable sight of salt flats, jagged mountains and sand dunes.

Jake heard Tony exclaim, "My God!"

Jake said, "The mountain range on our right is the Amargosa Range. Somewhere in that area Breyfogle was found wandering by a rancher. He told the rancher that somewhere in his wanderings of

Death Valley, in a thirst delirium, he found a ledge of gold. He showed the rancher a small piece of the ore. He told of how his two partners had been murdered earlier by a party of Indians, and of his escape through Death Valley. After regaining his health, he tried on several occasions to relocate his lost ledge, but was unsuccessful."

While the Roberts were digesting this story, Jake pointed out, "Below us is the salt flats. It covers forty square miles. Apparently Death Valley at one time had been an inland sea. Death Valley is the lowest point in America—282 feet below sea level. That structure you see ahead is Scotty's Castle, an interesting place to visit. The castle walls are thick, to insulate it from the outside temperatures that can range from 120 to 140°F in summertime."

After a brief moment of silence, Tony remarked, "You said something about another lost ore?"

"You mean the lost gunsight outcrop?"

"Yes. What was that story?"

"A group of Mormons on their way to California decided to take a shortcut through Death Valley. One of their members had broken off the front sight of his rifle. Near where the group camped the man found a small outcrop of silver ore. He took out enough silver to make a new gun sight for his rifle, thus the name."

"Did he try to relocate it later?"

"I've never read of his trying to find it again."

"Bloody strange."

As Jake's plane traversed the valley, all gazed at the terrain. Mountain ranges had jagged peaks interspersed with deep winding canyons, devoid of any noticeable vegetation or water, and large sand dunes. When Jake headed his plane south he flew along the Panamint mountain range located on the west side of Death Valley. Once clear of Death Valley, he took a southwesterly course towards Santa Monica Airport.

Along the way Jake pointed out Apple Valley, a development of Roy Rogers. The flight and all that the Roberts had seen were discussed en route. The rest of the day all relaxed around Jake's pool. Jake did his usual daily call to his office, conferring with his partner.

Next day Jake and the Roberts picked up Charlie. Although tired he was a good sport and agreed to spend more time on an airplane, flying to Catalina Island. Jake and Tony sat up front on the flight, and Charlie sat with Lady Jane in back. Upon landing, Jake was amused that Tony had white knuckles from the landing.

The airstrip doesn't have a tower, and when touching down one cannot see the far end of the runway—due to a slight rise in the middle of the runway. Tony was concerned that the runway was too short and they were going to crash.

Jake had set up a guided tour of the island. The guide gave a brief history of the island, why there was a small herd of buffalo on the island, talked about famous actors and actresses that had visited the island, how the pavilion with its large dance floor of 180 feet in diameter with great ocean view came into being, and the many well-known orchestras that had played there. At the conclusion of the tour, Jake took his guests to dinner. On the flight back to Santa Monica, the talk was on the tour. Jake noticed that Charlie kept dozing off.

On the short flight back to Santa Monica airport, Jake tried to size up Charlie, thinking, "Will you be a help or a hindrance?" Charlie was tall, had very dark hair with touches of grey around the temples. On the tour of Catalina, Jake could see that he was very attentive, and at times pleasant. He sensed that behind that poker-faced front was a pleasant person. He hoped that he was right in thinking Charlie would not torpedo his sales.

While Charlie and the Roberts relaxed by the pool enjoying a cocktail, Jake made an appointment to again show the property purchased by the Roberts. He made the appointment for one o'clock the next afternoon. Since the showing was for Charlie's benefit, it would give Jake a better chance to size up the man. This done, he joined the others. The heated pool refreshed all. The Roberts were enjoying telling Charlie of their many adventures. It was a relaxing conversation shared by all. Marie appeared and announced that dinner was almost ready. All hastened to their rooms and changed for dinner. Charlie retired shortly after dinner.

Next day, Jake felt uneasy on the way to show the Beverly Hills property. He took the long way to the property so he could point out properties and let Charlie know what they sold for. If Charlie convinced the Roberts to pull the sale out of escrow, his out-of-pocket cost would be substantial and he'd lose a large commission.

Arriving at the property, Jake was glad that an enthusiastic Roberts conducted the tour, pointing out the things they enjoyed. Back in the car, Charlie said, "I think you made a good choice. The price you paid is about in the middle range for the area, which is good. It will give you room to make a profit when or if you decide to sell. I can tell that you really like the property."

Jake felt relieved. Tomorrow morning it was off to Montana and ranch properties.

CHAPTER 4

Bright and early the next morning, after breakfast, Jake, the Roberts and Charlie boarded Jake's plane in Santa Monica. Before takeoff, Jake made sure his plane's oxygen system was fully charged and working. To give the Roberts and Charlie a better idea of the vastness of the West, his planned route was Santa Monica to Cheyenne, Wyoming over an area that had peaks over 14,000 feet. He would need to carefully monitor the weather. At this time of the year, and at this altitude, it was possible to run into snow or ice, and Jake wasn't approved for instrument flight rule (IFR); then to Billings, Montana, and finally to Missoula, Montana.

Climbing to altitude, Jake headed towards Las Vegas. Varying his course slightly, he pointed out to his passengers Las Vegas to their left and the Grand Canyon to the right, just ahead. Flying over the canyon, getting a bird's eye view of the canyon's vastness and beauty, Jake heard his passengers expressing their awe. Even though Jake had visited the Grand Canyon on other occasions it was still an awesome sight to behold.

Jake told his passengers, "From this elevation you get an overview of the canyon. It's an awesome sight. To really appreciate its magnificent grandeur it needs to be seen on the ground. A person can walk down to the canyon floor, or take the mule ride."

Sir Roberts said, "I've read that one can take a tour of the canyon by rafting. From what I see below that must be an awesome ride?"

"It probably is. I've never had the desire to try that," Jake replied with a grin. Continuing, he said, "We're climbing to 15,000 feet. Since Mt. Wilson is 14,200-plus, we need to give it a safe margin. We'll be going over the Rocky Mountain Range which has several other peaks of similar altitudes. When we reach the Hartsel area on our approach to Denver we drop down to a lower altitude. We've picked up some strong headwinds and I've modified our original flight plan. We'll have lunch in Denver and top off our fuel tanks. This will allow me more time to give you an aerial view of some huge Wyoming ranches."

Homing in on the Colorado Telluride Airport beacon, Jake began his climb to 15,000 feet to be sure he was high enough to clear Mount Wilson. He could tell by his ground navigational charts he had picked up stronger headwinds than he had estimated. At 15,000 feet he began running in and out of feathery clouds that held moisture. Some produced snow flurries and others a freezing mist. Jake turned on carburetor heat. He didn't want the carburetor to ice up. He could see that fine sheets of ice were forming on the wings. He was glad his passengers were enjoying the beautiful scenery below, not aware of his safety concern.

At least the weather was reasonably good and visibility was better than a mile. Mt. Wilson was a beautiful sight as they passed over. At the Telluride beacon Jake took a new direction, heading for the Denver beacon. He thought, "If I've adjusted enough for the strong winds, we should see Mt. Uncompahgre go by close off our right wing." He had hardly phrased the thought when he could see Uncompahgre approaching on the right. His next major peaks over 14,000 feet were Princeton, Yale, Harvard, Shavano and Antero. Once over these Jake breathed easier. He was now able to descend to a lower altitude, and clear the wings and control surfaces of ice.

At the Denver airport all got out, stretched their legs and went into the terminal for some lunch, while their plane was being refueled. When their orders were given, Jake was amused at the choices. His British passengers chose fish, chips and iced tea—a favorite British dish; Jake chose his favorite, cheeseburger, fries and Dr. Pepper—a favorite American dish.

While enjoying their lunch, Sir Roberts remarked, "Jake, your America has it all. It has plenty of natural resources and beauty. The Rockies we just flew over are reminiscent of the Alps. Knott's Berry Farm gives a glimpse of your Old West. Disneyland gives an insight into both past and future. This has been a remarkable trip for us."

Jake replied, "Just wait until you see what's ahead."

"Do you mean there's something better than what we've seen?"

"I'll let you be the judge."

Meal finished, the group returned to their plane. Jake paid for the fuel and they were off to Wyoming. Homing in on the Cheyenne, Wyoming beacon, Jake said, "In Wyoming, you'll see some of the finest and largest cattle operations in America. Both today and in the past, Wyoming, eastern Montana and the Dakotas were known for raising beef, as was Texas. In the 1800s millions of buffalo roamed this area. During the Ice Age glaciers ground under forests in the area, which are now a huge resource for coal. When the glaciers receded, that land was covered with grass. Both buffalo and cattle do well in these areas."

While his passengers watched the scenery below and Cheyenne off to their left, Jake reset his radio compass for Billings' beacon. He slightly altered his course so that his passengers would get a good look at the vast grasslands of Wyoming.

He was momentarily startled when he heard Sir Roberts in an emphatic voice say, "Smashing! All that land and no people!" Continuing, he asked, "What are those tiny structures I see below?"

Jake replied, "Those are line cabins. Ranches send out ranch hands to keep an eye on their cattle. Each cabin is usually occupied by only one person. Each day he will ride out to check on the cattle to see how they are doing and to determine if they need to be moved to a different pasture. It's a lonely job, but there doesn't seem to be a shortage of those that enjoy the solitude. In winter they move the cattle closer to ranch headquarters."

Sir Roberts replied, "I enjoy peace and quiet, but I would never be able to stand that kind of life. I'd be quick to say that looking at all that land with bunches of cattle grazing on it is very soothing." Continuing, he shouted, "Look!"

Sounds from the airplane had stampeded a herd of wild Mustangs. It was a beautiful sight. The stallion guiding the herd was magnificent with spirit to match.

Before reaching Billings, Montana, Jake handed Tony a map he had brought along. It was a reproduction of a 1937 map for old-timers.

Tony looked at the map, gasped and said, "Where did you find this map? Are any still available?"

"Yes. When we stop over in Helena, I'll get you one. I thought you might enjoy checking out the area we'll be flying over." He told his passengers they were now passing over the famous historical ranches of Hash-knife, YT and Pitch Fork.

Reaching Billings, Montana, Jake set his radio compass heading for a radio station in Helena, Montana. Banking left he heard Sir Roberts ask, "Do you know the name of the river on our right?"

Looking down, Jake replied, "It's the Yellowstone. A short distance ahead of us three rivers come together. They are the Gallatin, Jefferson and Madison. They flow into the Missouri River.

"I don't know if I mentioned it, but I went a semester at a college in Bozeman. I've always enjoyed Montana's history."

With his passengers taking in the sights below and their approach to the town of Three Forks, Jake called their attention to Buffalo Jump.

Circling the jump he explained to his passengers, "Indians would cut out a few head of buffalo and drive them over that cliff. Those not killed by the fall would be killed by the Indians. Buffalo hides and the meat would be carried on travois back to the tribe. Women would cure the hides to be used as robes. Much of the meat would be sun-dried or smoked into small strips called jerky. This would keep them from starving during the long winters. From deer, women would cure the hide and chew it to make it soft for clothing."

Sir Roberts asked, "Why just the women?"

"Men were considered warriors and providers of game; women were required to butcher the meat, prepare meals, make clothes for their families, rear children, carry firewood, and gather nuts and berries.

Indian women were treated more like chattel, to be sold or traded off at the whim of their husbands, be it Indian or mountain man."

Lady Jane exclaimed, "That's not fair!"

"I agree Lady Jane, but that was their custom."

Glancing off to his left, Jake said, "Remember the three rivers I mentioned? They're on our left."

His passengers looked down on their left. It showed the convergence of the three rivers into the Missouri. Jake switched his radio compass to home in on a radio station in Missoula. This course would take them north of Butte and south of Helena. Approaching Missoula, he announced, "The canyon you see below, with the highway running through it, is called Hellgate. This was a main route in the 1800s. Indians used the canyon to attack travelers. The attacks were so violent that travelers began to refer to it as Hell's Gate. This was shortened to Hellgate."

Clearing the canyon, they could see Missoula.

Jake called in to the control tower and was cleared for a direct approach. Landing, the tower directed them to a parking place. All got out. Jake tied down his plane and removed everyone's luggage. The foursome then went inside the airport terminal and to the Hertz rental car section. Jake rented a car and drove to a close-by motel. After checking in, the group went to dinner and then retired to their rooms. Jake called the local realtor he had been working with to set up an appointment to see the ranching properties next day. That out of the way, he went to bed early.

After breakfast next morning, all got into their rental car and drove forty-seven miles to St. Ignatius. They met the realtor at his office. He drove them to the ranch.

It was a brilliantly bright and beautiful Indian summer day. The Mission Mountain range with snow-crested tops rose majestically to the east. Quaking aspen leaves were turning from bright yellow to golden brown. Streams ran clear and cold. Magpies were screeching at one another. Riding with the realtor, Jake could sense that his clients were taken by the beauty.

Arriving at the ranch, the owner allowed the realtor to show the property. The realtor began his tour.

"This is a purebred Angus seeding ranch and it also raises good cattle-herding horses. The owner has built a two-bedroom two-bath living quarters over the rustic log stable. There are additional quarters for a ranch hand. The owner has poured a concrete slab for a house of 5,000 square feet to be built. There's a machine shed, mechanic shop and an insulated calving barn. The property has 120 acres and leases 2,200 from the federal government. The asking price is $995,000."

Inspecting all the improvements the group was driven to the realtor's office. After some polite conversation, Jake and his party left for Missoula. On the way, he asked what they thought of the property.

Tony stated, "The setting is beautiful. It would be more desirable if the planned house was already built."

"I thought by seeing this property it would give you some feel for land and improvement prices. As you said it has a beautiful setting. It is forty-seven miles to Missoula with easy access to commercial aviation, a travel asset for your many businesses. I think you'll like the property I've set up for you tomorrow."

The rest of the day the group looked around Missoula and the University of Montana near Blackfoot River. Sir Roberts and Lady Jane enjoyed looking into the many shops. They bought Levis, western shirts, Stetsons and cowboy boots.

Turning to see a smiling Jake, they returned the smile and said, "Don't laugh."

Next morning Jake drove his guests to Stevensville, stopping at the local real estate office. John Melhouse greeted them. Going into his office, the group got acquainted. As any good realtor would do, John sized up the Roberts to get a feel of their interests and determine if they were financially able to purchase properties such as he was about to show. Satisfied, all got in his car and drove out Ravalli Street to the property.

Pulling into the ranch, he said, "This ranch home was built in 1915. It's been totally restored. Just wait until you see what was done on the inside."

He knocked on the front door and then used his key to let everyone in. The inside was a shock to all. It was beautiful.

He began the tour through the house. While leading the tour, he commented, "As you can see, the interior has been totally updated and all new top-of-the-line appliances installed—all in new condition. The house has five bedrooms, two and a half baths and a fireplace. The square footage is 4,500. Now let me show you the guest house."

Leading the way, they went back of the main house to an attractive cottage, shaded by huge elm and oak trees. Their realtor pointed out that it had also been updated with top-of-the-line appliances. It was a two-bedroom, 1,400 square foot house with one and a half baths. Next they were shown the caretaker's cabin. Again, everything was in new condition. It was a one-bedroom one-bath 900 square foot cabin built of logs. They were then shown a spacious barn with hay loft. The realtor explained that a small section of the barn was heated for calving purposes. While looking at some of the outbuildings near a small clear running stream, Sir Roberts, who had been eyeing the stream, called out, "Look!"

A nice brook trout was swimming upstream. John, the realtor smiled and said, "The stream has some nice brook, cutthroat and brown trout. Do you enjoy fishing?"

Sir Roberts replied, "I love fly fishing. We have a couple of nice trout streams on my English estate."

"You'll enjoy this stream, then. Do you do any hunting?"

"Yes."

Pointing to the mountain to the west, John said, "That's the Bitterroots. There you'll find herds of elk, mule deer and bears. You'll also find grouse and other upland birds. The Bitterroot River is about a mile west of here. Ducks and geese use it as a stopover on their way south in the fall. Whitetail deer and moose roam the marshes along the river. So, if you enjoy outdoor life there's plenty of it here. About two miles from here, along the river, is a State Park. It's open from April until October. It has several numbered parking places, BBQ grills on steel posts, water faucet and an area to pitch a tent."

Pausing, he asked, "Is there anything else I can help you with?"

Sir Roberts remarked, "I don't think you've mentioned the asking price."

"For all the improvements on this irrigated 600 acres, the owner is asking $3,950,000."

Suspense hung heavy. Sir Roberts looked over at Charlie.

Charlie said, "I'd like to see some listing and sales data."

The realtor replied, "That's back at the office. If you're finished here we can go to my office and I can show the information you've requested. I have it for one year; two or more if you wish."

All got into the realtor's car. He stated, "Since we're so close, let me show you that park I mentioned."

Jake and his group could see how well the park was laid out. The realtor drove down and parked along the Bitterroot River. It was a beautiful spot. Jake surmised the realtor had been here often, using the setting to help close a deal.

He pointed to a deep cut in the majestic Bitterroot mountain range, stating, "That's Blodgett Canyon. There's a nice hiking path in that canyon that leads to a vast wilderness area."

That said, he drove all back to his office. Going into his office, Jake and his clients took a seat while the realtor went for his real estate data. Returning, he and Charlie went over several sales and listings. Charlie asked several probing questions while Jake and the Roberts listened in.

Finally Charlie said, "John, would you step outside for a moment while I talk to my clients?"

"Sure, take your time."

When the realtor left and closed the door, Charlie asked the Roberts, "What are your thoughts on the property?"

"Personally I like it. It's a little small but we could add on. Jane, what's your impression?"

"It's very charming and has such a beautiful setting. What do you plan to do with the property?"

"I like the idea we saw at the property in St. Ignatius. We could run a few head of registered Angus cattle. Charlie, what do you think?"

"I think you have a good idea. It would be easy for a cattleman caretaker to handle. After going over all the sales and listing data that John gave us, the asking price is about right. Like the house you bought in Beverly Hills, this property is about mid-range in local prices."

Sir Roberts said, "Then I think we should make an offer."

John, the realtor, was called back in and notified the Roberts wished to make an offer.

Getting out a sales contract, John asked questions of Sir Roberts, filling in on the contract form the data he sought. When it got to the offer price, Sir Roberts offered $3,300,000.

John stopped writing and said, "My client will never accept such a low offer."

Sir Roberts replied, "It'll be an all cash offer. He'll not have to wait to see if we qualify for a bank loan. At close of escrow he'll be paid all cash in one lump sum."

John said, "I don't know. He might get angry at an offer $600,000 below his asking price."

"Why not try and see?"

"Alright, I'll give it a try. How much earnest money are you putting down?"

"Sixty thousand."

John filled in the contract and passed it to the Roberts. In turn, they passed it to Charlie who carefully read the entire contract. He nodded his approval to the Roberts and turned it over to them to sign.

John looked over the completed purchase contract and said, "The owner in presently in Hawaii. He left me a number to call. How long will you be staying in Missoula?"

Jake replied, "We had planned to leave tomorrow for Helena."

"How long do you plan to stay there?"

"Probably a couple of days, more or less."

"Give me call and let me know where I can reach you. I'll call the owner in Hawaii and let you know his answer. I wish you luck on your offer and your trip."

With that, all got up, shook hands and Jake's group left.

Next morning, Jake called the realtor in Stevensville, "John, were you able to reach the owner?"

"Yes, he's thinking it over. Hopefully I'll have an answer for you today or tomorrow. Are you getting ready to go to Helena?"

"Yes, we are checking out right now."

"Be sure to call and let me know where you'll be staying in Helena."

Jake told his group what was said. All checked out of their motel and went to the airport. The short flight to Helena was one of sightseeing and small talk about the ranch.

Arriving in Helena, Jake rented a car and drove all to the Best Western Motel. Rooms were rented. Once settled in Jake called the realtor in Stevensville, leaving a number where he could be reached. He then called Sir Roberts' room, "Tony, since it's early in the day, would you like to take that tour train I told you about?"

"Sure, I'll call and tell Charlie. Any word yet from the realtor?"

"No, but I left our number here."

"We'll meet you in the lobby in fifteen minutes."

The foursome met in the motel lobby and drove to the tour train waiting area, next to the Lewis and Clark Museum. On the way there, Jake told them some of Helena's history.

"Helena was founded by the Four Georgians. They were a group of prospectors looking for gold. They had searched several other places in Montana, but found nothing. Spotting the area where Helena now stands, they decided to take one last chance to find gold before returning home to Georgia. They struck it rich. When we ride the tour train we'll cross a street called Last Chance Gulch. It got its name from the little stream that once flowed down that area. In the late 1800s, Helena had more millionaires per capita than any other city in America. The tour train takes us past the old mansions, one of which Teddy Roosevelt spent a night at."

The foursome arrived as the tour train pulled out. Jake let his group know it'd return in an hour and suggested they use their waiting time to go through the museum next door.

While going through the museum, Jake bought Sir Roberts a copy of the history map he had shown him earlier, and a copy of a book telling of Helena's early history. Leaving the museum, they joined a group of tourists now loading on the train. The "train" was pulled by a World War II jeep that was made to look like a steam locomotive. It pulled three cars that resembled old-time passenger cars. The driver told about Last Chance Gulch, identified the original owners of large mansions, drove by Reader's Alley and told of Chinese mine workers that used to live there. Going by the Montana Club he told about how the wealthy elite had met there. The train drove by the State Capitol Building and back to its parking space, and another trip.

Arriving back at their motel, Jake was informed he had a message. It was a call from the realtor in Stevensville.

From his room he returned the call. "Hi, John. What's up?"

"I heard back from the owner. He agreed to reduce the price to $3,600,000 and said he'd go no lower."

"Okay. Let me check with the Roberts and call you back."

Calling the Roberts' room, he said, "Tony, I just heard from the realtor. The owner of the ranch reduced the price to $3,600,000 and said he'd go no lower. What should I tell the realtor?"

"Let him know we accept his counter price. Thanks, Jake, for all your help. What do we do next?"

"I'll let the realtor know we're in agreement and will send a telegram confirming the deal. The realtor will let me know the escrow company that will handle this and you'll need to wire in your earnest money, and notify your bank in England the amount they will eventually need to send to finish transfer of property."

To celebrate the deal, all had dinner that night at the Black Angus Restaurant. Sir Roberts talked about what he had read, so far, of the history of Helena, and that he had found it interesting. During the meal, light conversation was carried on about Helena and some thoughts about what they might do with their new ranch.

At the conclusion of the meal, Sir Roberts asked, "Well Jake, knowing you and the amazing ideas you come up with, should I ask what's in store for tomorrow?"

"In the morning, after we get off your telegram, I thought we might go on the Gates of the Mountain tour. In the afternoon you can try your luck at sapphire panning."

"That sounds like a smashing good idea! Panning for sapphires! What a story I'll have to tell when we get back to England."

Next day went as planned. The tour guide for the Gates of the Mountain told his passengers how it got its name. How it looks like the huge rock cliffs open, like a gate, when traveling down the Missouri River.

That afternoon they went to a local sapphire mining company. The Roberts and Charlie bought a bucket of concentrated soil for five dollars. They had fun sifting it through a screened pan. Jake was happy that each found some small Yogo sapphires, of varying colors. Sir Roberts found the best one— a light blue sapphire about the size of a pencil eraser.

At dinner that night, it was determined that with business concluded it was time to return to California. The Roberts planned to return to England with Charlie, and then off to South Africa. Jake let the group know that on the return trip to California he would take them over Yellowstone National Park and the Great Salt Lake in Utah, skirting desert military proving grounds.

Next morning the group left for Santa Monica, California. Over Yellowstone Park, Jake circled a couple of times so his passengers could see its enormity, telling them, "It's a caldera." Smoke columns could be seen rising from several sites. Sir Roberts called everyone's attention to a large herd of buffalo and elk.

Heading in a new direction, they soon flew over the Great Salt Lake, vast desert areas and landed at Santa Monica Airport. It was the conclusion of an interesting and rewarding trip.

At Jake's home, the Roberts said it was time for them to return to England, stating their trip to America would be long remembered.

CHAPTER 5

Two days later, Jake drove his guests to Los Angeles Airport.

Before getting on their plane, Sir Roberts said, "Jake, be sure to visit us, and let us show you around England."

Jake nodded yes, and saw them off. Driving home he felt sad. He had become so used to showing them around. Their being gone was like a large void in his life. Rachel being on location in Africa made the loneliness all the more intense. He thought, "I'll just throw myself into work at the office."

Next day he drove to his office. It seemed the traffic was worse than before. He chalked it up as a mood thing. At the office he and Bert Owen, his partner, went over some potential real estate listings. For Jake it seemed like the day would never end. Arriving home Marie told Jake a package had arrived for him. She informed him it had arrived by special courier and that she had to sign for it.

Opening the package and the box inside, Jake was shocked. It was a Rolex Oyster Perpetual wristwatch. The note accompanying the gift stated, "Please accept this gift as a small token of our appreciation—The Roberts."

While Jake was looking at the gift the phone rang.

Marie answered, "Yes, he's here."

Handing the phone to Jake, she said, "Rachel for you."

He was surprised, but managed to say, "Hi Rachel, how's the movie going?"

"We just finished today; several of us are staying over to go on a real safari with Philip. How did it turn out with your English clients?"

"Fine! They bought both the houses I showed them. That one in Beverly Hills I told you about, and a gentleman's ranch in Montana. They left for England two days ago."

"Why not celebrate and join us in Africa?"

"I don't know."

"I thought you loved me and would want to be with me?"

"Oh, okay. I'll check on the next flight to Africa. Where am I to go and how can I reach you to let you know what flight I'll be on?"

"Got a pencil?"

Grabbing a pencil and a pad from the lamp table, he said, "Go ahead." He wrote down her instructions. She told him she'd be at that number until tomorrow night; that his best connection would be to fly South African Airways to Johannesburg, and then Zambia Airways to Lusaka. She said, "Philip and I can meet you."

Hanging up the phone, Jake felt a tinge of jealousy. Rachel's tone of voice when mentioning Philip's name indicated a more familiar personal tone.

Jake called Los Angeles Airport and made reservations with South African Airlines. He called Rachel and let her know. He told her he'd have a two-hour layover in Rio de Janeiro and, if all went well, would be in Lusaka on Saturday at 5:30 p.m.

With that and some light conversation, he hung up the phone and began making arrangements with Bert at the office, letting him know about the planned trip, and packed.

After a flight on South African Airway's Constellation and Zambia Airways Beechcraft 1900 for a total of almost thirty hours in the air, Jake finally arrived at Lusaka airport. While his luggage was being unloaded, he was met by Philip Zambrowski, Rachel and a man named Allen Fritz-Robin. He learned that Allen was a Game Management Ranger; also their professional hunter. Jake guessed Allen to be in his late fifties, due to streaks of white around his temples that stood out against his black hair. Jake took an instant liking to Allen and his easygoing smile.

Luggage now in Jake's hand, Allen gave a good natured smile and said, "Shall we get underway?"

With Rachel carrying on a lively question and answer conversation with Jake, they arrived at an old WWII Dodge 4x4 Weapons Carrier, with benches lining each side. Jake, with his luggage, was accompanied by Rachel to the benches. Rachel, as usual, carried on most of the conversation while a bone-tired Jake mostly listened.

Lusaka was a modern-looking city with several tall buildings, about fourteen stories. This quickly changed to rural farm shacks made of mud bricks. It made Jake think of what it must have looked like when the ancient Israelites made mud bricks of straw. It looked somewhat similar.

It was dark when they reached the hunting camp. The camp cooks gave Jake a sandwich and, to his shock, a Dr. Pepper.

Seeing the surprised look on Jake's face. Allen asked, "Would you prefer another type of beverage?"

"No. I was just surprised to see a Dr. Pepper here."

Allen laughed, "I visited your country a few years back and got hooked on Dr. Pepper. A local importer keeps me well-supplied. He ships in several cases each month."

Both got a good laugh. His meal finished, Allen accompanied Jake to the men's dorm. Entering, Jake was pleased to see his cameraman friend, Bruce Culp.

The dorm had several individual beds and a common bath with two showers at the end of the building. There were two ceiling fans, a large screened-in front window and three smaller type windows on the opposite wall, for cross ventilation. Since that wall formed the outside wall of the compound, the regular screens were reinforced with heavy-duty wire bars. The dorm's only door led to the compound. It was a glass storm door whose upper part could be slid down to allow additional ventilation. Jake managed to take a quick shower and then went to bed. He was instantly asleep.

Next morning he was awakened by the camp sounds and people talking. After getting dressed he joined the group in a canopied, screened-in dining area. The dining area had several wooden park tables with benches. He returned waves to Allen and Bruce, and then joined Rachel. A member of Allen's workforce brought him breakfast and a cup of coffee.

Jake said, "Good morning!"

Rachel returned the greeting and asked, "Did you get a good night's rest?"

"Yes." Continuing he commented, "This is quite a layout; not what I expected of a safari camp. It has the luxuries one might expect in town."

"Philip told us it's the best in the area."

The two continued a light conversation, catching up on each other's happenings while apart. This was interrupted by the clinking of a spoon on a glass. Allen was standing.

He said, "I'm informed by Philip that all are now present. Today will be a day of relaxation and enjoying our camp compound. I'll be checking out herds east and north of our compound in search for a good trophy animal for Philip. If you need anything let my crew know. Enjoy."

With that Allen left the dining area. Conversation resumed. While talking to Rachel, Jake paused. He heard the all-familiar sound of an aircraft engine being started. Both Rachel and he looked towards the main gate entrance. A bright yellow Piper Super Cub—a two-seat single-engine monoplane—went zipping by.

Jake thought to himself, "What a clever way to cover lots of ground in a short period of time."

The realtor in Jake took over. He let Rachel know he planned to take a tour of the compound, asking if she would like to go with him.

She declined, saying, "I think I'll do some reading and rest."

With that the two left the dining room for their separate interests.

Jake noticed the huge compound was shaped like a corral, with buildings forming the outside walls. Each building was made of colored cinder block. The side facing the compound had an added cobblestone veneer. The roof tiling resembled shake shingles.

Jake thought to himself, "Pretty elaborate for a permanent hunting camp."

Jake noticed that between each building was a cinder block wall that reached the eaves of the building. Instead of a cinder block capstone the top was concrete with sharp shards of glass embedded. The main gate was built of heady-duty wire, twelve feet high, and heavy-duty screen mesh to keep out unwanted small visitors—snakes.

The north side of the building compound was comprised of a machine/maintenance shop with an entry door to the compound and double doors to the outside. Going to those outside doors, Jake could see a small metal hangar for the plane and a garage for motor vehicles. Continuing around the compound, on the north side, he saw the private quarters of Allen Fritz-Robin and barracks-like buildings that housed the work crew. Next came some storage buildings.

On the south side were quarters for his hunting clients/guests, dorms for men and another for women. The center of the compound held the large dining tent, screen enclosed. Along the western part of the tent was a concrete block wall with a large commercial cook stove, with pots hanging from pegs overhead and two large refrigeration boxes. At the other end of the compound was a fire pit surrounded by several lounge chairs. For shade and comfort was a huge Mopane tree, he later learned.

Jake thought, "Yep, this is quite a layout."

Sitting down in a lounge chair, he was approached by one of Allen's crew. Jake was asked, "Sir, would you care for something cool to drink?"

"Yes, thank you. I'd like a Dr. Pepper."

From his vantage point, he could see that some were in the dining tent. It seemed that Philip was captivating them with some of his tales. While considering what that might be, he heard the return of the plane. He was soon joined by Allen who ordered a glass of iced tea. When that arrived and Allen had taken a sip, Jake said, "You have a great setup here."

Allen responded, "It has taken a few years to achieve, but, it's very comfortable."

"Do you ever get lonely living out here?"

"No. Right now we're in the dry season with many animals on the move for water and food. You should see this country in the rainy season. For miles you'll see a vast carpet of green. The Zambezi River overflows and saturates the ground. You'll see huge herds of wildebeest, Cape buffalo, Zebra, sable antelope, gazelles and impalas. Shadowing these herds will be packs of African dogs, hyenas and lion prides. It's a sight that always thrills me.

"I never could stand the noise and crowds of the cities. When things are slow the crew and I will go to Lusaka to unwind for awhile. It's very peaceful here.

"A few years ago I had installed a large propane tank. The cook stove and refrigeration boxes are run by propane gas. I then had installed an electrical power generator, gas pump and storage tank for our vehicles and my plane. Water wells supply all the water we need. A septic tank was installed two years ago. So, you see we have all the conveniences of the city without the noise. At night I'm lulled to sleep by sounds of lion prides and other night hunters, or that silly laughter of a hyena. Who would want to live in a crowded city and give up this peaceful way of life?"

Changing the subject, he asked Jake, "Do you plan to hunt big game?"

"No. I basically came to spend some time with Rachel. I brought along my camera, hoping I might get some nice photos of Africa. Any big game hunting for me will be done by camera."

"What camera did you bring?"

"A Minolta and a telephoto lens."

"Good camera. I use a Nikon myself. I didn't see any trophy-quality animals for Philip today. I plan to fly south tomorrow to checkout herds there. Care to come along?"

"Love to."

With that, Allen headed to the dining room. Jake reflected on what Allen had said about this country. He could see the point Allen made. The rest of the day things were quiet. Philip dominated those that had come with him. He talked about the movie just completed and how he could improve on it. Then he talked about some new scripts he was considering for a movie.

Jake thought, "Yep. You have all those about you hoping they'll get a part in your future movies—all brown-noses." Seeing Rachel among them didn't make him happy, or was he only being jealous? He was seeing a side of Rachel he had never seen before.

That evening Bruce and he seemed to gravitate to each other by the fire pit. Allen joined them. While Philip dominated much of the conversation, Bruce, Allen and Jake carried on a muted conversation about Africa, its beauty and what it had to offer, and its peoples. Rachel joined them for awhile, but went back to the movie group. Jake finally said, "I think I'll turn in early."

Bruce said, "I think I'll do the same."

Allen said, "Jake, we'll leave tomorrow at 9 a.m."

Jake replied, "I'll be ready," and left for bed.

At breakfast next morning Jake visited with Rachel, and let her know he planned to accompany Allen on a flight to look for trophy specimens for Philip. She seemed peeved, but, what the heck, so was he. He was tired of the Philip-worshipers.

At a signal from Allen, Jake went to his quarters and picked up his camera case, checking to be sure he had everything, and several rolls of film. That done, he joined Allen who was checking out his plane. Both got aboard and were quickly airborne. The view of so much green below, as they followed the Zambezi, soon became dotted with grazing herds of animals. The stark contrast between green land near the river and the dry parts just a few hundred yards inland was shocking. The animals grazed along the river. Allen made low passes over the herd, looking for a trophy animal. Jake was snapping photos. Not spotting what he was looking for, Allen followed the Zambezi River down to where it emptied into Lake Arriba.

Allen headed for a large herd of Cape buffalo that he had spotted. Zooming over the herd, he scanned the buffalo with his binoculars. Jake heard him say, "Smashing" and was startled when Allen put the plane in a short steep climb, did a banking turn at the higher elevation and headed back for the herd. Passing his binoculars to Jake, he said, "Look at the herd at three o'clock! See that big bull! That's our target for tomorrow."

Jake saw what he was talking about. The bull had a massive set of horns. At their higher altitude, so as to not startle the herd, Allen circled the herd and made some notations on his aerial map. He also took notice of ground cover and markers to pinpoint the herd.

That done, he said, "Now that we've located our trophy and we're close to Victoria Falls, would you like to see them?"

"Yes. That would be great."

Allen altered his course. Jake put the telephoto lens on his camera. The falls came into sight. It was awesome. Allen suggested that Jake raise the plane's window to get a clearer shot. While Allen made some varying paths and circles above the falls, Jake took a bunch of shots. He let Allen know that he had all that he wanted. Allen now headed for the compound, arriving mid-afternoon. Philip was notified. Allen asked Philip how many of his party would be going on the hunt, so he could make transportation plans.

Philip checked with those of his party. He told Allen that only he, Rachel, Bruce and Jake would be going on the hunt. There was a great deal of excitement about the hunt that evening.

Allen joined Jake and Bruce at the fire pit. He asked Jake, "What type of rifle do you prefer?"

"I hadn't planned on any. I was going to take some pictures."

"In the bush it's wise to always carry a rifle. One never knows what might happen; Africa is unforgiving. What type of rifle do you use in the States for big game?"

"I use a Bolt-Action Winchester .270."

"Tomorrow I'll loan you my .375 Remington. It has action similar to your .270—just carries a bigger punch. Since I'll be backing up

Philip, I'll be using my H&H .600 double rifle. It can bring down an elephant at close range. If faced with a charging bull buffalo, it's the gun to have. We'll leave tomorrow morning at eight-thirty."

Next morning the group had breakfast and went to their vehicles. Allen would drive the four-by-four with Philip in the passenger's seat. Jake, Bruce and Rachel would ride on the benches in back. Guns, in their carrying cases, were placed on the floor next to the front seats, for easy access. Allen's assistant game ranger backed out a flatbed truck with sideboards and a robotic arm over the cab. Allen explained that the arm would be used to load the bull onto the truck. Four of Allen's ground crew got into the back of the truck. Allen led the way towards the herd, stopping only briefly for a luncheon sandwich.

They spotted the herd at around 2 p.m. After parking the vehicles, all dismounted. Allen took some loose dust and let it fall. It indicated they were downwind of the animals, who were casually grazing. In a muffled voice, he told the truck crew, "Wait here." Rifles were uncased and loaded. Allen, leading the way, cautiously eased the group to a better viewing position. At this point he gave a hand signal for Jake, Bruce and Rachel to stand still. Bruce had his Bell & Howell 16mm camera going. With guns at ready, Philip in the lead, Allen and he moved closer to the herd. Tensions increased. They saw Allen point to the herd and Philip's rifle come up. With the explosion of the gun being fired, they noticed the big bull stagger and then follow the direction taken by the herd, towards a dense grove of miombo trees with thick underbrush.

Allen signaled for Jake, Bruce and Rachel to come forward. When they joined Allen and Philip, Allen pointed to the ground and said,

"The bull's hard hit, by the amount of blood spilled. He's the most dangerous at this point. We'll wait for awhile, hoping he will die and we can track his blood trail to the carcass. He's probably in that grove up ahead. Philip and I will go forward while you stay here, clear of any immediate danger."

After a short pause, Philip led the way forward with Allen slightly behind and to his right, following the blood trail. As the two men neared the grove, Jake caught movement to their left. He yelled, "Look out!"

Sight of the angry bull clearing the grove's undergrowth, beginning its charge, frightened Philip who dropped his rifle and turned to run, knocking Allen off balance. Out of instinct, Jake in split second action brought his rifle down on the charging bull and fired. The animal's front legs gave way and the bull went down.

Allen cautiously inspected the animal to be sure it was dead and motioned Philip over to stand by the animal, big game hunter style. While Bruce was taking his photos of "Big Bwana," Allen came over to Jake and said, "Thanks. That was a great shot. For a moment that was a real sticky wicket situation."

Seeing that Bruce had finished his photo shoot, Allen went over, measured the horns and signaled the truck to come forward. With the animal loaded, all headed back to camp. It was rather a somber group. Jake thought to himself, "Okay, Philip, let's see how you twist this one."

It was dark when they arrived back to camp. They had a light dinner. Those that hadn't gone on the hunt were excitedly asking questions. Jake noticed Philip's skirting of the details, and what happened on the hunt. Jake felt he had enough of this group and determined that tomorrow he would come up with a need to return to California on business. Even Rachel seemed to be caught up in this Hollywood make-believe. It was something he hadn't been aware of. In Hollywood she was in her element of make-believe. In real life she was lacking in what it takes to meet the real trials of life. Jake retired.

Next morning Jake had a talk with Allen. Allen listened and understood. He agreed to help Jake come up with a logical excuse to leave. The story was that Jake had used Allen's shortwave radio to be patched through to a telephone connection, and then to Jake's office. Jake would tell Rachel and the others that his business demanded immediate attention, and that he must return home.

The news didn't set well with Rachel. Just to be on the safe side, he used Allen's radio to contact Zambian Airways to make reservations for a flight to Los Angeles.

Bidding goodbye to all, Jake and Allen went to Allen's Super Cub and left for Lusaka. At the airport, Jake picked up his ticket. Allen accompanied him to the waiting room.

Allen said, "I'll miss you. We hunters have to put up with all kinds of individuals. The prima donnas and braggarts chap us the most. Your quick action with the Cape buffalo proves you're one of us, a good hunter and sportsman. Come visit us whenever you can."

Jake replied, "Thanks, Allen, for your compliment. It means a lot to me. I would like to come back and visit. If you're ever stateside, come visit me."

"That I'll do."

With that the two men shook hands and Allen went to his plane. Jake watched as the yellow Super Cub lifted off the runway. He felt a sense of depression come over him.

Jake's boarding call came. He was again flying to Johannesburg in a Beechcraft 1900. This time the plane was full—eighteen passengers. He spent the short flight observing the African landscape. It looked so peaceful, with few inhabitants. He felt it'd be his last visit to the continent, but he would try to return.

His wait in Johannesburg was short. He again was flying South African Airways on a Lockheed Constellation, with a short layover in Rio and Miami. He was glad when the Constellation touched down at Los Angeles Airport. Getting his luggage and going to his parked car he headed for home, stopping only once at a car wash to get all the dust off from being parked in the Los Angeles Airport parking lot. Marie, his housekeeper, was happy to see him. She made a quick meal for him. Being bone-tired, he went to bed at 7:30 p.m.

CHAPTER 6

Rising early the next morning, he had breakfast and brought Marie up on his trip to Africa. He tried to give a clear picture of what Africa looked like, the hunting compound, Rachel, the Hollywood crew and the buffalo hunt.

She listened intently and asked, "When is Rachel returning?"

"She didn't say."

Jake was suddenly aware that he really didn't know when Rachel planned to return, and even more surprised when he realized that it didn't matter.

Since he wasn't expected back so soon, he decided to lounge around his pool for a couple of days. The water felt good and took some of his tensions away.

Going to his living room he turned on the news channel. He wanted to see how the United Nations' war effort was going in Korea. The surprise attack by an overwhelming number of North Korean army troops was pushing American and South Korean forces south towards the Pusan peninsula. President Truman ordered General Douglas MacArthur to Korea where he was selected to be Supreme Commander of all Allied forces.

Turning off the TV, Jake left for his office. The war and its possible outcome was the major topic among the sales agents in his office. Jake got with his partner, Bret, to catch up on business. Business was doing well and Jake's percentage of the net profits was substantial.

Going to his office he began canvassing old clients on the phone. After several hours of calling he had made appointments to visit two properties in Beverly Hills. The owners were looking to trade up. Jake liked the thought of maybe getting a listing and a client, the seller, looking for property.

Going home for the day, he took his mind off the war by taking a swim and settling down to read a book called *Ivanhoe*. From his movie contacts he heard that it was being made into a movie. The book captivated his adventurous spirit. He thought to himself, "This will make a great movie."

Days slipped by. He figured that Rachel surely must be back from Africa by now. When he called her home, he was informed that she was back but not available to talk right now. He had the feeling he was being avoided.

The daily news told how General MacArthur made a huge amphibious landing at Incheon. This caused the North Korean forces to rapidly retreat from Pusan to avoid being cut off. With the recapture of Seoul, the capitol of South Korea, President Truman ordered MacArthur to advance above the 38th parallel.

Things were going well until the Chinese committed several divisions of their troops to assist North Korea, trapping and surrounding a marine force at Chosin Reservoir. Commander of the surrounded marine force ordered all his troops to do a breakout. One of his marines yelled out, "Are we retreating?" The officer quipped back, "Retreat, hell! We're not retreating; we're just advancing in a different direction." That statement made headlines in the newspapers. The news also said that the draft was being reinstated.

Jake and his partner Bert threw a Special Awards Party at the El Moroccan Restaurant in Hollywood to honor the office's top salesman. Jake noticed that Rachel, Philip and some of the Hollywood group were seated on the opposite side of the room. When Jake started to get up and go speak to them, Rachel saw him and turned her back to him. Jake sat back down with his group. He and Rachel avoided each other the rest of the evening.

In early December of 1950, Jake was in his office when his secretary brought in the mail. The one from the U. S. Department of Defense caught his attention. Opening it, he read, "Your number was called. This notice is to give you time to get your personal things in order. You are to report for active duty on January 15, 1951." It went on to give the Army base to report to. Jake sat upright in his chair. Going into Bert's office, he showed him the letter. Returning to his office, Jake called a friend that he knew on the local draft board.

"Russ, Jake here. I received notice that I'm to be drafted into the Army in January. Do you know about this?"

"Hi, Jake. I was just notified of that."

"Is there anything I can do? I'd make a lousy infantryman."

"What branch of the service would interest you?"

"Air Force."

"If I were you, I'd make as though I hadn't received a draft notice and quickly enlist in the Air Force. Remember you didn't hear me say that."

"Thanks, Russ."

When he hung up, he went to the nearest Air Force recruiter and enlisted, being assured he'd go to Undergraduate Pilot Training School. He was told to report for duty at Randolph Air Force Base (AFB), outside of Austin, Texas on January 10th.

While Jake went about getting his business, house and assets in order, he learned that his partner's notice had also come, but Bert had failed his medical. Bert and Jake agreed on terms of what percentage of the business' net income would go to Jake while he served in the Air Force. He made a deal with his bank and mortgage companies to keep his debts paid; with Marie to look after his home while he was away. His gardener was to keep his property up as usual and he would be paid by Jake's bank. With all arrangements made, he tried to relax around the pool. He tried to reach Rachel to tell her he was entering the Air Force, but was told she was at the studios or not available.

CHAPTER 7

Jake, along with several other recruits, caught a train to San Antonio. Their train was met by an Air Force private, who was driving a blue bus. The weather was bitterly cold. All hastened to get into the warm bus. Driven to the base, they were escorted to a building where they were met by a major.

"Welcome to Randolph. I'm Major Knight. You are now a part of the Operations Support Squadron (OSS). Tomorrow you will begin phase one of your training. This is made up of academic classes and pre-flight training. Each of your days will begin at 6 a.m. and end at 6 p.m. Expect to be studying and preparing for class at night. Don't forget to factor in class events such as class meetings, social events and group study sessions.

Your academic studies encompass aircraft systems, flight regulations, instrument flying, aerospace physiology, navigation, flight planning and aviation weather. Expect to know these topics thoroughly prior to finishing phase one. Phase two is flight line training which will be intense. Good luck on your training. You're now entering your undergraduate pilot training."

Pointing to a sergeant he continued, "Sergeant Boykin will show you to your dorm. You're dismissed." Jake's experience with the Air Force had begun. On the way to their dorm, Jake could hear some grumbling. He had the feeling that he would be glad that he took ROTC training, and held a private pilot's license.

Next morning, as promised, the training began. From ground school classes he had to get his private pilot license. He aced the classes on flight planning, navigation and weather. He also learned that undergraduate pilot training was a team effort. He helped his teammates with their nightly studies. They in turn helped him on aircraft systems and flight regulations. At the end of phase one only two percent of the class failed. Jake and the rest were passed on to phase two—flight line.

Each morning began with a briefing by a flight commander. He would go over weather topics, student trends, landing pattern tendencies, general knowledge questions and emergency procedures. On emergency procedures the flight commander would state the emergency scenario and have a student stand up at attention and recite what they would do in such a situation.

Following the briefing, Jake's fellow flight students executed the flight schedule. Jake first had flight simulator training. From his private pilot training, he had no problems with normal flying, but took some concentration when the instructor controlling the simulator induced a stall and spin maneuver, or an engine failure. These tests required instant action.

For flight training, Jake flew in a T-6 Texan trainer with a check pilot, pulling Gs and doing aerobatic maneuvers. He would receive instructions to pull up the nose and hold it there until the plane stalled and went into a spin. This required that Jake push the stick forward to gain airspeed and to use his rudder to oppose the spin.

Weeks and months went by. Those in his class became good friends, giving encouragement to each other. Phase two ended and phase three began. Students could state their preference to the type of aircraft that interested them. Jake put in for fighter/bomber.

Finishing their schooling, they were presented with their wings and given their second lieutenant bars. They were now proud American Air Force officers. Jake was disappointed to learn that he would be sent to Enid AFB in Oklahoma for multi-engine flight training. Even though Oklahoma was his native state, he had hoped to be a fighter pilot. He quickly earned his multi-engine rating.

Orders arrived notifying him that he was assigned to the 581st Air Resupply Wing at Mountain Home AFB in Idaho, but to report to Pensacola Naval Air Station to be trained on flying an SA-16 Grumman Albatross amphibian-type aircraft. He was told he'd be aircraft commander and would be met there by his fellow crew members.

Jake thought, "What in the hell have I got myself in for?"

Jake caught Military Air Transport Service (MATS) flight to Pensacola. He was introduced to his crew members: co-pilot Second Lieutenant John Jenkins, navigator Captain Doug Piper, radio operator Corporal Jack Bennett and flight engineer Technical Sergeant George Judkins.

Next morning Jake's crew was met at Base Operations by their Navy check pilot, Ensign Bill Cody who was nicknamed "Wild Bill."

Going to the plane parked on the tarmac, Bill took the group on a walk-around, telling Jake and his crew the features of the plane. Entering the plane, the crew was pointed out the internal features of the plane. With the flight engineer and radio operator seated in back, Jake took the command pilot seat, as instructed, while the check pilot took the co-pilot's seat.

Jake's co-pilot, John Jenkins, sat in the radio operator's seat, which was located behind the co-pilot's seat. The check pilot explained the plane's various instruments, switches and levers. To demonstrate proper procedures, the check pilot gave Jake a plastic-covered step-by-step procedures form, asking that he read each individual step out loud. As Jake read each step, the check pilot would do what was read. When finished, he'd call out "Check."

Finishing the list the checkout pilot started the two Wright Cyclone engines. Clearing with the tower, the overhead throttle controls were eased forward and the plane taxied to a concrete ramp and out into the bay. When the plane began to float, the check pilot moved the gear position lever to the up position. When the indicator showed the gears were up and locked, the check pilot selected part flaps and applied full power to the engines. He used the yoke to gradually get the plane, like a salmon swimming upstream, up on the wave crest and then airborne. Putting up flaps, he reached up to adjust the propeller pitch. Circling, he showed how to prepare and do a water landing; how to flare out at the proper time. He then turned the plane over to Jake to do touch-and-go water landings. Then, it became John's time to practice.

After a few weeks Jake and his crew were declared proficient and were released to fly #1017 to its new base in Idaho. On the flight,

Doug proved to be a good navigator. The crew touched down at their new base at 5 p.m. They were driven to their quarters and then to chow. Next morning all air crews were instructed to assemble in a hangar.

The assembled group was called to attention and Wing Commander Colonel James Armstrong addressed them.

He said, "At ease, gentlemen. You are now members of the newly created 581st Air Resupply Squadron. Our mission is psychological warfare, the infiltration and resupply of guerrilla-type personnel, and the aerial delivery of PSYWAR material—leaflets and similar material. To effectively do this, all crews must train for low-level flight, to get in under enemy radar. By low-level, I mean a fifty-foot altitude."

An audible gasp was heard from the group.

Colonel Armstrong continued, "I know this will be especially difficult for you B-29 crews. For this reason we have made your planes lighter and more maneuverable by removing all armament, the exception being the tail guns. Our wing consists of twelve B-29s, four C-119s and four SA-16 amphibians. Training will begin tomorrow. All pilots, co-pilots and navigators will report daily at Base Operations for flight scheduling and mission assignments. Gentlemen, you're dismissed."

Jake and his crew spent the next several weeks on low-level flights and navigation training. Low-level flying for Jake was fun but tiring. Flying at 124 MPH a plane weighing over 12,500 pounds required the pilot to concentrate fully on the terrain ahead, looking for any obstructions. The difficulty in seeing highline power transmission wires made these flights especially dangerous and nerve-wracking.

On one low-level flight, Jake called his navigator on the intercom and asked, "Doug, where are we?"

The response was, "Hell, I don't know. Read the road sign."

Jake glanced to his right. He was near a highway. A road sign said, "220 miles to Reno." All the crew, being on intercom, got a good laugh.

For the navigator to pass his requirements, he had to do cross-country navigation and be able to reach his target point within a five-minute span of time. He also had to be able to use Loran radar, and be able to do celestial navigation. Jake learned that Doug was exceptionally accurate in his navigation abilities. He also learned that John, his co-pilot, Jack, his radio operator, and George, his flight engineer, did their duties well.

To get in some water landing practice, Jake and his crew were ordered to Puget Sound in Washington for a full day of practice. Jake and John had to keep a close lookout for floating logs. When not flying, Jake and his crew, along with some other crews, attended lectures.

The lectures were about escape and evasion used by some in WWII, and low-level flight. A couple of escape and evasion stories were told that Jake enjoyed. One was about a pilot shot down deep inside Germany. The pilot, figuring he couldn't make it back to Allied forces, set up a tobacco shop in Germany. He played the part of a deaf and dumb mute. He was doing a thriving business by the time Allied forces captured the town. He ran out and said to the troops, "Thank God you finally made it!"

Another escape story was about a pilot shot down over Germany. With stolen clothes and papers, he was working his way back to his lines by using the railway. While in France, waiting on a train, he noticed two German soldiers studying him. As the soldiers started towards him, he turned to a nearby woman and said, "I'm an American. Will you help me?" It turned out that she was a member of the French underground, and she got him out.

The low-level flight story was told by a major. During World War II he was a pilot on a British Mesquite fighter-bomber. He explained that his radar man's seat was next to his. He said that in England when one flies low-level, he has to keep a sharp lookout for the many highline wires that cross the country. From those attending his lecture, one asked, "How were you able to see them?"

He replied, "I didn't. When I heard my radar man gasp, I immediately pulled back on the yoke and zoomed over." That got a chuckle from all in attendance.

Several weekends Jake would attend USO dances and activities in Boise, or go bowling or to a movie. It was good getting off base and relaxing. Weeks passed quickly.

Jake got his final check ride. His checkout pilot had Jake cover his eyes. The checkout pilot put the plane in several ups and downs and hard banks in differing directions, then told Jake, "It's all yours!"

Jake quickly uncovered his eyes and got the plane under control, flying on a straight and level course. The final test for Jake's crew was a night flight to San Francisco, then to the Farallon Islands, back to San Francisco and then return to base at Mountain Home, Idaho. Without a moon to give light the ocean at night becomes very dark. Thanks to his navigator, Doug, finding the islands posed no problem. On the way back towards San Francisco, Jake asked his radio operator to tune in to a San Francisco radio station. Jake planned to home-in on the radio station with his radio beacon direction finder. He would never forget that moment. The song that was playing was "Harbor Lights" by Sammy Kaye. Suddenly out of the vast expanse of the black ocean the harbor lights of San Francisco appeared on the horizon.

In late June the Wing was assembled. They were told that those wanting a two-week furlough would be given one; that the Wing was moving overseas. Jake took his leave to go home and see how things were going.

Marie was glad to see him. He was wearing his dress blues, his well-earned wings and his shiny silver bars on each shoulder. He was also well-greeted at the office. He tried calling Rachel at home and at the studio. He was always told that she wasn't available. Part of his leave was taken up by lounging by his pool and a couple of days' stay on Catalina Island at the Catalina Hotel. He took in a dance at the huge Catalina Ballroom, meeting an attractive blonde from San Diego. All too quickly his furlough was over and he returned to the base.

With all aircrews back on base, Colonel Armstrong got the group together, informing them that the base was in lockdown. No calls in or out were permitted. He then said the Wing was being deployed to Clark Field, on Luzon Island in the Philippines, a surprise to all. The grapevine had said it'd be Korea, another said Europe; still another had said the Middle East.

CHAPTER 8

B-29 and C-119 squadrons would fly the direct route, refueling in Hawaii. Jake's squadron would fly the Great Northern route, refueling in Great Falls, Montana; Fort Nelson, British Columbia; Anchorage, Alaska; Shemya in the Aleutian Islands; Tokyo, Japan and then to Clark Field in the Philippines.

On the day of departure all the crews stood in front of their planes. Colonel Armstrong went down the line taking a photograph of each crew standing next to its respective plane. That completed, all planes took their turn lining up on the runway and taking off. Jake had one passenger, a master sergeant who was head of maintenance for the Wing's aircrafts. Jake also realized his plane was carrying a load of tools in the hull of his plane. With a full load of fuel it made him close to the maximum allowable takeoff weight for his plane.

In Great Falls all planes in Jake's squadron refueled and left for Fort Nelson. The terrain below was mountainous with many lakes. Approaching Fort Nelson, he heard that one of the planes in his squadron had landed. In the river nearby he saw several float planes. He also noticed that at the far end of Fort Nelson's runway was a small ravine. Beginning his landing approach, he was notified by John that the facility had only a 5,000-foot runway. He nodded.

Dropping the plane's landing gears, he called on John for flaps down. Closing in on the runway, Jake noticed a small crosswind and crabbed the plane to just before touch down. The landing went well and on roll-out was directed by the tower to a parking area.

All disembarked the plane and went into the terminal. A refueling truck appeared and began the refueling process. Jake's group joined the first crew that had landed. In the terminal they awaited the rest of their squadron.

my plane. Flown by Wing Commander Col. Arnold. He scared the day lights out of us.

It was a short wait. They could see another squadron plane approaching. It was the plane with Colonel Armstrong. The plane was too high, hit the runway hard and bounced. Full throttle was applied as the plane quivered close to stalling. Gaining flying speed, the plane circled for another attempt. This time the landing was a good one.

When their crew entered, Jake overheard that the first approach was made by Colonel Armstrong. In the distance all saw the approach of the last plane in their squadron.

A British corporal, upon spotting the approaching plane, called to one of his buddies, "Hey! Here's another one of those planes. Let's see what this crazy S.O.B. is going to do." Colonel Armstrong, standing nearby, just smiled. *True story.*

All crews went to the small terminal restaurant to get some lunch. A matronly Scottish waitress asked, "'Ought would ye laddies have?" It caused Jake to smile. After finishing his meal of cheeseburger and fries, he went to pay his bill. The same waitress looked at his bill and said, "Laddy, ye bill comes to a shilling twenty pence."

Jake, not knowing how much that was, held out his hand with several U.S. dollars and with a grin said, "Take what you need."

Jake was second in line for takeoff. He did a quick run up of his engines and checked his instruments. Satisfied, he taxied to the end of the runway and lined up for takeoff. Concerned about the short runway, he used partial flaps and held the plane's brakes until his engine's RPM reached maximum. He then released the brakes. He needed seventy-four knots for takeoff. With the end of the runway closing rapidly, he eased back the yoke, calling for John to do gears up. On the verge of stalling, he lowered his plane's nose and took advantage of the small ravine to gain airspeed.

On the way to Anchorage, Doug came forward to the cockpit. He indicated on his map a pass they were to fly through. He told Jake that the most recent weather report indicated icing conditions in that area, and asked if he wished to go around the pass. Jake agreed even though it would delay their arrival in Anchorage.

Jake's was the last plane in their squadron to arrive. He and his crew were taken to the mess hall for chow, and then to their assigned sleeping quarters. Next morning after chow, Jake and his crew went to their plane. Jake checked with ground support to be sure that his wing, float and drop tanks were full and topped off. The flight to Shemya was 2,800 miles over water. On takeoff, he made a mental note of the tall mountain about a mile in front. He thought, "I'd sure as hell not try landing here during a bad snowstorm."

Jake's crew was supplied with box lunches before they left the base in Anchorage. In route to Shemya, he learned that his plane's heating system had failed. The cockpit was comfortable due to the heat generated by the plane's tube-operated radio equipment. He took a quick look at his passengers in back. All had donned their heavy winter overcoats and we wrapped in some wool blankets that were in the plane. The ham and cheese sandwiches were no problem, but the can of beans were to be heated. Glancing back, he saw his radio operator enjoying a can of warm beans. When questioned, he said, "I heated it up on top of my transmitter." Jake and John handed the radio operator their cans to be heated.

Other than the heating problem, the rest of the trip to Shemya was uneventful. Upon landing, all crews were picked up and taken inside. Even though it was mid-July the weather was cold. Enclosed hallways connected the buildings. When a crew member commented on this, their guide informed him that in winter snow covered these passageways. Jake thought, "Now I know what a mole must feel like."

Before takeoff next morning, Jake saw there was a thin coating of ice on the plane. While running up his engines he turned on the de-icer boots, and checked his control surfaces. Feeling the plane was safe to fly and knowing they were headed for warmer weather, he took off for Tokyo.

Tokyo was an overnight stop. Coming in to Tokyo, he could see remnants of WWII. Near the docks were bombed-out building shells. He got a surprise in the mess hall. Cute Japanese girls waited on the tables, taking orders from a written menu and bringing food.

Leaving early the next day, Jake was glad they were on their final leg to Clark Field. Jake was informed by his squadron commander that Colonel Armstrong would be the first to land at Clark Field. This ruffled Jake's feathers. To him, his commander was brown-nosing. Approaching Luzon Island, Jake called Doug forward.

"Doug, is there a shorter route we can fly and be first in? I'm tired of being told that the colonel is to be first."

Doug scanned his charts and said, pointing to his aerial map, "Yes, if we make a turn at this point and head direct for the base. You realize though that once we send in our hourly position report the other planes will realize what we're doing, and the race will be on."

Jake waited until his radio operator sent their position report, then changed to the more direct approach to Clark Field, knowing the other planes would not realize what he was doing for another hour. That hour-long lead made it possible to be the first of his squadron to land at their new base. He was given a strong lecture about that, but it was worth it. He never had much respect for those that brown- nose.

Bachelor Officers' Quarters at Clark Field were great. Century-old Mimosa trees and a few palm trees dotted the area and lined the streets. The country club and eighteen-hole golf course was nearby. Clark Field was a city within itself. It had a modern theater, a USO club called "Silver Wing," library, gym, base PX, bowling alley, skeet range, several food places run by Filipinos, Base Operations and Base Headquarters. Charlie Corn's food place became Jake's favorite place to have a piece of pie and iced tea.

He got his first introduction to life in the Philippines. Outside the base was a town called Angeles. Those going into Angeles were told to wear civilian clothing. Base transportation to the main gate was by what appeared to be a cattle truck. A diesel truck pulled a trailer with open window areas. Bench seating ran the length of the trailer on both sides. It picked up base personnel and drove them to the main base gate. It then let off its passengers and returned for the next trip.

Those going off base to Angeles caught a jeepney to Angeles. These converted WWII jeeps became minibuses, hauling up to thirteen passengers. There were always a dozen or more hawking for passengers going to Angeles. The price of the ride was ten centavos.

Entering town, both sides of the dirt street was lined with many bars and shops that sold beautifully carved 3D wooden coffee tables depicting Philippine life and other items and souvenirs. There were also restaurants that had American names, gas stations and a theater.

What amazed Jake was the absence of any streetlights. Jeepneys, old and new American cars, red-painted Filipino commercial buses, called Philippine Rabbits, and kalesas, Filipino horse-drawn carriages, worked their way through pedestrians. Horns reigned supreme. People crossed back and forth on the street. Horns were honked by driven vehicles working their way through the mass of milling people. Jake wondered to himself just how many, if any, were killed daily.

Taking in the sights he soon learned that the best places to hang out in town were the Esquire and High Hat Clubs. In these clubs he could get drinks. His favorite was a malt-liquor beer called San Miguel. He could also have the company of a cute Filipina hostess and enjoy American music played on a jukebox. He liked these clubs because no prostitutes and their solicitations were allowed.

Of the two clubs, he preferred the Esquire. It had a large enclosed area that had a concrete dance floor lit at night by colored Christmas tree lights. Music from a jukebox was piped into the area. Around the dance floor were several tables. Park-type wooden benches were placed farther back under arches covered by colorful green flowering vines.

These benches had small coffee tables and two wooden chairs in front of them. His favorite hostess was Eve. She was interesting to talk to. Like many Filipinos, she was interested in hearing about America. Jake had read a book that stated, "If you want to be considered a great conversationalist, learn to ask intelligent questions to those that you meet." Eve did that well and Jake enjoyed her company. When he needed a new drink she would get it for him. On other occasions she would bring out her guitar and play and sing American songs. Or, they would dance on the concrete dance floor. It made for a relaxing evening.

Along the outside concrete block wall, facing the street, was a row of several hibiscus plants of differing color. At night the air was cool and refreshing.

The High Hat Club was an old two-story mansion that had been converted into a club. It sat back from the street. Evenings he would sit at a table on the upper veranda and visit with Marina, or dance with her to some of the tunes played on a jukebox.

Jake became aware Filipinos were very curious about America, its customs, its lifestyle and places to see. That was fine with him; he was just as curious about the Philippines and their customs.

One night while visiting with Marina, he heard an approaching siren and the building began to shake. An American Sherman tank, given to the Philippine Army, went roaring by. When he asked Marina about this, she said they were trying to cut off the military arm of the communist party, guerilla fighters known as Huks.

One day in town he noticed that the book *Ivanhoe* had been made into a movie and was now showing at the local theater. He bought a ticket and enjoyed the movie. Going outside he noticed a crowd around a man that he later learned was Magsaysay, later to become President of the Philippines. Jake enjoyed the Philippine people. They were happy-go-lucky, fun-loving and artistically talented.

When not scheduled for a mission, Jake played golf. One day he saw a fast-approaching jeep. He was told to give his clubs to his caddy; that he and his crew were assigned a top secret mission. The driver said he knew nothing about the mission, only that it was top secret and he was sent to get Jake; and that the rest of the crew were at Base Operations.

At Base Operations he learned what the top secret was all about. His crew would be delivering four hundred pounds of ice to the base General, who was aboard the President of the Philippine's yacht, off of the island of Palawan.

Considering the type of mission, Jake filed a flight training mission to do water landings at Sangley Point in Manila Bay. When he entered his plane, he saw that his flight engineer had the four hundred pounds of ice secured to the floor in the plane's passenger compartment.

He informed his radio operator what was to be put in his radio log upon departure. Doug's navigation was accurate and Jake sat the plane down next to the yacht. He, his co-pilot and navigator were invited aboard the yacht for a cocktail, while Filipinos in a six-man raft ferried the ice over to the yacht. That done, Jake and his fellow officers were returned to their plane—mission accomplished.

Jake learned there would be several secret missions that he would be sent on. He would be sent to Hong Kong on "training missions." It really boiled down high-ranking base officers going on shopping sprees in Hong Kong, buying bicycles for their kids, jewelry, tailor-made clothes or a new Jaguar for family back home.

On one such mission Jake purchased a beautiful blue star sapphire ring. On another he purchased a tailor-made baby blue cashmere sport jacket from Mohan's. When he went into Mohan's, he was waited on by an attractive Chinese girl. She was wearing the typical Chinese form-fitting dress with high neck and skirt with splits to the knee. Jake expected to hear a regular sort of Chinese sing-song way of speech. She spoke in perfect British brogue. It caused Jake to smile.

On another trip he purchased a tailored gray flannel suit at Mohan's and shoes from Lee Kee Boot and Shoe Company. Each trip called for a night's stay at a five-star hotel on Kawloon.

Kawloon had more of a British feel about it. Their nightclubs had good food and great bands. In one he found the music was similar to that of Mantovani, with lots of stringed instruments. Mantovani was one of Jake's favorite orchestras. The music was soothing.

On what turned out to be his last trip to Hong Kong, he had engine runaway trouble. While running up the engine, to get ready for takeoff, the propellers at normal RPM began to run away, spinning too fast. His flight engineer checked out the engines and found they would hold at a lower RPM setting, and gave the go-ahead to return to base.

This and crossing bars, to keep traffic from crossing the runway while a plane is on takeoff, troubled Jake. He couldn't get his mind off how many cars, stateside, tried to beat the crossing bars before oncoming trains.

Just as Jake was getting used to this laid-back lifestyle, with frequent trips to Subic Bay for water landing practice, his plane and one other were given black coats of paint. They were then ordered to K-16 AFB outside Seoul, Korea.

CHAPTER 9

What a change. Crews were housed in four-man tents. The tents had wood floors and wood half walls. In the center of the tent were oil drum heaters. They were assigned "houseboys" to clean and do repairs on the tents. Jake's crew had a houseboy named Honcho. He was good but the only English he could say was, "Me fix." No matter what was conveyed by sign language when he realized what was wanted, he would say, "Me fix."

Both black SA-16s were parked near the crew's tent. At night sentries were selected to pull guard duty, to keep anyone from pilfering the planes. It was now winter and bitterly cold in Korea. Guards would make one round of their post and return to their tent to warm up, and then do another turn.

Jake was called in for a briefing. He was told he had a passenger to deliver, and none of his crew was allowed to talk to that person. The target site was indicated to Jake and Doug. They were to fly up the northern coast of North Korea, land offshore at the selected point, taxi to the beach, drop landing gear, roll up on the beach and turn around; then let their passenger off. Jake soon realized he was taking agents into or out of North Korea. It troubled him to think of what might happen if the enemy ever caught him and his crew. Later he was told that the Chinese had a dossier out on all crew members of the 581st.

On one occasion, when taking a "passenger" to Yo Do Island, they were tying up to a buoy. Their passenger had just reached his destination—a Navy destroyer—when an enemy battery on the mainland opened fire, trying to locate Jake's plane. The shell fell short and Jake was ordered by the destroyer to leave his passenger and go.

He was faced with swells almost eight feet high. Pouring full power to his plane, he raced down the trough of a swell, gradually getting up on the crest and airborne. Climbing for altitude and circling, he saw the two Navy destroyers, who had steamed around the island, open up a full barrage on the located shore batteries.

The two crews in Jake's squadron were only armed with Colt .45 automatics. He convinced his higher command that they should have at least a couple of M-1 carbines onboard for protection when unloading or picking up passengers on the beach.

He was issued the carbines with banana clips taped back-to-back. This proved to be a wise move. On one trip up the coast to pick up a passenger, they had just made the pick-up and returned to the water when enemy soldiers appeared and began firing at Jake's plane. Jake's enlisted personnel returned the fire while he was taking off. Bullets could be heard hitting the plane.

On one trip up the eastern coast, Jake heard a British pilot say on VHF, "Heads up, chaps! There are twelve bandits at two o'clock high. Would four of you chaps take care of that?"

This was amazing to Jake. Four against twelve. Days later at Base Operations he got the chance to talk to a British pilot and relate what he heard. The British pilot's response was, "Yes, old chap! That's the only way to fight. Anything that comes in front of your gun sights must be an enemy, and you shoot it down."

The rest of his tour in Korea was uneventful, the exception being ducking into cloud coverage to hide from a flight of MIG-15s.

During his brief tour in Korea, he went off base only once to a small town outside the base. Anyone leaving the base for that town was required to be armed, due to its closeness to the battle lines. At night flashes from big artillery guns, like lighting, could be seen to the north. Jake carried his .45 automatic in a shoulder holster under his flight jacket. Each time he entered a shop a sign said, "Remove clips from weapon." Each time he did that it reminded him of old gangster movies. Outside the shops he was always crowded by young shoeshine boys vying to shine his boots. When he zipped down his jacket and pulled his .45 to reinsert the clip, the young boys stepped back.

Jake and the command pilot of the other plane received orders to leave their planes at K-16 for rotating crews. A C-124 would pick up the two flight crews and their ground maintenance personnel, with all their tools and equipment.

The C-124 Globemaster was the Air Force's newest cargo plane. It was huge. The plane's cockpit was about two stories above ground. Its arrival at K-16 drew lots of attention. With all on board and buckled down, the pilot, proud of his plane, came in on his plane's intercom.

"For you pilots on board I thought you might like to hear our pre-flight checkout procedures."

With that he went through them. Upon completion of checkout, power was applied to the plane's four engines. He taxied the plane to the end of the runway. The pilot lined up with the runway, held the plane's brakes and applied full power to his engines. When they reached maximum RPM the pilot commenced his takeoff roll.

Jake, looking out a plane window, noticed the plane seemed to be moving slowly. They were now passing the first quarter of the runway. As the tower halfway down the runway was passed, the plane still was moving slowly. As Jake saw their old quarters coming into view three-fourths of the way down the runway the pilot who had forgotten to turn off the plane's intercom stated, "My God! I've misjudged the weight."

Jake and the rest of those sitting in the cargo compartment went pale. At the last moment the C-124 pilot bounced the plane and snapped up its landing gears. The plane barely cleared the base perimeter fence. Jake wondered what would happen when the plane was confronted with the two tall smokestacks that he knew it was approaching. Again at the last moment, the C-124 pilot did a steep left bank of his plane, flying between the smokestacks.

Jake's assessment of the plane was to never to fly on a C-124 again. The plane was so overloaded that instead of a nonstop flight to the Philippines it had to stop for refueling in Okinawa. When power was reduced on the plane's engines it dropped like an elevator. The runways on Okinawa were long, thank goodness. The plane was quickly refueled and left for Clark Field. The only good thing about the C-124 was its bailout procedures. If bailout became necessary, a square section of the plane's belly was jettisoned. Those bailing out would run, jump and grab the firemen's pole over the opening. When the person slid down and ran out of pole, it was time to open his parachute.

Arriving at Clark Field safely and stepping out on the tarmac, Jake was greeted by warm tropical air. What a relief from all the cold he had been through in Korea. The returning crews were driven to their quarters to rest for the remainder of the day. It was good being back.

Routine "training" began again, the one exception being the day the two aircrews that had been in Korea were honored by receiving Air Medals and Korean campaign ribbons with one battle star. They were also offered a short R&R.

Talking to some base officers, Jake was told that the prettiest island in the Philippines was Palawan. Their descriptions caused Jake to go see for himself. All had recommended the Kawsaysay Resort. Making his reservation, he caught the short flight to Palawan aboard Philippine Air Line (PAL).

Landing at Puerto Princesa City Airport, he caught a jeepney taxi to take him to the resort. Going through Puerto Princesa he noticed it was a thriving business city. It was like a small town in America, with several two-story buildings with similarities that reminded him of Angeles, the town outside Clark Field.

On the fringe of Rizal Street, the commercial main street, were several shops selling a variety of goods. In the center of the business district were two-story businesses that sold goods and services like in America. Again, the streets were crowded. At least here the streets are paved and pedestrians walked on sidewalks.

Arriving at the resort, he entered the compound through a main gate. It was like stepping into paradise. His eyes took in a jungle-like setting with beautiful landscaping, with wooden bamboo and cabins with thatched roofs, fountains, several cabanas that served as conversation places, small covered rustic rest areas with attached stools where refreshments could be enjoyed, and a huge outdoor swimming pool. He immediately loved the place. With its bamboo eight-foot-high walled-in compound to keep noise out and privacy in, he was very pleased.

Registering at the front desk and boutique, he received a key to his cabin. The inside was a rustic bamboo with a woven thatch motif. The bath had a shower that had hot water, a luxury item in Philippine hotels and resorts. The pool that he saw looked so inviting that he put on his swimsuit, terrycloth robe and wedgies, and with a towel went to the pool. The pool wasn't crowded. There were older and younger Filipino couples, and three young girls about Jake's age.

Jake struck up a conversation with those in the pool. They exchanged information about themselves. The one that drew Jake's attention the most was Mari de Escat. He learned that she was Spanish and her father was a financier in Manila. He also learned that she attended college at UCLA in Southern California. The two girls with her were from Venezuela, daughters of a wealthy oilman, and also attended UCLA. It was fun talking to the girls, recalling favorite places in Southern California. The older Filipino couple, Michael and Rosa Santoses, was from the island of Panay. He was captain of a cargo sloop, delivering supplies between the many islands.

Next day, while relaxing in one of the cabanas, he saw Mari and her two friends coming down the pathway. When they reached his cabana he smiled and asked, "Care to join me in some refreshments?"

The girls smiled and replied, "Sure."

Once they were seated, Jake ordered what they wanted—three cokes. Jake was drinking iced tea.

Striking up a conversation, Jake said, "If you don't mind my asking, what caused you to choose going to college at UCLA and not USC, or the University of the Philippines?"

In unison, they replied, "Our fathers." Continuing, Mari said, "Our fathers liked what they saw in the information packet sent by UCLA. It has a nice-looking campus and is located in what they considered a good neighborhood. My friends, Rebecca and Marian, share the same classes as me. Due to our fathers' wishes, we're all business majors."

"Do you always go by your father's wishes? Do you enjoy taking business courses?"

Mari, as a spokesman for Rebecca and Marian, replied, "We find the courses interesting and realize that our parents want us to know these things in hopes that one day we'll play a major role in running the family businesses. I take some classes in acting and drama for personal pleasure. Rebecca and Marian take some classes in ballet and music for pleasure. If I may ask, what brings you to Palawan?"

"Rest and relaxation. As I said yesterday, I'm an Air Force pilot on leave. Palawan was recommended by several base officers, especially Kawsaysay Resort."

"What type of plane do you fly?"

"An amphibian." Changing the subject, Mari asked, "You've said you live in the Hollywood area. Is California your native state?"

"No. I'm a native of Oklahoma."

Jake was bombarded with questions about Oklahoma. They asked if Indians were still hostile there. Jake laughed and told them that the

Osage tribes in Oklahoma were oilmen, owning oil fields and expensive cars. They were shocked, yet pleased. Time sped by as he tried to answer their questions. Rebecca finally interrupted the conversation, reminding the other two that they were to meet a person in Puerto Princesa. The girls left.

It had been an enjoyable and pleasant afternoon visiting with them in the cabana. It being rather warm, he decided to go for a cool swim in the resort pool. He got ready and went to the pool to relax and get some sun. He was joined by several couples. One couple was from India.

He had read many things about India and was interested in knowing what it was really like. He told them of the stories he had read about man-eating tigers. They confirmed they we true; that one of their grandfathers had been on one of the hunts with Jim Corbett. Jake hoped that Michael and Rosa would show up, but they didn't. He finally went back to his cabin, got dressed and went into town for dinner.

Next day he went for a stroll in the beautifully landscaped compound. Walking about, he admired the way the landscaper brought in the natural beauty of broad leafy plants, ferns, live bamboo groupings, colorful flowering vines, natural-looking waterfalls, stone paths and planters. It was like taking a stroll through a jungle. This combined with cabins and cabanas that used bamboo and thatch construction put a peaceful spell over Jake.

He noticed that Michael and Rosa were relaxing in a cabana.

Stopping, he said, "Hi."

They replied, "Hi. Won't you join us?"

Jake replied, "Thank you," and joined them.

It being a rather warm day, he asked, "May I order some iced tea for us?"

They agreed.

While waiting for the iced tea, Jake asked Michael, "At the pool you mentioned you're the captain of a cargo sloop. I don't know much about boats. How does a cargo sloop differ from a regular sloop?"

"Basically, they're just larger. On *Rosa*, my cargo sloop crew consists of myself, a mate and two deck hands."

"You mentioned you carried cargo between the islands on your sloop. Why not use a schooner?"

"Schooners have a deeper draft and can only be used on the larger islands that have deep harbors, and they are expensive. A sloop has a lesser draft and can clear the reefs on the smaller islands. A few own schooners but others do the same as I, own sloops. There's a lot more needed."

"Would you tell me more about what you do? How many islands do you take cargo to and what do they want?"

"There are thousands of islands scattered among the Philippines, Borneo and New Guinea. Many are populated. They need food supplies, grain, vegetable seeds, livestock and passage to other islands. I try to fill their needs.

"On islands too shallow even for sloops, the people use Philippine Banca boats to get to an island with a better harbor to get their supplies. We use the barter system. They pay for their goods with raw materials, such as tropical fruits, bamboo, lumber; sometimes precious metals or pearls. We receive a profit on delivering their needed goods, and a profit on their raw materials that we take back to market for them."

"How many boats do you have?"

"Just *Rosa*."

"Why not more?"

"Money. Sloops are expensive; schooners are even more expensive and crew size depends on the rigging. A schooner gaff-rigged can be crewed by five to eight."

"You mentioned Bancas. What's a Banca?"

"They're small canoe-type boats with outriggers and small sails for short open water travel."

"That sounds interesting."

Michael asked, "You said you were a pilot of an amphibian. Are you permitted to talk about your plane?"

"About the plane—yes. About what it's used for—no."

"I would like to know about the plane."

Jake went through how the plane could lower its landing gear for landing on dirt or concrete runways, or with gear up land on water. When he mentioned that after landing in the water he could lower the plane's gear and taxi up on the beach, he was interrupted by Michael.

"Your plane can do that?"

"Yes."

"A plane like that would be very useful here."

"In what way?"

"With a plane like that one could offer delivering needed supplies to smaller islands with poor harbors, passenger service to other islands and emergency medical transport, delivering small critical parts and supplies to the many oil rigs in our area. It could be a good business."

Taking a few swigs of his iced tea, Jake considered what Michael had said, and then replied, "I see your point."

Michael pressed his point, "Have you ever considered living in the Philippines?"

Again Jake thought about that question. He considered the type of life he'd return to in the States. His thoughts turned to all that traffic. Everybody seemed to be in one big hurry, how he cherished privacy from the mass of people, the many modern conveniences, his movie clients and the money he was making. Could he give up all that?

He then considered the traffic he has witnessed in the Philippines and the Filipinos with whom he had come in contact. The larger cities had traffic problems, probably worse that in the States. Filipinos, he found, were friendlier and good-natured in general. He realized that any place had its problems. It was the beauty of the tropics that captivated him. Once away from the city, it was relaxing and peaceful.

Jake's replied, "I don't know about living here. I do enjoy the tropics and the people, but there are many beautiful places in the States."

Michael said, "I can understand. Have you considered having a place in the States and in the Philippines?"

Jake realized he hadn't given that any thought. He replied, "I'll have to think about it." Glancing at his watch, he said, "It's been nice talking to you two. I think I'll get in a swim before dinner. I have to return to my base in the morning."

Michael said, "We'll miss your company. Keep in mind what we discussed."

With a smile, Jake said, "Will do."

Walking back to his cabin, he did think about it. Changing to his bathing suit, he went to the pool. The afternoon sun was pleasantly warm. Mari and her two friends were relaxed on chaise-lounge poolside chairs, sunning. He spoke to them and dived into the pool. The water was cool and refreshing. After a few laps, he joined the girls in an adjacent chaise lounge.

Striking up a conversation, he asked, "When do you leave for college?"

Mari, who seemed to dominate the other girls, said, "We leave about this time next month."

"I return back to my base tomorrow. Maybe I'll get a chance to visit with you and your friends before you leave for UCLA?"

"That would be nice. I'll leave a number at the desk where we can be reached in Manila." Continuing, Mari asked, "What will you do when you return to your base?"

"Training flights to Subic Bay and Sangley Point, in Manila Bay, to practice water landings and takeoff, some golf on base and USO entertainment."

"We found a nice restaurant in town. The food is good and they have a small five-piece band. Care to join us?"

"Thank you. I'd love to go along. Where shall we meet?"

"How about the front desk at six?"

"Sounds good. See you then."

With that Jake left and returned to his cabin for a short rest.

Shortly before meeting the girls he got dressed, putting on a white shirt and navy blue tie, his blue cashmere sport jacket, grey pants, black shoes and socks. Checking himself out in the mirror, he was satisfied.

Meeting the girls, who looked great in their cocktail dresses, they caught a taxi to town. The girls directed the driver to the Blue Dahlia. Jake took care of the taxi fare. Going inside the restaurant, they were escorted to a table near the dance floor, and their order was taken. Jake liked the atmosphere. Indirect lighting, lots of bamboo decorations for the tropical feeling, tables covered in white tablecloths with lit candles in the center gave off an intimate, romantic atmosphere.

During dinner, the foursome carried on a casual conversation. They asked Jake several questions about his home in Beverly Hills, Hollywood actors and actresses he had met and what they were like. In turn, Jake asked about their life in the Philippines and Venezuela. He learned that Mari's home was in a guarded subdivision in Manila; that they had maids, housekeepers and a cook and that a landscape company maintained their grounds. The girls from Venezuela lived on their father's rancho of two thousand acres near Ciudad Bolivar. They explained that Angel Falls was only a few kilometers from their home. The descriptive words the girls used of their compound layout, the plants and flowers, their staff of helpers, their thoroughbred horses, of horseback riding in the hills painted a beautiful picture in Jake's mind. He made a mental note that he must visit Venezuela someday.

He was so engrossed in these thoughts that he hadn't noticed the band had appeared. It became evident that American music was popular in the Philippines. He took turns dancing with the three girls. American songs such as "Purple Shades," "Smoke Gets In your Eyes,"

"Stardust," "In the Mood" and "I'll See You in My Dreams," sung by an attractive Filipina, set up a dreamy atmosphere. This was interspersed with lively jazz tunes, mambos, rumbas and trumpet and sax solos. It made a great evening that eventually came to an end. He escorted the girls back to the resort. Farewells were said and Jake returned to his cabin.

Next morning he had an early breakfast, packed and checked out. True to her word, Mari had left her Manila phone number and her number at UCLA. He was pleased to find that the girls from Venezuela had done the same.

His short flight to Manila and bus ride to the base gave him time to think about his wonderful experiences on Palawan.

CHAPTER 10

Back at base, it was difficult to get back in the groove again. It seemed there were more planned "secret" missions to Hong Kong than usual. Then there was the search mission for a downed PBM Navy plane and a couple of trips to Baguio. By the time water landing practice in Manila Bay came around Mari and her friends from Venezuela had left for UCLA. He busied himself learning French foil fencing, going on the skeet range, bowling and visiting the base library. Then there was the monthly base parade.

A truce was signed in Korea. Jake's time in the Philippines was coming to a close. While guessing where his next base would be, and wondering why he never received answers to his many letters to Rachel, he learned he had a letter from his business partner. Opening the letter, a newspaper clipping dropped out. Along with the clipping was a short note, "I regret being the bearer of bad news, but thought you should know."

It was a picture of Rachel and Philip, telling of their marriage. The news came as a surprise, not a shock. He supposed he had a hunch all along that this might happen. He was surprised that it didn't really bother him. Maybe the trip to Africa and how Rachel had acted were instrumental in his feelings now.

A few days later, at flight crews roll call, Colonel Armstrong notified the assembled flight crews that their wing was being deactivated, and that all would be rotated back to the States where they would be integrated into new units. He also let the pilots know that there was now an over-supply of pilots and that those interested in early discharges were to see him in his office.

Jake considered his situation. He had a good business and a nice home waiting stateside. It also meant that he would be back among the old crowd of Hollywood celebrities and would-be celebrities. No doubt he would bump into Rachel and Philip. Then there was the gossip group, always digging for spicy situations. The more he thought about how life would be in his old setting, the less it appealed to him.

Having mentally gone over that scenario, his mind switched to a new idea. Why not start over in a new business in the Philippines? If he sold his part of his real estate business to his partner Bert, his home in Beverly Hills, and some of his holdings, he would have a sizable amount of funds to go into the shipping business that Michael had talked about.

The picture he formed in his mind of sailing to numerous tropical islands, relaxing on his ship's deck, delivering needed supplies, meeting happy-go-lucky islanders and their daughters in brightly colored sarongs, sunning on an almost-vacant tropical beach beneath tall palm trees with one of the beauties, and feeling the cooling breeze blowing in off the ocean—yes, he felt he could easily adjust to that.

His mind made up, he went to Colonel Armstrong and told of his plans.

The Colonel smiled and said, "You paint an interesting picture. I wish you luck in your plans. However, you'll need to return stateside to muster out of the service. A month from today all C-119 and SA-16 crews and their ground personnel will board the USS Morton bound for San Francisco. There you can receive an early discharge."

"Sir, you mentioned that only the C-119 and SA-16 crews were returning by boat."

"Yes, the B-29 crews will fly back."

"May I ask what will happen to C-119 and SA-16 planes left behind?"

"They'll be offered to the Philippine government or sold to the highest bidder."

Instantly a thought popped into Jake's mind and he asked, "Can I place a bid on my plane—AF 1017?"

A questioning expression came on the Colonel's face, but he replied, "I'll see what I can do about that. Leave me a number where you can be reached."

With that, Jake stood up to leave, gave the colonel a salute and said, "Thanks, Sir."

The month went by quickly. He contacted Michael on Panay. "Michael this is Jake Moore. We met on Palawan. Do you remember our discussion on shipping needs? I've decided to try that. I'll need to return stateside to be discharged from the Air Force and clear up some personal things, then I'll return to Palawan. Would you keep an eye out for a good used sloop or schooner for me?"

"Sure, Jake. Maybe we can work out some business deals when you return."

"Thanks, Michael. I'll keep in touch."

On the long voyage back to stateside the USS Morton ran into the edge of a tropical storm. When he had gotten on the USS Morton, he was amazed at how tall it was and figured it would be an easy trip to San Francisco. When the storm hit Jake saw waves that looked like mountains next to the ship. He became seasick and began to question his idea about going into the shipping business.

He was glad that the ship had a stopover in Honolulu to get supplies and take on some new Hawaiian naval recruits. He took the short stop as an opportunity to go ashore with two of his crew members. They went to a dockside bar and ordered drinks. The waitress asked his crew members, John and Doug, what they wished to order, and wrote it down. She then turned to Jake and spoke what he assumed to be Spanish.

Seeing the puzzled expression on Jake's face, she asked, "Aren't you Portuguese?"

"Heavens no!"

She replied, "I'm sorry. You're so dark but have blue eyes. I thought you must be Portuguese."

"Nope. Just lots of sun from playing golf."

The waitress took his order. He was teased by his two friends. Too soon they were back aboard the ship. The thoughts of being cooped up aboard the ship again for the remaining miles to San Francisco didn't please Jake, but he had no choice.

At the San Francisco reassignment base, Jake was given credit for unused furlough time in cash plus an airline ticket to Los Angeles and an Honorable Discharge. He learned his co-pilot, John, was assigned to Dow AFB at Bangor, Maine, and that his navigator, Doug, was being sent to Wright-Patterson AFB in Ohio. That night the threesome went out for dinner one last time before going their separate ways.

Next day Jake arrived at Los Angeles Airport at two in the afternoon. He called Bert to see if he could pick him up. It would give them some time to talk. Bert was happy that Jake was back and said he'd pick him up at the airport. On the way to Jake's house, Jake announced his intentions.

Bert was shocked and asked, "Are you sure this is what you want to do?"

"Yes, I've had plenty of time to go over this, and feel I should try it."

"Is this because of Rachel?"

Jake had to admit, "Partly that and the Korean War. I just feel that I need to try another way of life—to find myself. Can you understand that?"

"I think so. If you're dead-set upon on this idea of yours, come to the office and we'll see what we can work out. Take the rest of the day at home and seriously consider what you're planning to do."

Arriving at Jake's home, the two friends shook hands and Jake went inside. Marie was happy to see Jake. His home and the grounds were as he remembered them from almost fours years ago. He held off telling her his plans. He'd wait until he was sure he could put everything together. While having a snack of cookies and milk, he went over some of his Air Force adventures, the places he had been and what it was like. Marie was a good listener. She would interrupt on several occasions to clear something up.

Finishing his stories, he got up and said, "I think I'll take a swim and get a little sun before dinner."

Marie replied, "I'd like to again say it's great that you're back home. Is there anything special I can fix you for dinner?"

"Yes, I'd like a nice chef's salad. They were in short supply in the Philippines, unless I went to a Navy base. They always had fresh salad greens, vegetables and milk shipped in. I gained a healthy desire for fresh salads."

"Then that's what you'll get for dinner."

Hanging up his Air Force clothes, he then put on his bathing suit and went to the pool. The water was refreshing. After a few pool laps, he got out, dried himself and stretched out on a lounge chair. The sun was warm and felt good. Again, for the umpteenth time he considered his decision. Was he willing to give up all this and live in a foreign country? He couldn't put the blame solely on Rachel and her crowd. There were many pretty girls that he could date, and things to see and do. These thoughts and others were spinning around in his head, broken only by Marie's letting him know dinner was ready.

After dinner Jake thought he should call Michael to see how things looked there. Looking at his watch, he realized that he would need to wait until 9 p.m. That would be noon the next day in the Philippines. Waiting to place the call he jotted down some questions and went over some business reports from his investments.

At the selected time, he called Michael. He was lucky that Michael had just finished his lunch and was about leave back to his office near the docks.

"Michael, this Jake Moore. How are things in the Philippines?"

"Hi, Jake! Things are going well. I've located a good used sloop and schooner. Both are gaff-rigged like you requested."

"Great! Tell me about them."

"The cargo sloop is thirty-six feet in length. It has an auxiliary power unit that hosts the main sail and jib, and can be used for inland water passage. For stability on open seas it has a keel fin, which can be retracted for shallow water areas. If given a new paint job it would look great. The owner is asking $42,000 but I think I can get him down to $38,000."

"Michael, since I know very little about boats, if you think it's a good buy, make the offer for me and let me know where and how to send the purchase price. What about the schooner?"

"It's a beauty with great lines. Its length is fifty-seven feet. It has an auxiliary power unit also. With the gaff-rigging it can be handled by a crew of five to seven. For size it's in the middle range and would be good for longer hauls among the islands or tourists interested in sightseeing on a sailing ship. It's in good condition. The owner wants $138,000 but I think he might accept $125,000."

"I can handle buying both boats. Go ahead and make the offer. Thanks so much for all your help. Where are they moored?"

"Both are in Manila. The sloop is presently named *Swan* and the schooner *Sea Hawk*. If I can get them for the price mentioned, do you want to change their names?"

"They're okay for now. I may change them later."

Hanging up, he realized he had committed himself to a new adventure. In his mind he conjured up standing at the helm of his ship with a refreshing sea breeze cooling him, under full sail on a sea of blue-green water among the thousands of islands, visiting such exciting places he had only read about in books or heard about in WWII newsreels—Borneo, Mindanao, Indonesia, New Guinea, New Britain, Bougainville, Saipan, the Solomon Islands and so many more.

With the excitement of the new adventure on his mind, it was difficult to sleep that night.

Next morning he let Marie know of his decision. He told her he would give her and her husband a good letter of recommendation, and see if he could help her get employed by one of his many Hollywood friends before he left for the Philippines in four weeks. The announcement came as a surprise to her, but she understood. He put his Beechcraft plane and house up for sale, worked out a purchase price for his part of the real estate partnership with Bert, converted some of his assets into cash and made arrangements for shipping some things to Palawan. His decision came as a surprise to some of his friends. Like true friends, they wished him well.

Two days before he was to leave for Manila, he received notice that his plane had sold. He also received a call from his old Wing commander, Colonel Armstrong.

"Jake. Colonel Armstrong here. The Philippine government took the C-119s and all SA-16s, except yours. According to the paperwork you won it by a bid for $50,000. Can you handle that?"

"Yes. Thank you so much, Sir."

"Do you know when you can pick up the plane?"

"Sir, I'm leaving for Manila in two days. I can pick it up then."

"Good luck on your venture. I'll see you in a couple of days." Colonel Armstrong hung up the phone.

To Jake it seemed like his adventure was meant to be. Everything was falling into place. His spirits ran high, until the day he bid friends goodbye at Los Angeles Airport. As his plane took off, he felt some doubts at leaving. It stuck with him all the way to Manila.

CHAPTER 11

Michael met Jake at the airport in Manila and they drove to the docks on Manila Bay. An excited Jake got his first look at the boats he had bought. They were beautiful. Michael took him on a tour of his boats. From the two's discussion, Michael had taken it upon himself to make arrangements for mooring the boats in Palawan, and had made tentative arrangements for crews for the boats. Michael let Jake know that he knew the crew members, that they were good seamen and loyal, and vouched that they would serve Jake well.

Jake then brought up something he had been considering. "Michael, would you consider forming a partnership with me? I'm new at this shipping business. I have good financial resources and you have the contacts and experience. I think that we'd make a good team. What are your thoughts on this?"

Michael was silent for a moment and then said, "It would mean my having to move my business from Panay to Palawan. I don't think that would be a problem. We'd be adding your two ships, getting more business."

Jake interrupted him, "And my amphibian aircraft."

An excited Michael asked, "You bought your plane?"

"Yes. I'm to pick it up today at Clark Field. I also think that if we agree on a partnership, you should be the President."

Michael could see the potentials, and agreed in principle. It was agreed that Jake would pick up his plane and fly to Palawan and that the crews that Michael had chosen would sail Jake's boats to Palawan. The two agreed to meet with an attorney to work out the details, and then parted. Jake caught a jeepney to Clark Field. He settled with Colonel Armstrong for his old plane and received permission to remain on base a couple of days to visit friends on base and in town.

At the end of that time, with purchase papers in hand, a set of flight maps for the area and full fuel tanks, he told Colonel Armstrong that if he ever was in the area of Palawan, he would enjoy having him as a guest. With that he boarded his plane and flew to Palawan.

His boats had arrived earlier, as well as Michael's boat *Rosa*. Michael and Jake went to an attorney and their company, Island Limited, was formed. Michael told Jake that between him and the two captains of Jake's ships they would teach him how to handle a sailing ship. Jake was introduced to his two crews. The captain of the sloop was Ignacio Santos; and the captain of the schooner was Pascual Labadia. Since the captains and crews were from Palawan and had their own homes, Jake decided he would live aboard the sloop or schooner until he had a home built.

Next day he went to the local bank and opened a personal account. He was helped by a cute teller named Maya. She always had a smile and talking with her was pleasant. He decided that he would like to know more about her.

A few days later Jake had his first consignment of supplies and machine parts to be delivered to the Topaz Mining Company in Papua, New Guinea. The machine parts had been trucked down from their operations in Baguio on Luzon Island, Philippines to Manila. On their return trip they were to pick up a cargo of palm oil, coffee and cocoa at Port Moresby.

Under Captain Santos' guidance he would get a chance to learn sailing and become familiar with the area. After the pick-up in Manila, the planned course was to go down the Sulu Sea, passing the port of Zamboanga, on Mindanao, off their portside. They would then make their way past the Sulu Archipelago into the Celebes Sea. From there they would pass through the passageway of the Molucca Sea into the Banda and Arafua Seas to Daru, New Guinea.

From Daru they would travel up the Fly River to one of its tributaries—the Alice River. From that convergence, they were told that twenty miles further up the Fly River they would see a dock on the right side of the river. There they would off-load their cargo to be trucked to the mine. Captain Santos and Jake were to accompany the trucks while the crew guarded the boat.

Looking at the sea charts, Jake asked Captain Santos, "How long do you think this voyage will take?"

"With good winds, about a week each way."

Jake was eager to learn what he could about sailing. He became Santos' shadow. On their way to Manila, with their keel fin extended for ballast, they sailed a zigzag tacking path into the wind, blowing from their starboard side. Docking in Manila, Captain Santos supervised the loading of their cargo, making notations on his manifest chart. Crates were stacked on deck and tied down. Making a final inspection of the cargo and being satisfied, Captain Santos cast off for New Guinea. With favorable winds blowing from the aft, Santos ran up the jib.

Santos, at the helm, asked Jake, "Would you like to take the helm?"

"Yes, I'd like that."

Santos, turning the helm over to Jake, said, "Watch the compass and keep that heading."

Jake had a feeling of exuberance and felt a sense of freedom that would be hard to put into words. Standing on deck at the helm, sails billowing, the sound of the sloop cutting bow waves, the blue-green sea, the sun bearing down but cooled by a sea breeze blowing against you, seeing different small islands in the distance slip by formed a picture of paradise in his mind. No wonder sailors were drawn to the sea.

Santos appeared on deck and instructed a crew member to relieve Jake at the helm. How long he had been at the helm, Jake didn't know. When one is in a blissful state of pleasure, time is insignificant.

Santos said, "I thought you might enjoy learning about the sextant and how we navigate."

"That I would."

Standing on the deck and facing east, Santos took the sextant from its case. Holding the sextant in his right hand, he looked through an eyepiece, made a few adjustments, jotted down a reading and the time. He readjusted the instrument back to zero.

Handing the instrument to Jake, he explained the parts of the instrument and how it worked. "Hold the frame in your right hand, look through the eyepiece telescope at the horizon, move the index arm until you have the sun setting on top of the horizon, judge your wave pattern so that you can fine-tune the instrument to take a reading when you're at the crest of a wave, use the locking device so that you don't lose your settings; then read the time and setting. Try it."

Jake followed the instructions that Santos gave him and got his reading. Both Santos and Jake went down into the cabin. Santos pulled out a nautical chart, looked at the readings he had written down and made a mark on the course that he had lain out. He then took Jake's reading taken only a few minutes later and marked them on the chart. Jake was amazed that the two marks were so close.

Santos, with a smile, said, "Jake, you're a good seaman. You caught on quickly."

Each time Santos checked their position, day and night, Jake practiced. He learned how to plot a compass course and use a divider caliper to tell how many nautical miles they had covered since their last reading, and how to determine surface wind direction. He watched with keen interest as they passed by Indonesia's Molucca Islands. The group of islands slipped by on both port and starboard side.

Arriving at Daru and beginning their assent up the Fly River, Captain Santos radioed Topaz Mining to let them know their cargo was now on the Fly River. Topaz Mining let Santos know they would be met at the dock.

Jake watched the dense vegetation on green-covered mountains go by on both sides of the river. There was a musty smell in the air. The high humidity caused the crew to sweat stains into their shirts. Spotting the dock ahead, Santos retracted the keel fin and used his auxiliary engine to lower the sail and powered up to the dock.

Men from two old WWII trucks assisted in securing the boat to the dock. A Filipino man in charge told his crew to move their supplies to the two trucks. Santos oversaw the operation to be sure no damage was done to the boat. When everything had been transferred to the trucks, Santos instructed his crew members on guarding the boat, letting them know to use the WWII Browning Automatic Rifles (BAR) to ward off any threats if it became necessary.

Jake got in the truck cab with the Filipino driver who bossed the crew, and Santos rode in the other truck. The men who had unloaded the boat got in back on both trucks with the supplies.

Jake and the driver made light conversation on the way to the mine. Jake was interested in the road. It had apparently been built by a bulldozer-driver who wasn't all that interested in building a good road. The trucks barely cleared several large rocks that had been pushed to the edge of the single-lane road; then there were the switchbacks over hills with a large drop on one side of the road. Discharged tailings from the mine's ore crusher were used to cap the road and keep down mud during the rainy season.

It took almost an hour to reach the mine. Jake felt it wasn't all that far "as a crow flies" but all the switchbacks seemed to make the distance much greater. He welcomed the sight of the mine operations in a small mountain valley. There was a large one-story building which he assumed was the milling and refinery operations, and two smaller buildings—probably office and machine shop. Santos and he were let out at a small building. A bookkeeper directed them to the manager's office. A name plate on the door stated, "Bruce O'Donnell, Manager." Upon their knock, a voice said, "Enter!" Entering, they met O'Donnell. He appeared to be in his late fifties with dark hair and eyes. His appearance seemed mild but Jake felt that underneath that façade was a man who demanded respect.

Bruce stood up and shook hands with Jake and Santos. "Have a seat." When all were seated, he continued, "I hope you had a pleasant voyage and had no run-ins with sea pirates or river thieves?"

Santos replied, "None, sir." Handing over a copy of the boat's manifest to Bruce, he said, "This is a copy of your order and what we delivered."

Bruce scanned the list of items and the shipping cost. Calling in his bookkeeper he instructed him to make out a check to Island Ltd.

While the check was being written, Bruce said, "The reason I asked about sea pirates or river thieves is that we've been having trouble shipping our gold and silver bullion to our Manila bank to be put on the world market. Thieves and pirates seem to know exactly when we plan a shipment. Although the shipment is insured, our insurance premiums have increased in cost due to the many hits on our shipments."

Jake asked, "Why not ship your bullion bars to a bank in Port Moresby or one in Darwin, and have them converted to cash and do a wire transfer? They're closer."

Bruce explained, "They are not familiar with gold and silver bullion bars, and are skeptical as to their value. The gold market fluctuates and they don't have the capacity in their vaults to store our bullion bars. Basically, they're just not interested. Our bank in Manila is Bank of the Philippines, where the Philippine government has its treasury stored. They have a huge underground storage vault. They trade worldwide in gold and silver bullion."

While Bruce was talking an idea came to Jake.

He asked, "Have you considered shipping your bullion bars by air?"

Bruce thought for a moment and said, "What do you have in mind?"

"I own an amphibian aircraft. I could fly out your bullion in small amounts. I could land on the river near your dock, or if a runway was build I could load your bars here. Your bars would arrive in Manila in one day instead of six, and no worries about sea pirates or river thieves."

It was plain to see that the idea appealed to Bruce.

Bruce asked, "What would your fee be?"

"It would be a fourteen-hour flight each way, with refueling stops at the airport in Ternate City, Indonesia. You would be getting your shipment to your bank in one day. I think four percent of the total value shipped is reasonable."

Bruce considered the cost of insurance and shipment costs by boat, and the danger due to delays and pirates. To ship by Jake and his plane would lower shipping costs and he'd get faster service.

Addressing Jake, "I like the idea. We'll give it a try. How much weight will your plane carry?"

"Maximum weight would be three and a half tons, but I'd feel more comfortable with half a ton less, at least on the first run."

Bruce considered this and asked, "Can you take a load at the end of this month?"

"Yes."

"Okay, let us know three hours before you land at our dock and we'll give it a try," instructed Bruce.

Jake responded, "Okay. Since we'd need a day of rest can you furnish guards for our plane?"

"Yes, and quarters for your crew. We could take the bullion to your plane the day you leave," continued Bruce.

"We'd need to leave the mine by 3 a.m. and have the plane loaded by 4:30 a.m.," said Jake.

"That can be arranged. I can send the bullion under heavy guard a half hour behind you, at 3:30 a.m.," answered Bruce.

The bookkeeper knocked and entered the room. He handed the check to Bruce, who handed it to Santos. Bruce went on to say they would be driven back to their boat. Jake and Santos rose, shook hands with Bruce and left. A driver in a WWII jeep drove them to their boat.

Casting off, Santos sailed to Port Moresby to pick up their load for Manila. With that loaded, he gave Jake the opportunity to test his seamanship that was taught to him on their voyage to New Guinea, under Santos' watchful eye. Jake did well on following the plotted course and again was wrapped in the rapture of the sea and islands. However, he couldn't keep his mind from straying to the deal he had made with Bruce. It was exciting. He'd make around $109,000 per load.

Arriving back at Palawan, he told Michael the good news. Michael also had some good news. They had cargo to be delivered to Borneo and Bali on the schooner, and sloop supply trips to Mindanao and Cebu. Their company, Island Ltd., had taken off.

In preparation for his flight to New Guinea to pick up the shipment of bullion bars, Jake quickly hired and trained a Filipino commercial pilot, Miguel Marcos, in the art of water landing, to act as his co-pilot. He also hired Filipino flight engineer Samuel Thomas, familiar with the Grumman Albatross, to be his flight engineer. It took some doing to get Matthew Aquino away from Philippine Air Lines (PAL) to be his navigator. He had a great record with PAL.

Bolstered by his success in acquiring his flight crew, he asked Maya for a dinner date. She accepted and they had an enjoyable evening, each realizing they had many similar interests.

Jake had hardly finished training of his crew when he received a radio message from Topaz Mining that they had a shipment ready. Leaving at four in the morning, flying Matt's plotted course to Ternate City by homing in on the radio beacon, he did a quick refueling and was off for Port Moresby, where he landed and refueled.

From the mouth of the Fly River at Daru, he flew a more direct route rather than following the winding route of the river. At the convergence of the Alice and Fly Rivers, he could see from the air a dock on his left. From the dock he could see a road that paralleled the Fly River for several miles before veering off to the left.

Dusk was setting in when he reached the Topaz Mine dock on the right bank of the Fly. Putting down full flaps and easing back on the throttles he made his water landing, hoping there were no floating obstructions. He was glad to see that a jeep and truck with armed guards were waiting for them. He taxied close to the dock and his flight engineer threw out a line to the men on the dock. Sam, his flight engineer, made sure the plane was secured to the dock. With guards posted to protect the plane, Jake and his crew rode back to the mine with the jeep driver. It was dark when they arrived. Bruce welcomed them, took them to the mess hall and later to their quarters.

Next day Jake and his crew were given a tour of the plant. Bruce was a good host. He explained each step of the mining process, from ore crushing in the stamp mill to the finished product—gold and silver bullion bars.

The tour over, they went with Bruce to his office. When all were seated, Bruce said, "Now that you've seen the finished product, this is how we ship them." Reaching by his desk, he picked up a small wooden crate, with effort, and continued, "Each crate like this will carry ten gold or silver bars. Total weight of each crate will be fifty pounds. If the shipment is gold ingots each crate is worth $27,200 USD—a total value of $3,808,000. If the shipment is silver each crate will be the same weight, with a total value of $750,000 USD. We'll load them on to your plane, 140 crates, designating which type of bullion is being shipped on our shipping list. We have alerted the Bank of the

Philippines. They'll be at Manila International Airport to meet you upon your arrival. Any questions?"

Hearing no questions, Bruce said, "I'll be available at any time, if you have any questions. So, relax and enjoy your rest."

In looking around, Jake and his crew found the mine's air-conditioned recreation room. The cool air was a refreshing relief from humid outside air. It had a pool, billiard tables, a radio and a library. While Miguel and Sam played pool, Jake found a fact book on New Guinea and a refrigerator with a cold Cokes. Taking the book and a Coke to an overstuffed armchair, he sat down and scanned through the book, reading short articles. He glanced up and saw Bruce approaching.

Bruce said, "Glad to see you found our recreation room. I'll get a beer and join you." When Bruce joined him, he continued, "I see you're reading about New Guinea. Quite a place, isn't it? Some call it the Green Hell. We have to give our employees some time off each quarter to unwind in Daru or Port Moresby."

"Yes. Do they still have headhunters and cannibals here?"

Bruce said, "Maybe you can meet Dirk von Housen on one of your trips. He and his wife are Dutch missionaries. They live with one tribe of cannibals a few miles up the Fly River from us. They're very interesting to talk to."

Jake replied, "I would think they might fear for their life, living among cannibals?"

"They claim that teaching religion to the tribe and having a couple of tribal ministers has stopped cannibalism, at least openly. They're quick to admit that if it wasn't for religion, they would probably revert back to old tribal ways and wars."

Jake thought about this for a moment and answered, "I'd like to meet von Housen."

"You probably will on one of your trips. His supplies are shipped to our dock. People are still afraid to venture into cannibal country. He picks them up in a pirogue powered by an outboard motor. Well, I'd best get to work. I've instructed the cooks in our mess hall to fix whatever you want for your lunch and dinner, and a box lunch for your trip to Manila."

At three the next morning, Jake and Santos were driven to their plane. The truck that brought the guards the night before and the jeep turned their lights on while Jake and his crew readied the plane for flight. They had just finished when the truck carrying the bullion arrived. Jake's flight engineer, Sam, supervised the loading and strapping down of the 140 wooden crates.

Starting the plane's engines, Jake checked his instruments. Satisfied, he had Sam bring in their docking ropes. Easing the throttles forward, he headed for the middle of the river. A sliver of a moon helped. Reaching the middle, he swung the nose of the plane downstream and applied full throttle. With the river flow and full power to the engines, they were quickly airborne. With a sigh of relief, Jake throttled back the engines and climbed for altitude, heading north for Ternate City for refueling and then on to Manila.

Placing the plane on autopilot, he and Miguel, his co-pilot, relaxed and took turns taking small catnaps. By the time they reached Ternate City it was midmorning and a bright, sunny day. A refueling truck Jake had called for was waiting by the parking place they were directed to, by the tower. They were refueled and off again in half an hour.

When they got in range of Manila's radio station, Jake tuned on their radio direction compass and followed it to Manila and a landing. The trip was uneventful, but long. An armored truck from the bank met them and unloaded the crates. When the transfer was completed and his plane refueled, Jake and his crew flew to Palawan. He learned from the secretary that all boats were out delivering supplies. Jake then checked in at the Kawsaysay Resort. This became a pattern.

It became apparent to Michael and Jake that they needed additional ships for their business. Demand for their services was increasing. With Jake's line of credit, they added two more sloops and crews to Island Ltd. Topaz Mining asked for bimonthly shipments for their bullion. With business booming, Jake decided it was now safe to buy some land and get his house built. He was tired of living in ships' cabins or aboard the Albatross in one of their bolted-down bunk bed cots.

He learned that the architect for Kawsaysay was a local named Daniel Lu. With Michael's help and a local realtor, Jake purchased five acres across Honda Bay from Puerto Princesa City. The acreage's location was on a small peninsula that had 300 feet of white sandy beach.

At Lu's office, Jake described the type of house he was looking to have built. "I like the layout of Kawsaysay, using local ingredients of bamboo, thatch work and roof cover, and plenty of tropical plants.

"Since the property has several coconut palm trees, I would like to save as many as I can when my house is built. The house will have three bedrooms, two and a half baths, living room, a kitchen with a pantry, a family room and an office. Off of the office I'd like an atrium with tropical plants and a fountain.

"I'll need a separate cabin for caretakers of my property when I'm gone on trips. The whole acreage needs to be enclosed by a bamboo fence, similar to that at Kawsaysay."

"Okay. I'll give you a call when I have the design ready."

Jake stood up, shook hands with Lu and left. It was a relief to know that he would soon have a new home. He was also impressed by Lu. He felt that here was a friend.

Returning to the office, he was happy to see that Michael had returned from his trip. They talked about the other sloop's trip to the Spratly Islands, under Captain Batu, and the schooner's trip, under Captain Lucas, to Kota Baharu, Malaysia with oil company passengers and drill bits. The captains of these two boats were instructed to use their radios and contact the home office before their return trip. Their discussion was interrupted by their secretary stating there was an urgent call on the radio from the schooner; that they were being pursued by a Chinese pirate ship.

Michael picked up the radio microphone and spoke to the schooner's Captain, "Lucas! Can you outrun the pirates?"

"We're adding more canvas to see if we can. Their ship is a Chinese junk and fast."

"Break out the BARs. If they get within range, fire some warning shots in their direction and send a radio distress signal out on your radio. We'll stand by."

"Aye aye!"

A few moments later Captain Lucas radioed that the shots from the BARs discouraged the pirates and they broke off the chase.

Going back into their office, Michael and Jake discussed the situation.

Michael said, "Pirating is increasing. I've talked to some of the other shippers. They say they're getting more reports of ships being attacked and crews being killed and dumped overboard. The pirates then steal the ship, paint on new names and sell both the stolen goods and the ship. Most pirating is done in the South China, Sulu and Celebes Seas."

Jake replied, "Any ideas on what we can do to protect our ships and crews?"

"Our cargo sloops are fast. BARs or maybe a .50 caliber machine gun would discourage the pirates. Our schooners would also need a .50 caliber machine gun or maybe a WWII Orelikon 20 mm cannon. The Orelikon has a sixty-round drum of ammo, but can sometimes jam. Also, its shells are more expensive than a .50 caliber round. I think that for overall protection and cost, the .50 caliber machine gun, with canisters of a hundred rounds, is the best and easiest to obtain. It has a range of about one and a quarter miles, it can fire a single shot, good for warning off a potential attacker, or a sustained fire of a hundred rounds per metal canister. The .50 caliber would be my choice."

"Sounds reasonable. Could you look around and see if we can purchase some for our ships?"

"Yes. I bet some of my old friends in the Philippine Army can find us some."

At that moment, their secretary appeared and told Jake he had a radio message from Topaz Mining.

Going to the radio room, Jake answered the call. It was Bruce.

"Jake, we have a shipment ready. Can you pick it up?"

"Sure, Bruce. Would day after tomorrow be okay?"

"That would be fine. I'll see you then."

Checking back with Michael, he let Michael know about the trip and went to check on the plane. Finding that his plane was airworthy, he let his flight engineer know that the plane needed to be serviced and ready for flight early on the second morning. From the hangar he called his co-pilot and navigator to alert them of the early morning takeoff.

After their many trips to New Guinea, Jake and his co-pilot had worked out a rest pattern. When flying these long missions they would take turns using the bolted-down bunk cots to get some sleep. This allowed them to rest and be alert. Refueling at Ternate, Indonesia and Port Moresby, New Guinea, they arrived at the Topaz Mining dock on the Fly River.

Their ride to the mine was waiting. Jake noticed that a pirogue with an outboard motor was also tied up at the dock. With guards posted to protect the plane, Jake and his crew were driven to the mine. Along the way Jake surmised that the pirogue belonged to Dirk von Housen, the Dutch missionary that Bruce had mentioned.

Arriving at the mine, Jake and his crew were introduced to Dirk while having a late-night snack.

Jake said, "I'm glad I finally got to meet you. I understand you live with a tribe of cannibals."

"Yes. I live among a branch of the Asmat tribe."

"I'd like to hear about your life among them."

"I return to their village in the morning. Would you care to stay a night with my wife and me at their village? I can introduce you to them and we can talk about their culture."

Jake hesitated. Some of the scenarios that popped into his mind weren't pleasant. Jake's hesitation caused Dirk to smile and say, "Surely you don't think I'd leave my wife there alone if she would be in any danger?"

Jake's reply was more in the line of reluctant agreement. He said, "I would spend the night, but I'm here on a business trip."

Bruce said, "Our shipment can wait a day, so go ahead."

Jake thought, "You would have to say that. Just when I had a possible out," and then replied, "Okay Dirk, I'll go with you." Turning towards his crew, Jake continued, "Miguel, Sam, care to come along?"

Both men shook their heads in an emphatic no. Jake didn't sleep very well that night. He kept thinking, "What have I gotten myself into?"

Next morning after breakfast, as Dirk and he were driven to the dock, he wrestled with whether to really do this or not.

To Jake it seemed like they arrived quickly at the dock. Dirk's supplies were loaded in his pirogue and, with Jake aboard, they set off up river. Dirk used the time to tell Jake some things about the tribe.

He said, "The tribesmen call all light-skinned peoples Laleos. There are some tribes, like the Korowais and Kombis, who live further upstream and have never seen white people. In the upper river areas there's a pacification line that's unsafe to cross. How many unidentified tribes that live in that area are unknown. It's just too dangerous to go beyond that point. In the tribe I live with I've trained a couple of them for missionary work. I'm hoping they will be able to convert others to Christianity among the many tribes. Even they won't venture into another tribe or clan's territory until they make a friend in that tribe. My work here is very slow."

Jake asked, "Do they ever talk about eating human flesh?"

"Yes. They have mentioned that they don't eat humans, but only Khakhoa—witches. They believe death is caused by an evil witch that is in human form. They kill and eat that person. This custom of eating your enemy has been practiced by many cultures. Look at your American Donner Party or some of your Indian tribes."

"Do they tell what human flesh tastes like?"

"Yes. I asked them that question. They say human flesh tastes like pig meat. They dress-out humans as they do wild animals. They eat everything but the victim's bones."

The picture of all this graphic description almost made Jake sick at his stomach. Yelling and shouting from a group of people on the river bank caused the nausea to go away.

Dirk nosed his pirogue into the bank. He talked to them in their language. Several of the men helped Dirk with the supplies, while studying Jake. Jake thought, "Am I being studied as their potential evening meal?"

Jake observed that the men were about five and a half feet tall, had dark, almost black, brown skin, kinky black hair and were naked except for the woven protection they had over their male organs.

Jake stayed close to Dirk. He noticed that houses of the tribe were on stilts about six feet high, and their houses were constructed of forest materials. He learned from Dirk that their floors were made of bamboo, the walls bark and their roofs were made of the leaves of sego palms. All men carried small bows and a handful of long arrows made from small bamboo that been dried. Each arrow tip was barbed. All the men were muscular, like young trained athletes.

Arriving at the von Housen house, Jake met Dirk's wife, Anne-Marie. She was a pleasant person with a warm smile. Dirk took Jake to meet with the tribe's leader and his clansmen, in the leader's house. Using an interpreter Jake learned that their neighbor clan was the Korowais who build their houses in the tops of banyan trees, some as high as 150 feet from the ground. When Jake asked how that was done and about their children's welfare, he was told.

"First a good climber goes up the tree and cuts away unwanted branches, at the direction of the house owner. Then with the help of fellow tribesmen a ladder is built to the area. Then bamboo, bark and sego palm leaves are hauled up by vines. Once the house is completed, the family moves in."

Jake asked, "Being so high up, how do young children get to the house?"

"Their parents carry them up and any pets."

"Aren't they afraid they might fall?"

"No, children seem to know at an early age the danger of falling."

"Does the family come down to prepare their meals?"

"No. Food is prepared over a clay pot hanging by a vine to the ceiling."

"Aren't they afraid that it might start a fire in their house?"

"No. A hole is cut in the floor underneath the pot at the time the house is built. If fire in the pot gets out of control its cut loose from the ceiling and drops to the jungle floor."

Jake was almost afraid to ask his next question. Everybody seemed relaxed and he didn't sense any danger, so he asked, "Do you hunt for food or grow it?"

"We hunt and we grow sweet potatoes."

"What do you hunt?"

"Monkeys, snakes, some spiders, sego worms and birds."

"How do you treat sickness?"

"Jungle plants. The von Housens help us."

Dirk broke in and said, "We're finding that many different jungle plants have medicinal uses. There are about 126 or more plants that are used for that purpose. For instance the young plant leaves of the Benth are squeezed into water and the solution drunk to treat diarrhea and dysentery. Then there's the Devil's Tree, used to treat malaria, combat anemia or used as an abortion drug. Or, Ranbutan Amomum, a perennial herb used to treat bleeding injuries, and to wash patients suffering from fever. The list and uses go on and on. I've cataloged many plants and have photos of them and their medicinal uses, if you'd like to see them."

The village, located next to the river, offered some relief from the stifling heat and humidity. Jake was glad the building they were in had a thick sego palm roof and open sides, allowing air to circulate.

Going outside male members of the tribe demonstrated their proficiency using bow and arrows, and the blow gun. They had Jake try their weapons. They had a good laugh at his lack of skill with the weapons. This whole adventure would forever be part of Jake's memory.

Since Dirk would be returning Jake back to the Topaz Mine compound early in the morning, he went to bed early. Between thoughts about sleeping in the midst of a tribe of cannibals and jungle noises, especially the racket put out by cicadas, he didn't sleep all that well.

When Jake arrived back at Topaz he told of his experience to Bruce, Miguel and Sam. When he brought up that Dirk talked of other tribes, further north, that had never been contacted by outside civilization, Bruce commented, "I've talked to some of the other mine operators and know this to be the truth. They find it difficult at times to get their bullion shipped out, the same as us."

Jake thought for a moment. He was presently working his plane to the limit. He could possibly buy a used C-119 cargo plane that can carry a maximum load of fifteen tons, but that would require building a runway at the sites.

"Where do they ship their bullion?"

Bruce studied Jake a moment and asked, "You're not thinking about transporting their bullion, are you?"

"Possible. Our ships will be armed with a .50 caliber machine gun and two BARs. That should discourage any pirate. For faster service, I might be able to purchase a used C-119. They can carry a fifteen-ton load, but would need a 7,000-foot runway built. Our schooner can carry twenty-eight tons. Yes, Island Ltd. might be able to help with shipping their bullion."

Bruce thought about Jake's idea and said, "I'll check with the other mine operators and see what they have to say, then I'll contact you."

"Thanks, Bruce."

Jake and his crew spent the day relaxing in the mine's recreation room. After dinner they went to bed early, since they would be driven back to the dock and their plane around 4 a.m. It was another restless night for Jake. He couldn't get his mind off the idea he had brought up to Bruce. The last thought he had before dozing off was that he would do the takeoff in the morning and then turn the plane over to Miguel while he used one of the bunk beds. He'd relieve Miguel at Ternate City, when they stopped for refueling.

The flight to Manila was long and tiring. It did give Jake plenty of time to consider what he needed to do, if he received positive word from Bruce. Since his old Wing sold their four C-119s to the Philippine government, he'd get Michael to check out the possibility of buying one. If that didn't work out, he'd do some looking around for one. One other thing he needed to check out was the cost to maintain the plane and the necessary ground crew to keep it airworthy. All this would need to be determined before he could make a bid; to see if he could offer mine owners a good deal.

After a good day's rest at his cabin at Kawsaysay, Jake went to the office. He discussed with Michael his idea. Michael let out a low whistle and said, "That's big stuff. Do you really think we can do that?"

"I don't know. We'd need to do a lot of checking to see if it's feasible. Would you check with your Philippine Army friend on the plane while I check into the cost to maintain it—if we get a C-119? By the way, did you find out anything on the machine guns?"

Michael smiled and said, "Yes. I bought the guns and they are being mounted at this moment. I hope you agree with the purchase. I thought I'd better buy them before my friend might change his mind."

With a big grin, Jake said, "You did the right thing. Let's go see how they're doing in mounting them on our ships."

On the way to the docks, Michael added, "My friend said he could supply us canisters of .50 caliber shells." With a sly smile Michael continued, "I think that he's putting all this under supplying Philippine military forces fighting the Huks, and fattening his bank account."

At the dock, Michael and Jake went aboard each of their ships. On each ship they were met by Filipino security guards, a precaution they had taken when Island Ltd. was formed. Jake noticed that each machine gun mounted on a raised mount in the stern could cover a wide range.

Michael explained, "I had the guns mounted this way because I figured any pirate ship would approach from the rear. The raised mounting will allow the gun to cover every possible approach except a head-on encounter. If that were the case we'd need to do some tacking. The locked bench seat next to the gun houses canisters full of shells."

Jake looked inside. There were four canisters. Picking up one to check inside, he found them heavy. Stating this, he was informed by Michael, "Each canister contains a hundred belt-fed .50 caliber ammo. Each canister weighs thirty-wo pounds."

Jake said, "That should discourage any pirate. It would be our way of telling them we intend to keep what we have."

Completing inspection of their ships and having a brief discussion with the guards on duty, Michael and Jake returned to the office.

Their secretary informed Jake that Daniel Lu had called. Returning his call, Jake learned that he wanted to go over the plans for Jake's house, for his approval.

When Jake arrived at Lu's office, Lu had the plans laid out on a drafting table. Before going over the plans, Daniel informed Jake that he had ordered a water well drilled, to be sure there was enough water for the property. He was pleased to inform Jake that the driller had hit an underground artesian water source. First he went over the floor plan of Jake's house and that of the caretaker's cabin. Having seen many floor plans in selling homes in Beverly Hills, he was pleased at the design's traffic flow pattern on both structures.

Daniel then laid out the landscaping plan. In the attached climate-controlled atrium according to the plan, several orchids of different varieties would be hanging down from artificial trees near the designed waterfall. The catch basin of the waterfall would hold some water plants. For some additional plants small planters were located on the floor. Daniel showed a picture of the plants he had in mind, asking Jake if he had any ideas on what he wanted.

Jake said, "I think your ideas are great. With the glass wall and sliding glass door of my office, the atrium will give a peaceful vision to enjoy. What's planned for the outside landscaping?"

Daniel pulled out another sheet of the project. Using a pencil as a pointer, he identified objects on the drawing. "This is a scaled-down version of the house, swimming pool with patio decking and caretaker's cabin as they will appear when finished.

Here is your property perimeter boundary, built of bamboo similar to that at Kawsaysay. These tall coconut palm trees will be left to give filtered sunlight to the house and pool area. Around their base will be tropical plants. I thought an elephant ear plant and some Australian fern would go well near the power generator shed and top of the water well. Then they won't stand out and distract from the beauty of your lawn. I think along this part of your perimeter fence some bougainvillea vines would look good."

Pointing to another area along the fence, he continued, "This area would be good for a vegetable garden, if you desire. Over here I sketched in some possible locations for mass plantings of bird-of-paradise plants, and here for daylilies. The entire compound will have a sprinkler system.

"On your beach front area you might consider a bath house. You might also consider using male peacocks as your 'watchdogs.' They would add beauty to your compound, warn you of strangers, and will kill any snake that enters your property. Well, that about covers my tentative plans for your site. Any questions?"

"Peacocks kill snakes?"

"Yes. They work as a team. One will distract the snake while the other attacks with his beak. Their calls give a jungle sound and add to the elusion you're creating in your compound. Their droppings fertilize your lawn. With a little grain they become pets, like a dog."

"I like your ideas. You've done a great job. My house and compound would be a paradise on earth to me. The really big question is the cost. What will all this run?"

"By using local labor and materials, this is the figure I came up with," showing Jake a pad of paper with calculations and sum at the bottom.

Jake was shocked. It wasn't as expensive as he had guessed. In California that would have cost a small fortune. He eagerly agreed on the project and signed a contract with Daniel.

That evening he took Maya, the attractive Filipino teller at the local bank, with him to the Blue Dahlia to celebrate. Her white formal dress with the large Filipino short sleeves accented her dark tan-like skin. She was a real beauty.

After ordering their dinner, she asked, "What are we celebrating?"

With a smile, he replied, "Who said anything about celebrating?"

"You did. Your actions and demeanor indicate something good has happened. Care to tell me?"

Jake told her about his house and how pleased he was with the plans. Maya was easy to talk to and he enjoyed her company. Since their first meeting at the bank they had become good friends. Tonight was an enjoyable evening of dancing and carrying on a light conversation.

Leaving the club, he hailed a taxi, took her home to her parent's house, kissed her goodnight and then had the taxi let him out at the Kawsaysay.

Several days passed. A call came in on the radio for Jake from the Topaz mine. "Jake, Bruce here. I talked to some mine owners in our area. They're interested in hearing your proposal and would like to meet with you. Are you available?"

"Let me check my schedule."

Jake checked to see if he was scheduled for any shipping deliveries. Seeing none and needing some time to check into the cost of purchasing a C-119, if available, he replied, "Bruce I can meet with the mine owners on a Saturday, three weeks from today."

"Fine. I'll let them know. I'll reserve a room at the Marauder Hotel in Port Moresby."

"Thanks, Bruce."

Jake went to Michael's office to let him know about the meeting.

Jake asked, "Would you contact your friend in the Philippine Army and see if he knows where we could buy a C-119? I know that my old Wing transferred four C-119s to the Philippines when our unit was decommissioned. Could you check on this before I meet with the mine owners at Port Moresby?"

"I'll see what I can do."

The two weeks went by quickly. After many phone calls he located a C-119. The Philippine military decided to sell the C-119s given to them and upgrade to the newer C-130s. Jake asked for and received the sales price of the plane and its maintenance records. He figured that with this he could determine the upkeep costs and the extent of ground maintenance personnel that would be needed. Then he would know what quote he'd have to give the mine owners to ship their goods by air. If his charges were acceptable, he would then buy the C-119 and hire a ground maintenance crew.

Captain Ignacio Santos and his crew transported Jake on his sloop, the *Swan*, to New Guinea. During much of the trip Jake went over his proposal to the mine owners. Going on deck occasionally to rest his mind, he enjoyed the sea and sight of distant islands, and the feeling of a cooling breeze blowing over him.

When he arrived at the Marauder Hotel he was ushered to one of the hotel's meeting rooms, where Jake found Bruce talking to two men.

At Jake's entrance, Bruce introduced him. "Henry and Charles, I'd like to introduce you to Jake Moore. Jake, I'd like for you to meet Henry Jones, owner of Kiwi Mine upriver on the Fly River from the Alice River. His is gold and copper mining. This other gentleman is Charles Christensen, owner of the Walkabout Platinum Mine. His mine is about fifteen miles inland from Sepik River."

Jake told the men he was glad to meet them and they shook hands.

Charles replied, "G'day mate! Glad to make your acquaintance."

That reply momentarily stumped Jake until he realized he was from Australia. He thought, "We both speak English, yet we both have trouble understanding what's being said."

Jake, getting down to business, told the group, "Island Ltd. has sloops that are capable of hauling up to fifteen tons; our schooner can carry twenty-five tons. Our plane, the amphibian, can carry up to three tons. I have access to purchase a C-119 capable of carrying fifteen tons—same as the sloop but allows for faster service. Shall we call it 'airmail delivery'?" The mine owners laughed. Continuing, Jake said, "If we're to pick up at your mine, a landing strip would have to be built."

He concluded by stating their costs for the different methods of shipping, including the cost for the number of miles to cover in delivering the product. Jake learned that Charles Christensen sent his platinum ingots to a bank in Brisbane, Australia, and Henry Jones ships to a bank in Sydney. There was a discussion on the means of protecting their shipments and insurance requirements. The Aussies were impressed with the ships being armed with .50 caliber machine guns.

Charles had questions about the cost of building a runway and its construction requirements. Jake told him it could be a flat surface about 7,000 feet long and could be surfaced with the mine tailings gravel from the mine to keep down costs and the runway from being muddy.

Jake concluded by asking Charles, "Since you're only a few miles from the river, have you considered building a road to a dock on Sepik River, similar to Bruce's or Henry's?"

Charles replied, "Bloke, we're back of beyond. It's truly 'whoop whoop' country with lots of mozzies. It's raw, thick jungle and so muddy we had to cut bamboo poles to get through some places with our mule pack trains. If it weren't for the poles a man could sink to his waist in mud.

"We're only twenty four kilometers from the river. As a raven flies that's a short distance, but with the muddy, slippery terrain trail, thick jungle with lots of mozzies, temperatures around 45° Celsius with high humidity and possible attacks by cannibals, it has earned the trail name Devil's Passage by our workers.

"To get them to make that trip with our bullion, we have to pay a heavy hazard fee. We've lost several men on that trail. That's just to get our bullion to our dock on the river. Because of fear of cannibals, we have to pay a substantial fee to a shipper to come this far to our dock. In this country, it's away with the pixies."

Seeing the puzzled expression on Jake's face, Bruce translated, "Charles was letting you know that his mine is a long way from civilization, through thick jungle with lots of mud and mosquitoes. That it's no place for daydreaming."

The group laughed at needing an interpreter to convert Australian slang English to American English. The humor of it lightened up the meeting and Jake gained two good friends. Jake could also see that he needed to learn what some of the slang words meant, if he was to do business in Australia. The rest of the meeting was cordial, the men trying to see if they can help each other solve problems.

Jake first asked Henry, "How are you presently shipping ore?"

Henry replied, "We presently separate gold from copper ore. We smelter the gold and pour into ingots. Our copper ore is concentrated and then hauled by trucks to our dock. At the dock we dump the copper concentrate onto a barge to be taken to Daru. At Daru our ore is off-loaded to large storage bins. When we have enough ore concentrate in storage, we arrange to have a cargo ship pick it up and transport it to our facilities in Sydney, where it'll be refined and sold on the world market.

"Our gold bars are our biggest concern, as I'm sure Bruce will agree. We have to hire a licensed powered gunboat crew, like your American Brink's service, to take the bars to Port Moresby. They are then flown to our bank in Sydney. Since we're shipping what is worth millions in USD, that 450-mile trip down the Fly is our biggest concern."

Jake asked, "What type of gunboat?"

"It's a Japanese gunboat that was captured during WWII."

"That would seem to be as good as Island Ltd. can offer, unless you built a runway for our C-119. Another possibility would be for Island Ltd. to set up a field office at Port Moresby and use our amphibian as a shuttle service between your docks and Bruce's docks to Port Moresby. The amphibian can haul only three tons per trip, but flying out of Port Moresby it could make several trips per day if a new building with a large underground storage vault was built in Port Moresby. It could be protected by armed security forces like Brink's in America. From there it can be flown by us or commercial airlines such as Flying Tigers to any destination you desire."

Bruce and Henry liked the idea of building a vault in Port Moresby, and said so.

Charles said, "Oy! What about me?"

Jake smiled and said, "I haven't forgotten you. Your problem is a difficult one. What are your present operations?"

"Our platinum is in the form of oxides. We concentrate it and then refine into ingots. These are taken by mules to our dock. They are then picked up by ship and taken to our Brisbane bank."

"Hmmm. Are you satisfied with your shipping company?"

"They argo me at times. Those nongs are afraid of the natives and are too damn stickybeaks for me."

Jake again had to use a translator who said, "Charles is saying that the shipping company angers him at times; that they're too afraid of cannibals and too damned nosy."

Jake smiled and said, "Island Ltd. could pick up your ingots at the dock, similar to what you already are doing. Since Bruce and Harry are considering going in on a storage vault in Port Moresby, you might consider going in with them for your ingots. Island Ltd. could use either one of our ships to ship, or amphibian aircraft to fly, your ingots to Port Moresby. To pick up the ingots at the mine would require a runway. With a runway either the amphibian or the C-119, depending on size of load, can land and fly your product to Port Moresby, or a destination of your choice. Does this answer your question?"

"Aye. I'm happy as Larry."

Jake learned that meant Charles was happy with the idea.

With that the meeting broke up and Jake took the group on a tour of his armed sloop. The group was pleased with what they saw. They invited Captain Santos to dinner that evening, or as Charles put it, "Tea." After a good meal, Jake informed the group he would be heading back to Island Ltd. on Palawan, and that they could give him their decisions there. Trying to be the one to pay their meal tab was an enjoyable tussle, but Charles took the day with, "Oy! It's my shout!"

Sailing back to Palawan, Jake had time and opportunity to think about what was said at the meeting. Sailing was great. No engine noises, just a refreshingly cool breeze and the occasional flapping of the sail. It was a world of its own. He was just a tiny dot on a blue-green sea. As distant islands went past he wondered what it might be like on that palm-tree-lined piece of land. Was it inhabited? Was it ever visited by man? Would it support humans, animals or birds?

Captain Santos interrupted his thoughts, "I'll relieve you for a spell."

Jake turned the helm over to Santos, went down the stairs to the cabin and stretched out on a bunk. While looking at the cabin ceiling, he went back to his thoughts. The meeting with the mine owners had gone well. If they took him up on his idea it could amount to a lot of money. He also reasoned that to give better service, Island Ltd. should open up a branch office in Port Moresby. Based on what the mine owners decided, he might need to purchase the C-119, or maybe two.

His mind switched to personal thoughts. He was building his dream home on Palawan, but had no one with whom to share it and his business ventures with. He was in his early thirties and successful but missed the closeness that a wife companion would bring. He had no one to give him a warm embrace when he succeeded, or to cheer him up when things went wrong. He thought about Rachel. At the same time he also realized that life with her wouldn't have worked out, and besides she was now married. He thought about Maya. He enjoyed going out with her. She was a lot of fun, but he sensed that there was something missing.

Hurried footsteps came down the steps into the cabin. He saw it was one of the crew.

"Sir! Captain Santos wants you on deck, quickly!"

Jake hurried after him and joined Santos. Santos pointed to two boats approaching from behind. He handed Jake his binoculars and said, "I think they may be pirates."

Jake took the binoculars and looked at the approaching boats. They were fast sailing Chinese junks under full sail and slowly closing the distance.

Jake asked, "Can we add more sail and outrun them?"

"We're tacking into the wind right now and can't add more sail. Each time I tack they do the same. The junk has a larger sail and is making more knots."

Looking through the binoculars again, Jake could now make out hurried movements on the decks of the two boats. He thought, "Maybe the mine owners were correct in thinking that one or more of their employees might be in league with pirates, letting them know

151

valuable cargo might be on board. The mine owners meeting in Port Moresby might suggest to the pirates that such cargo was on board the *Swan*."

Jake removed the canvas covering the .50 caliber machine gun and locked in a canister taken from the bench seat.

Levering a shell into the gun, he told Santos, "I'll give a pattern burst across their bows." With that he fired the bursts and watched water spray up when they hit. The small geysers were about fifty yards in front of the pirate's boat. The pirate boats opened up with a machine gun. Their shells hit the water well shy of Jake's boat. Their gun must be .30-caliber with lesser range. For Jake that solved the question of whether they were pirates.

Tilting the barrel slightly upward, he raked the decks of both pirate ships. Santos jerked off the empty canister and mounted a new one before grabbing the helm. All took place in a short time. Through binoculars, Jake could see havoc aboard the pirate ships. The pirate ships quickly broke off the chase. It was clear to see that Jake's gun had caught them off guard. They were now in full retreat.

Santos gave out a slight chuckle and said, "They didn't like your response. They'll remember to not try the *Swan* again."

For future reference, Jake would always remember to be alert for possible pirate action in the Celebes Sea area.

Arriving back at home port on Palawan, he left the crew and went to his office. He was glad to see that Michael was there. He gave Michael a detailed account of the trip and the pirate attack.

Jake said, "Michael, if the mine owners go with us I think we should set up a field office at the airport in Port Moresby. We can offer better service and not such a long flight or sail time. Coming back here I thought it might be a good idea to advertise in travel magazines in the U.S. that we can offer island cruising or charter our schooner. This might get us some tourist trade. What do you think?"

"It means going big time. Count me in."

About three weeks later, Jake heard from the mine owners. His proposed idea was accepted. Charles asked how he should go about building a runway. Jake described what would be needed. He let Charles know it should be facing normal wind currents, scraped level by a bulldozer, no mountains in front, have a six-inch cap of mine tailing on top to keep the runway dry, and preferably be near the mine. He also let the mine owners know Island Ltd. planned to open a field office in Port Moresby, for faster and better service. This was great news to the mine owners.

Island Ltd. went to the local bank with a yearly contract, received from the mine owners and received a line of credit so they could purchase the C-119 and another used schooner. Things were really looking up.

The next three months were busy ones. Island Ltd. bought a bank building that was in receivership, near the Port Moresby airport. It was renamed Island Security Bank. A construction company was hired to expand its underground vault. Armed guards were hired after extensive background checks. Bullion bars from the Topaz and Kiwi mines were shipped to the bank and stored in its vault. From there it would be flown out, under guard, by C-119 to Brisbane, Sydney or Manila. Jake made the first few flights and then, after extensive background checks, hired a crew for the plane. Each shipment was insured by a London firm.

Island Ltd. sloops were used to carry bullion bars from the Walkabout mine dock to Port Moresby and Island Security Bank vaults. The bars were transported from the mine as usual to their dock on the Sepik River. Charles finally called to let Jake know the runway was finished. Jake let him know that he was coming by sloop and would need to inspect the runway. He let Charles know that when he entered the Sepik River channel he'd call him on the radio and that he'd need a guide and way to the mine.

Jake went on the sloop for the next bullion shipment and was met by mine guards on mules. He told his crew he would be gone overnight and to stand guard over the boat.

He was given a saddled mule and escorted back to the mine. He quickly understood Charles' problem. Even the mules had trouble in places, due to the slippery trail. The heat and humidity was almost unbearable. The mosquitoes and an assortment of many other bugs made the trip pure hell. Thick jungle kept trying to close in on the trail. Warning calls of jungle birds kept everyone, especially Jake, uneasy.

It was a great relief to finally see the mine compound. The open area seemed like an oasis. Charles was there to greet Jake.

"Oy mate. Glad to see you made it to our whoop whoop outpost. How were the mozzies?"

Jake with a grin said, "You know damn well how it was."

Charles let out a huge laugh and said, "Would you like some liquid refreshment? Say some grog or a glass of iced tea? Once fortified I'll show you the runway."

"I'll take you up on the iced tea."

On the way to the mess hall, Jake got a chance to familiarize himself with the mining layout, while also trying to understand what Charles was talking about. He again thought to himself, "I've got to learn some of their slang expressions."

The mess hall was air-conditioned and a comfort. Between it and the iced tea, he was ready to see the runway.

The runway was built on top of a knoll. The crest of the knoll had been scraped down to form a nice flat surface. It had been capped with gravel tailings from the mine and had been packed down.

Jake said, "Charles, you've done a great job here. Only one thing is missing."

"What's that?"

"A wind sock so a pilot can see the way the wind is blowing."

"Why is that important?"

"A pilot lands and takes off into the wind. The wind sock will tell him which approach to take in landing or taking off. It'll also indicate if there are any crosswinds to compensate for."

"Okay mate, it'll be done."

"We'll take your shipment tomorrow to Brisbane. Let me know when you have another shipment ready. I'll fly in and try the runway."

"Jolly good, mate. This I have to see."

Jake left with the pack train of ore early the next morning. He hoped the early hour would make the trip to his boat more pleasant. It wasn't. The bullion bars were loaded onto the boat. The sail was hoisted and the crew quickly maneuvered the boat to mid-channel. Jake learned that the crew had spent a miserable night alongside the dock.

They said the mosquitoes were the worst they had experienced. On previous runs the bullion bars, in wooden crates, had been quickly loaded onto the boat, and the boat got underway before mosquitoes became a pest.

The cool breezes off the river and then the sea made the trip to Port Moresby pleasant. Jake radioed ahead to have an armored truck waiting for them to take the bullion bars to the vaults.

After a couple of days, Jake rode along on the C-119 bank delivery trip. First stop was Sydney and then Brisbane for an overnight stay. The plane, with its load of bullion bars for Manila, was kept in a heavily-guarded hangar overnight. Early next morning Jake and the crew flew to Manila. Once the crates of bars were off-loaded into an armored car, Jake was flown to Palawan. The crew would spend the night in Palawan, load some supplies destined for Port Moresby and fly a direct route to the port town.

CHAPTER 12

Island Ltd.'s expansion caused the two partners to conclude that at least one of them should be in the office daily during business hours. It wouldn't do if both were on the sea and killed. Even though both loved the sea, one needed to be a "desk jockey" to efficiently run the business.

This worked well for Jake. His house and compound had just been completed and he was using his office time to get it furnished as well as taking business orders.

He was pleased at the great job done by his architect, Daniel Lu. The house and grounds were as Daniel had described on the blueprints. He had added some additional planters near the house and did some mass plantings of colorful blooming flowers. Only yesterday Jake had purchased the basic furnishings for the house and moved in. His friend Maya helped him choose bedroom, living room, office, bathroom and kitchen furnishings.

He had hired Evelyn and her husband Frank to occupy the caretaker's cabin. This morning Evelyn had fixed his first breakfast in his new home. Evelyn and Frank were Filipinos in their early sixties. She reminded him of Marie, in his old home stateside. She was a motherly type and was always cheery. She helped organize the household furnishings. Her husband, Frank, immediately took charge of the grounds. When Jake left for the office this morning, Frank was working on one of the flower planters. He waved as Jake went by in his office WWII jeep. Jake took an immediate liking to the couple.

While looking over an ad he had placed in two American travel magazines, where he offered island cruises and charter service, he noticed an ad for a Harvard collection of great books, another ad for American Classic novels and one of international classics. All were leather bound. In the past he had read some of them, but to have the complete collection would greatly enhance his office library, and give him the opportunity to read books by the masters. He called and ordered the complete sets.

Jake's secretary buzzed his office, saying, "Mr. Moore, there's a lady here that requests to see you."

"Send her in."

Looking up when the door opened, he was shocked to see Rachel.

Under the circumstances, he could only stammer out, "Hi, Rachel. This is a pleasant surprise. Won't you have a seat?"

She seemed different in a way he couldn't quite place. She was more subdued and not her usual "rattle on" self that he remembered so well.

"I'm glad to see you again. I read where you and Philip were married. What brings you to Palawan?"

She began, "I had a devil of a time finding where you had moved to. I finally found out from your partner Bret. I'm on my way to a movie festival in Sydney and decided to stop by. What made you decide to move here?"

"I enjoy the laid-back way of life here. I bought a couple of ships and went into a shipping partnership. I was tired of the Hollywood scene and never-ending partying. Things have gone well here and I enjoy sailing. I also own two planes."

Changing the subject, he asked, "Is the festival celebrating one of Philip's movies?"

Her features changed as she said, "No it's one that I starred in. Philip and I separated last year. He was chasing after a young starlet."

"I'm sorry to hear that. I wish you well at the festival. How long will you be in Palawan?"

"I have a flight out tomorrow morning."

"I just moved into my new home. I have a housekeeper and ground caretaker. They have a cabin inside my compound. There's a guest bedroom if you would like to use it, and I'd enjoy showing you around the place. The architect did a great job."

"I'd like that. It'd give us time to talk about the past."

Jake let his secretary know he could be reached at his home. He and Rachel went to the airport in his jeep to pick up her luggage and then to his home. Opening his gate by remote, he drove inside and parked near his garage.

"Jake, your place is gorgeous. I've not seen any Hollywood set or tropical setting as pretty as this. How did you do it?"

"When I first visited Palawan, I stayed at the local Kawsaysay Resort. It has a beautiful tropical setting, very relaxing. I loved it. When I moved here I got their architect to do my compound improvements. Let me get your things to your room and I'll show you around."

Carrying her luggage with Rachel following, Jake entered his home. He introduced Evelyn, his housekeeper, to Rachel and then took Rachel to her room.

He said, "Would you like a tour now, or would you rather relax for awhile?"

"The tour."

First, Jake showed her through his house. When he showed her his office with glass wall and attached atrium she let out a gasp, saying, "It's absolutely beautiful. What a great and relaxing setting."

Jake replied, "Yes, it's my favorite room."

Going through the atrium, on the way to his swimming pool, the two peacocks welcomed them and displayed their beautiful tail feathers. With all the landscaping around the pool and filtered sun from tall palm trees, it was like a jungle oasis. He showed her the bamboo caretaker's cabin. Going around the side of Jake's house they found Frank, the groundskeeper, planting flowers. Jake introduced Rachel to him. He then took Rachel to his private beach on the Sulu Sea.

He said, "Tour complete. Since it's rather warm today, would you care to take a swim?"

"I'd love to. With what you've shown me, I can see why you love it here. It's beautiful beyond description."

"Thank you for your kind words. Shall we swim in the sea or my private pool?"

"The pool. It's like a tropical dream. You have done wonders. I really mean that. Again, I can see why you'd love it here."

Going back to the house and changing into swimsuits, they went to the pool. Diving in, they swam for awhile, got out and dried off, then stretched out on lounge chairs to take in some filtered sunlight.

After enjoying the sun for a moment, Rachel asked, "Why have you not married?"

"Too busy starting a business in an unfamiliar field. Other than what you said, what happened between Philip and you?"

"Ever since Africa and the incident with the Cape buffalo, he hasn't liked you. I sometimes think he married me because he knew you and I were close. I was starstruck and he was a wealthy producer that could help my career. I fell for his advances and we were married.

"Married life was good for awhile, then he would stay over on a set, he claimed, to work out details for a shoot the next day. I learned he was having an affair with a young starlet and divorced him. Now I need to ask a question. What really caused you to not marry?"

"What I've told you is true. My time in the Air Force and the Korean War changed my outlook on life. I took some R&R time on Palawan. I enjoy Filipinos. They are intelligent, artistic and have a good sense of humor. They enjoy being rather laid-back, fun-loving and living one day at a time. It's very contagious.

"While on Palawan I met my partner Michael. He told me about his shipping business. We agreed to become partners when I added two ships, a sloop and a schooner, to the business. I also bought my plane that I flew during the war.

"Business was good and we added another sloop and a larger schooner. I've learned to become a good sailor and enjoy the feeling of freedom that the sea gives. Our shipping business takes supplies and goods to many islands, New Guinea, Australia and Borneo. It's a great way to meet people of different cultures and customs."

"Does that mean you never date anyone?"

"No. I enjoyed the company of women in Angeles on Luzon, and I have a good friend here."

"Have you ever thought of me, or missed me?"

"Ever since Africa I have considered you to be a good friend. I realized there that our interests were too different, and that marriage wouldn't work for us."

Rachel was silent for a moment. Then, like Rachel of old, began telling about her acting career, the festival in Sydney and some scripts she was considering.

Ending her monolog, she said, "I'll race you two laps in the pool."

After the laps, they went inside. While waiting for dinner, Jake told Rachel, "Our company has purchased a used large schooner and we're refurbishing it. We plan on offering small party cruises aboard a sailing ship in the South Pacific and Southeast Asia, as well as cargo. The ship has twelve cabins. Carrying cargo will make the cruises less expensive while giving passengers an idea of what life aboard a sailing vessel was like for their ancestors. Do you think any of the Hollywood crowd might be interested?"

"Yes. It would appeal to their creative imagination."

"Perhaps tomorrow, before you catch your plane to Sydney, you'll let me give you a quick tour of our new schooner. It's in dock and being refurbished. You can then tell your friends about the ship. We've renamed the ship *Adventurer*."

"I'd like that."

Over dinner and the balance of the evening, Jake and Rachel talked about Southern California, how it was changing, places they used to visit, the Rose Parade and college football. She touted USC and the Trojans. He touted OU and the Sooners. It was a friendly rivalry. It was late when they adjourned to their rooms for the night.

Next morning after breakfast, Jake took Rachel on a tour of the large schooner and then to the airport. While waiting for her plane to arrive, she said, "I almost forgot. I saw Sir Roberts and Lady Jane at the farmer's market. They asked about you. I didn't know where you had moved to at that time. I'll let them know when I return home." `

"Thanks. I probably should call Bret and give him my new address and phone number, in case anyone else is looking for me."

Rachel's plane arrived. She kissed Jake and was off for Sydney. Driving to the office, Jake went over Rachel's visit in his mind. He had to admit it was pleasant and that he enjoyed hearing about familiar places and people he remembered. The more he thought about Rachel and their good times together the more melancholy he became. Although he realized marriage with her wouldn't work, her visit made him realize his loneliness. He had achieved success in business, but what good is that if there isn't someone to share it with?

Arriving at the office, he went over the office log blackboard, hoping it might change his mood. It let him know where each ship was on a trip, the date it left, estimated time of arrival (ETA) back to home port, general cargo information and the name of the captain. Their office in Port Moresby called in a daily report on their activities, which was posted on the board by the secretary. He checked with his secretary to see if any orders had come in. Any orders were then logged in on the blackboard. This method allowed he and Michael to know instantly what was going on day by day.

He noted that the schooner, *Sea Hawk*, captained by Michael, was taking a load of supplies to Zamboanga on the island of Mindanao. His ETA back to Palawan was in four days. He was bringing back a load of copra from Cebu. On the action board he saw an offshore oil rig's request for a replacement part and some tools, setting in Manila. Jake called the address in Manila to get an idea of size and weight. He was informed it was an expedited item. He realized that it would fit in his plane and that Island Ltd. could deliver the order in six hours by plane. He let Manila know he would do a pick-up next morning.

Calling the hangar and his flight crew, Jake alerted them to next day's mission. He radioed Michael and informed him of the mission, and was informed when Michael would reach home port. Jake would pick up the requested oil rig part in Manila, in his albatross sea plane, and fly to a rig off the coast of Bandar Seri, Malaysia. He checked with some of his sources and learned that he could get a return cargo of pharmaceuticals destined for Manila in Kota Kinabalu, Malaysia.

According to the action board, the schooner *Adventurer* would be completely refurbished in three weeks, ready to take passengers and cargo on longer voyages. Jake tested his adverting skills from real estate days. He wrote an ad and had his secretary call it in to three stateside travel magazines. In a few short words he painted a beautiful south sea adventure aboard a sailing ship to Sydney, Sri Lanka, Bali, Bangkok, New Guinea or Fiji.

Before leaving the office for the day, he called his old partner and college buddy. He had forgotten the time difference and woke up Bret at five in the morning.

Jake, realizing by Bret's sleepy-sounding voice, apologized and said, "Hi, Bret this is your old buddy Jake. I'm sorry to wake you so early. I forgot the time difference. Shall I call you back later?"

"No. I'm glad you called. What's up?"

"Rachel stopped by and said Sir Roberts was trying to locate me. Would you see that they get my new address and phone number?"

"Sure. Let me grab a pencil and pad. How in the hell are you, and what are you doing?"

Jake gave a brief update on what he was doing. At the conclusion, Bret said, "Man, you live quite the life. I envy you. Okay, go ahead with your address and phone number."

After that the two friends talked for a while longer before Jake said goodbye.

Next day Jake and his flight crew picked up the oil rig parts in Manila and flew to the offshore rig. Flying helped to keep his mind occupied. Radio contact with the rig helped him find the right rig among the many in that area. With the sea being calm, he made an easy landing and taxied up to the rig's small dock. Oil rig workers helped secure his amphibian to the dock and off-loaded their equipment.

Taking off, he set course for the short hop to Kota Kinabalu to pick up the pharmaceuticals. Having flown eight hours that day, Jake and his crew stayed the night. Next morning with a full load of pharmaceuticals on board they flew to Manila, unloaded their cargo and flew to Palawan.

He was glad to see Michael had returned from his voyage. The two friends chatted about their trips. The next few days were pleasant. Having a close friend to talk to eased somewhat his feeling of loneliness. Michael could tell that something was bothering Jake; he just wasn't his old self. Michael learned from the secretary that Jake had a female visitor from where he had lived in California, and that Jake hadn't been his old self since.

Michael went into Jake's office. Jake looked up as Michael entered and took a seat. Michael said, "Jake, I don't want to pry into your personal life, but you seem troubled. Remember I'm your friend. Can I help you?"

Jake smiled and replied, "I didn't realize I was showing my feelings so openly. I had a visit from my old girlfriend. Her visit brought up old memories and friends, making me realize my loneliness. I'll get over it."

Michael sensed the truthfulness of Jake's reply and said, "Through one of my contacts I've received a shipping contract to pick up a large cargo of black tea in Sri Lanka, destined for Darwin, Australia. This would be a good maiden voyage for our schooner *Adventurer*. There's a good chance of getting paying passengers for such ports as Singapore, Colombo, Bali and Darwin. The trip will take about three months to complete. Santos will be the ship's captain on this maiden voyage of *Adventurer*. He knows that area well, and you two are good friends. Why not go along on this voyage? The sea might do you some good."

Jake thought for a moment. Michael was right about the sea. Barring bad weather the sea had always had a calming effect. There is such a feeling of freedom and being at one with nature. The thoughts of feeling a cool ocean breeze and hearing the wind in the sails were overpowering.

Jake replied, "Thanks, Michael. I'll take you up on that offer. When do I set sail?"

"Captain Santos is provisioning the ship at this moment. He plans to catch the evening tide in four days. In the meantime I have some calls to make to see if we can get passengers. *Adventurer* will be carrying electrical parts and equipment cargo bound for Singapore. There we'll pick up finished electronic units destined for Colombo." By the time Michael left Jake's office, Jake was in a better mood and excitedly looked forward to the voyage.

Jake boarded early. He was happy to again be sailing with Captain Santos. From Santos he learned the names of their passengers and something about them.

A young couple, Matthew and Linda de Cordoba from Manila, would be making the full voyage in cabin one. The owner of a large import/export company was giving them the voyage as a wedding present. Cabin two was assigned to two Catholic nuns, Sisters Frances and Ester, on their way to Colombo to serve in a hospital. A Manila jeweler, Joseph Nino, and his wife Angelina would occupy cabin three.

He was on a trip to Colombo to buy jewels and complete the rest of the trip as a vacation jaunt.

A young graduate engineering technician from the University of the Philippines, Lucas Trias, would be in cabin four. He was heading to his new job in the tea industry in the highlands of Sri Lanka. A middle-aged couple, Mr. and Mrs. Salvador Roxas, were assigned to cabin five. They wanted to take a leisurely trip to Sri Lanka before Mr. Roxas became a branch bank manager there.

Cabin six was the cabin assigned to a middle-aged couple, Mr. and Mrs. Manuel Benigno. He was a botanist, soil scientist and tea expert hired by Ridderzaal Tea Plantation, which was supplying their tea cargo. A couple from the State of Oklahoma, Gene and Margaret Stephens, were assigned cabin seven. Jake thought, "It'll be interesting to visit with someone from my native state." They were on a South Sea adventure trip. The remaining cabins were vacant.

Jake noticed his name was assigned to the captain's cabin. He told Santos, "I'm a passenger on this voyage. I'll take cabin eight." Santos started to object but Jake held up his hand to signal the decision was made.

Santos smiled and said, "Okay. Just know we can change anytime you wish."

The two friends went to see how everything was being loaded and greet their passengers as they came on board. That evening at nine the *Adventurer* set sail. Jake's cabin was small and compact. He retired early. The soft rolling motion and creak of the ship put him to sleep.

Next morning at the captain's table he had the chance to meet and get acquainted with the other passengers. Conversation at the breakfast table was brisk. Jake mostly listened to them discussing what they do for a living and the thrill of sailing versus flying or riding aboard a power-driven ship. It was a friendly group. The young couple, the de Cordobas, asked Jake, "Are you on a cruise like us?"

"In a way, yes. I'm with Island Ltd., the owner of this ship."

Jake was bombarded with questions. He answered as best he could, then excused himself and went topside.

He was greeted by a smiling Captain Santos at the helm, who said, "They're a curious group. I see you managed to slip away."

Jake returned the smile and said, "Luckily, yes. They're a good and interesting group to listen to." Continuing, he asked, "Where are we now?"

Santos said, "Care to try your hand with the sextant?"

"Sure." Going down to the captain's cabin, Jake came topside with the sextant. He took a quick reading and then went to check the nautical chart. He came up with their location approaching Malaysia and the port of Kota Kinabalu. He relayed his findings to the captain.

"Very good, Jake. I took my reading just before you arrived. You're right about our position. Would you like to take the helm for awhile?"

"Yes."

Taking the helm, he got the feel of steering a large ship. He noticed it didn't respond as quickly as his sloop. It was like the difference of a large family car and that of a sports car. Passengers from below drifted up to stand at the ship's railing to get fresh air and look out over the expanse of water.

From Jake's position on the bridge, he studied them. The youngsters of the group, the Cordobas and Lucas Trias, were together, talking and laughing. The Ninos, Roxas and Benigno were clustered together and appeared to be having a thoughtful discussion. The two nuns strolled about the ship, enjoying sun and sea. Jake, always alert to possibilities, decided that getting to know these people might lead to future business. With Captain Santos leaving to work in his cabin on charting their course, Jake got the attention of their helmsman to take over the helm.

Going to the younger group, he asked, "Are you enjoying your trip aboard a sailing ship?"

The group in unison answered, "Yes!" Matthew added, "I've been on powered steamers and commercial airlines with all their noise. I can't get over how quiet it is aboard a sailing ship."

Jake smiled and replied, "I know what you mean. I was a pilot in the Korean War. The quietness of a sailing ship and being as one with nature is calming and relaxing." Continuing, Jake asked Matthew, "I saw on the ship's manifest your parents are listed as an import and export company. What type of business do they handle?"

"Industrial equipment. We import machines that improve production on such things as making ice cream, dairy equipment, cannery equipment, soft drink dispensers and things along these lines. We also export similar types of machines to other countries."

"Interesting. Maybe we can do some business with your company. Have a good trip. If you need anything let me know."

Turning to Lucas, Jake asked, "I understand that you're an engineering technician going to a Sri Lankan tea plantation."

"Yes. I'll actually be working for the Ridderzaal Plantation in the highlands near Nuwara Eliya."

"I'm not familiar with that area. Have you been there?"

"Yes. I was flown up for my interview. It's beautiful hill country, similar to Baguio in the Philippines. The hills in that area are covered with tea plantations. Ridderzaal is the largest. The town looks like what you'd expect in England. In fact it's referred to as Little England or City of Lights."

"That's really interesting. I'll remember to visit there one day. As an engineering technician, what would you be doing there?"

"When the pickers bring in tea leaves there are machines that grind, roll, and dry them. My job is to keep them repaired and look for improvements."

"How do they get the different varieties of teas?"

"I'm not sure."

"I can answer that." Jake turned to see that it was Manuel Benigno that had spoken. Manuel continued, "I'm a tea botanist and soil scientist hired by the Sri Lankan government to inspect tea plantations. Answering your question, there are four basic teas: white, green, black and oolong.

White tea is really a light green color and is the most expensive. To harvest white tea a picker has to select two leaves and a bud from tea plants, before sunrise, while dew is still fresh on the plants. They are steamed and dried. Due to the early morning hour, pickers can usually pick only two and a half pounds each before they have to stop. It's before the morning dew is gone.

Green tea leaves are younger leaves. They are steamed to destroy enzymes and rolled to bring out juices, then fired to dry. This is repeated until totally dry.

Black tea is the most widely consumed. The leaves are fermented until they turn black. This is rolled and dried under a hot drier.

Oolong tea is similar to black. The leaves are partially fermented, rolled and dried over charcoal."

Jake, the Cordobas and other passengers that had gathered to listen were amazed.

Jake said, "I never knew that. I'm not a tea drinker, other than some iced tea, but this is fascinating. I think you've made me a tea fan."

Manuel continued, "Drinking three cups of tea per day will keep the doctor away. Tea is a great antioxidant."

Jake smiled and said, "I'm sold."

He listened in for awhile, as others plied Manuel with questions on tea manufacturing, then took a stroll on deck.

The next few days he had a chance to talk with the Ninos, Roxas and the nuns. From the Ninos he learned about the fine gems located in Sri Lanka. He was told that Sri Lanka had the best and most beautiful rubies that can be found. From the Roxas he got an insight into the economy of Sri Lanka and that tea and rice were its major industries. The two nuns talked about the hospital they would serve in, and made several scriptural references from the Bible.

The Stephens were from Oklahoma on a world jaunt. They had recently visited Egypt and India, visiting Abu Simbel, Luxor's ancient Valley of the Kings, and Bombay. Jake had always been interested in ancient Egypt and hoped to learn more from the Stephens. All in all, Jake found the group to be interesting.

The *Adventurer* docked in Singapore on the evening tide. Since the unloading of electrical parts and loading of such items as television sets, radios, dry goods and other items scheduled for Sri Lanka would take an estimated two hours, passengers were told they could go ashore if they so desired.

Captain Santos directed his crew on stacking the cargo goods and securing them. Jake was topside near the gangplank observing the dockworkers. The ship's older passengers spent but a short time in Singapore and had returned to the ship. The dockworkers finished their loading job and all but two left. Jake could see they were drinking. He didn't like that. It could spell trouble. He hoped the young passengers would return and the ship could get underway. By the dock lighting, Jake checked his watch. It indicated the two-hour shore leave was about up. He became concerned his young passengers might have run into trouble, and wondered if he'd need to get the ship's crew to go look for them.

Soon he was relieved to see Matthew, Linda and Lucas heading for the ship. Then one of the drunken dockhands made a vulgar remark about Linda de Cordoba, knocked her husband down, grabbed her by the arm and was struggling with her. His friend was in a scuffle with Lucas.

Jake grabbed a belaying pin from its rack and ran down the gangplank. Reaching the lout struggling with Linda, Jake used the belaying pin to knock the guy unconscious. When the guy struggling with Lucas saw what happened to his friend he let go of Lucas and swung at Jake. Jake ducked the blow and with full force drove the belaying pin into the guy's stomach, knocking the breath out of him. As the guy bent over, Jake used the belaying pin on his head, knocking the dazed man to the dock floor.

Hearing an approaching sound from behind, Jake spun around, with belaying pin ready to strike. It was Captain Santos and crew members coming to aid him. Lowering the belaying pin, Jake said to the dazed dockworker, "Get your friend up and get the hell out of my sight!" Jake made sure they left while Captain Santos and the crew escorted their young passengers back on board and cast off for Sri Lanka.

Matthew and Linda de Cordoba and Lucas Trias were asked if they were okay. Assuring all they were not hurt, they retired to their cabins. Jake stayed on the bridge with Captain Santos as their ship began its passage up the narrow strait between Indonesia and Malaysia. Well up the strait, Captain Santos turned the helm over to his helmsman, giving him the compass heading. It was now near midnight. Jake and Santos went to their individual cabins. Next morning the adventure was widely talked about.

Jake went up on deck, enjoying the scenery through which the ship was sailing. He was approached by Linda and her husband Matthew. Jake couldn't help but notice that Linda, in the morning light, was very attractive. Her skin coloring was like a mild tan, making her blue eyes and light brown hair stand out.

She said, "We want to thank you for coming to our aid last night."

"My pleasure. How are you two today?"

Matthew replied, "My chin is sore but other than that I'm okay. My wife has gotten over her scare. If ever I can repay your help in any way, let me know."

"You're my passenger. Your being okay is payment enough."

The conversation turned to a casual discussion of many things. Jake learned that Matthew was a polo player. Jake had been to the Manila Polo Club only once, as a guest. Matthew and Linda talked excitedly about their many games.

Lucas joined them. He talked about his studies at University of the Philippines. Jake enjoyed listening to the chatter among the young passengers. Although Jake was only in his early thirties, he felt much older—a father figure.

Listening and joining in on shipboard talk made the voyage to Sri Lanka seem short. Manuel Benigno and the Roxas joined the gathering, anxious to hear about the last night's adventure. This gave Jake a chance to talk to the Stephens.

Jake asked, "Are you enjoying your trip?"

Gene replied, "Yes. What happened last night?"

"Two dockhand louts gave the Cordobas a bad time." Changing the subject, Jake asked, "I hear that you visited the Valley of the Kings at Luxor? I've always liked what I've read about ancient Egypt, and the pictures I've seen of Abu Simbel. I'd like to hear more about your trip."

Gene replied, "Pictures don't do Abu Simbel justice. It's hard for the human mind to take in the enormous size of the statues. The Egyptians seem to be motivated in doing everything in giant size. Luxor, Abu Simbel and the pyramids make humans appear as mere ants in comparison."

Gene's wife Margaret spoke up, "The Temple of Karnak impressed me the most. Our guild told us those massive columns are about sixty-nine feet high, and that there are 134 of them. The Temple of Luxor is beautiful and huge, but, I think Karnak was my favorite."

Jake would have loved to hear more but some of the other passengers had joined the Stephens and were as curious about ancient Egypt as Jake. He used the interruption to slip away to the bridge and talk to Captain Santos.

Arriving in the Port of Colombo, they bid farewell to Lucas, Manuel and the Roxas. The ship would be in port for a full day to unload their cargo and take on a huge shipment of boxes of black tea bound for Darwin. Captain Santos called the office in Palawan. Michael informed the captain that he had passengers to pick up: Colonel Mark Beckett and his wife Kathleen, and Frank Bain, a Northern Territory cattle station owner, going to Darwin. He was told Adinda and Osoka Putu, a Balinese husband and wife dance team returning to Bali would be passengers also. Michael told Santos where to contact his passengers.

Jake watched as their new passengers boarded the ship. He mused to himself that the colonel looked so stiff he must have a steel rod running down his back. His wife, Kathleen, had bright red hair, and was well-mannered and well-groomed—a real lady. Frank Bain reminded Jake of Old West cowboys, loose and easygoing in nature. In a way he reminded Jake of Charles Christensen, the mine owner on New Guinea. The passengers that most interested Jake were the Balinese couple. Both were slender and graceful in their walks. Osoka Putu was very pretty, with a cameo face and ready smile.

Cargo onboard and secured, the *Adventurer* struck sails and headed for their first stop, Bali. The nine-day voyage would give the passengers time to get acquainted.

Next morning over breakfast the new passengers got acquainted with the old passengers, the Cordoba, Nino and Stephens couples. After breakfast, with the passengers chatting among themselves, Jake and Captain Santos went to the captain's cabin to study the navigation charts.

Santos pulled out a chart and laid it out on a table. Pointing at the chart, he told Jake, "We'll strike the Sumatra coast here around Medan and follow the coastline to Bali." Pointing to a spot on the chart, he continued, "If our winds hold out we should pass between Christmas Island and Java in about six days."

Jake acknowledged and commented, "While growing up I read a lot about Java and Bali. I was always fascinated by their culture. Maybe our two passengers for Bali can fill me in on their island."

Going topside Santos went to talk to the helmsman on the bridge, and Jake went to join the passengers gathered together near the portside bow. It was clear to see that the Balinese couple was the center of attention. Knowing they lived in Bali, with all that was written about Bali, triggered the interest of the other passengers, especially the Stephens from Oklahoma.

When Jake joined the group Osoka was telling the group about her home in Denpasar. She said, "Denpasar has many beautiful temples, palaces and museums. It's a large city. We entertain mostly in Kuta which has many tourist resorts, only an hour's drive from Denpasar. Our costumes are made from Batik cloth, made to look gold-like and silky, like a sarong. Our dances are based upon ancient Hindu mythology."

Margaret Stephens interrupted, "How long have you been a dancer?"

"In Bali, girls begin learning the various dances at age five. They perform these dances before puberty. My husband and I demonstrate the dances and act as instructors to our young people."

Colonel Beckett asked, "What is the interior of Bali like?"

Adinda replied, "Tropical growth with unspoiled nature, flowers and fruits of many kinds. The Ayung River is beautiful. It has waterfalls, great tropical pools to swim in or go white water rafting.

"There are many terraced rice fields and some coffee plantations. Everywhere is lush green. The climate is similar to that in Darwin."

The colonel replied, "Sounds interesting. I served with Merrill's Marauders in Burma. It was hot and humid."

Linda Cordoba asked, "Could you and your husband show us one of your dances while on our trip to Bali?"

"Yes. Give us a few days to clear our minds. We found it brings peace to our minds by practicing yoga. It helps to do this before we perform. It brings us in harmony with the Hindu spirit God.

"At breakfast this morning you said you're from the Philippines. Do you do the Bamboo Stick dance?"

Linda smiled and replied, "I know and enjoy the dance you mentioned, but I'm not that skilled or graceful."

Both young women laughed. Jake left the happy group and went up on the bridge. Captain Santos said, "Seems as though our passengers are enjoying themselves?"

Jake replied, "Yes. They are full of questions for the Balinese couple. From what I overheard, I made a mental note to one day spend some time on Bali."

Days passed. Most of the passengers shared experiences and places they had visited. Jake noticed that the cattleman from Darwin, Frank Bain, listened in but didn't get involved. He and Colonel Beckett would occasionally talk and they were polite with the other passengers, but they kept mostly to themselves. Colonel Beckett's wife, Kathleen, socialized with the other passengers, and her fellow passengers appeared to enjoy her presence.

Seeing Frank standing at the bow, looking out over the sea, Jake joined him. Jake commented, "In less than a week we should arrive in Darwin. Have you enjoyed you trip?"

"Happy as Larry, mate."

From his association with Charles of the Walkabout mine, Jake realized Frank was telling him he was very happy, and called him friend.

Jake asked, "From where we dock in Darwin, is your station far?"

"Naw. We dock off Bullocky Point. It and a river are named after the owner of the Bullo River Station. Victoria River also crosses the property. Their station runs about 9,000 head of cattle on a half million acres. My station is small. It's half that size. They're a good mate."

Jake said, "I've always had a love of my country's Old West, as dramatized by our movies. I would guess that there are a lot of mundane and boring tasks in the cattle business?"

"Bloke, there's a lot of blatters in the bush. Blow-ins come and goes. Cattle get stuck in a billabong and have to be pulled out. Then there are bities, blowies and crocs to contend with. The bush is no place for a bludger. I know my fellow passengers are good blokes and sheilas, but I'm not an ear basher."

Jake, trying to understand, surmised that Frank was telling him that there were many struggling financially against the odds in his area; that newcomers come and go. Cattle get stuck in watering holes and have to be pulled out while contending with all sorts of insects, blow flies and crocodiles. That the bush is no place for a lazy person. And, Frank wasn't one for non-stop chatter.

Jake took an immediate liking to Frank. He was friendly and expressed his feelings openly. No fancy airs with him. As a person, you either like him or you don't.

Talking with Frank, Jake got an insight into life on a cattle station. A station was independent and self-sustaining. The shortwave radio was their major contact with the world. If there were kids in the family, they used the radio for class participation with their teacher. If any on the station became ill, they contacted their doctor by radio. They would describe their ailments and the doctor would tell them what medication to take from a small chest that contained several numbered drawers filled with pills. The doctor would tell them to take a certain amount of number five or any of the other numbers. If their symptoms indicated that a doctor's visit was necessary, the doctor would fly to the station in his Piper Super Cub and examine the patient.

All stations had small runways. Some stations used aircraft to check on their herds and relay instructions to ground crews traveling in Land Rovers. Once a month someone from the station would drive a large truck into Darwin for supplies. This gave the station owner and his family a chance to enjoy some of the niceties of a big city.

Learning this, Jake now understood why the Aussies were highly respected fighters in WWII and Korea. They were fearless and independent. While flying in Korea, Jake heard how an Aussie in a prop-driven P-51 fighter plane took on five MIG-15 enemy jets. The MIG-15s, figuring an easy kill, swooped down like five fingers of a hand. The Aussie pilot applied full power to his P-51, went head-on toward the MIGs and used his rudder peddle to sweep his plane's machine guns at the oncoming MIGs. He shot down four and wounded the fifth. When asked why he didn't finish off the fifth, the Aussie said, "He still had enough power to outrun me back across the Yalu River."

Jake excused himself from Frank and went to talk to Captain Santos on the bridge. Santos let him know that they should be docking in Benoa Harbor, Bali the day after tomorrow.

Next day at breakfast, Osoka asked, "Would any of you that are interested in the Balinese dances like my husband and I to do a dance for you?"

The group gave an excited, "Yes!"

The group went up on deck while the Putus went to their cabin to change into their dance clothes. When they appeared on deck Osoka wore a long gold-colored batik cloth sarong with an elaborate crown-like headpiece. Adinda wore a men's batik sarong that covered his body from torso to feet, leaving the upper part of his body bare. He carried a small drum to give the proper rhythm for the dance.

Osoka explained, "Our dance costumes are of batik cloth. It's a form of waxing and dyeing that has been passed down for centuries. The basic principles which guide Balinese life are the concepts of mutual assistance or "gotong royong" and consultations "Musyawarah" to arrive at a consensus "Mufakat." Our dances primarily are about Hindu mythology or Balinese way of life. The dance we'll do for you is the Barong.

The Barong dance is the most popular dance in Bali. It's a myth and history blend. Basically it's a dance of strife between good and evil."

Nodding to her husband the dance began. She danced to the beat of his small drum. While the dance was going on Jake noticed that everyone on board the ship watched intently. At the conclusion of the dance there was a huge round of applause from the audience for the dancers, who returned to their cabin to change back into their regular clothes. Jake smiled at all the attention the young couple received when they again came on deck. They were bombarded with questions. The young Balinese couple went over the entire story of the Barong who fought against the forces of evil demons.

Next day at noon *Adventurer* sailed into Benoa Harbor and docked. All on board said their goodbyes to the Putus. The ship took on a few provisions and left two hours later for Darwin.

Sailing off the Lesser Sunda Islands, Jake had an opportunity to talk privately with Colonel Beckett. Jake learned that Beckett was a native of Brisbane, Queensland. He had graduated from Southern Cross University at Toowoomba with an engineering degree, then attended the Royal Military College at Sandhurst, England. While studying at

Sandhurst he met his wife Kathleen, an Irish lass, a business major attending Oxford University. They were married before he left to join Merrill's Marauders in Burma during WWII. While her husband served in Burma, Kathleen moved to Brisbane to be reasonably close to her husband.

Colonel Beckett mentioned some actions he had seen in Burma, working behind Japanese lines. He also mentioned that both he and his son had served in Korea, at the same time. His son was a P-51 pilot. Having also served in Korea, Jake found it easy to talk to Colonel Beckett and share military experiences.

Arriving in Darwin, well wishes were given to Frank Bain, Colonel Beckett and his wife Kathleen as they disembarked from the ship. The Cordobas, Stephens and Niños went ashore to look around while dock crew workers helped unload *Adventurer*'s black tea cargo. Four hours later, *Adventurer* set sail on the final leg of their journey.

As a learning observer, Jake watched Santos plot a course for home. They would be crossing through five seas: Timor, Banda, Molucca, Celebes and Sulu, passing near several islands. The voyage would take over a week to complete. Threading their way past the many islands would give Jake a chance to sharpen his skills as a navigator, using the sextant. He would also take turns at the helm and feel the freedom that gives. It caused him to remember an old quote, "Captain of my ship; master of my soul."

Now having only three couples as passengers, it gave Jake a chance to visit them more often. They appeared to be enjoying their trip, frequently asking him about islands in the distance. This was the case when they spotted the Tanimbar and Kai Islands off the starboard side.

Jake could tell them the name of the island but referred them to Captain Santos for detailed information. Santos knew the islands well. In his youth he had been a cabin boy. Later he became a seaman, first mate and then captain. From all the years at sea he knew much about the various islands in Southeast Asia.

Dropping off their passengers in Manila, it was a great relief to again see home port on Palawan after the months at sea. They had made good time.

CHAPTER 13

Being late in the afternoon, he went home, leaving the reporting to Michael at the office up to Captain Santos. Evelyn, his housekeeper, and her husband, Frank, were glad to greet Jake. Evelyn fixed Jake his favorite dish for dinner—spaghetti and meatballs with garlic bread and a green salad. It was great to be home again. After dinner he took a stroll around his compound to let his dinner settle, then went to his office to read before going to bed.

Selecting the book *The Count of Monte Cristo*, he sat down, put his feet on his desk and began to read. He didn't get very far in the book when fatigue and the sound of the waterfall in his atrium caused him to doze off. Evelyn woke him before leaving for her cabin. Jake took a quick shower and went to bed.

Next morning he arrived at the office early, arriving at the same time as Michael. Inside they talked about the trip.

Michael told Jake, "You look rested and refreshed. By the looks of it the sea air and sun helped you. Has it cleared your head?"

"Yes." Jake then went over his version of the voyage, people that he met, their passengers, possible business deals, what he learned about their cargo and the excitement of learning so much about all the islands they saw from Santos.

When Jake had finished, Michael informed Jake, "We make a good profit on that trip. Your mine owner friends called and said they hope you visit them soon. You also had a call from Napa Pharmaceuticals of Boise, Idaho. Cynthia Cowan requested that you call when you return."

"Did she say what it's about?"

"No. Since it's a pharmaceutical company, I thought it might be important."

"Okay, I'll call her from home. To get her during business hours I'll need to call around midnight."

Leaving Michael's office, Jake checked their action board to see where their ships were and when they'd return. That complete, he went to his office. The rest of the afternoon he couldn't keep his mind away from the call from Idaho, wondering why they had personally asked for him.

That night he called Napa Pharmaceutical, identified himself and that he was to call Cynthia Cowan. There was a short pause and Cynthia answered, "Mr. Moore, I noticed in your ad that you offered a charter service in the Southeast Asian area."

"Yes."

"My father, who owns our company, and I would like to charter one of your ships for a month. What would be the cost, and will you captain the ship?"

This was an odd request. It got Jake's full attention. He liked the sound of her voice, and guessed she was young. He thought to himself, "Yeah, she's probably married or an unattractive old maid." He replied, "I would need to know more about your planned trip and where our ship would be going, and why me."

There was a slight laugh from Cynthia. He liked that. She replied, "I'm sorry. Let's begin at the top. Being in the business of developing new medical drugs, my father read an article published by Dirk von Housen. In the article Mr. von Housen told how certain native plants help those with illnesses in his tribe. My father wrote Mr. von Housen and was invited for a visit, offering to show his material on the plants. Mr. Von Housen mentioned your name, and that he showed his reports to you. This is why we're requesting you. I didn't know how to locate you. Even von Housen didn't know. By accident I came across your ad in a travel magazine. When I called I was told you were on a voyage. I asked that you call. Does that clear things up?"

Jake liked the way she expressed herself. She was factual, with a soothing coaxing tone in her voice. He looked forward to meeting her.

He replied, "Yes, that clears up many things. When were you planning to make the trip, and where do you want to go? I assume you want to visit Dirk, but that doesn't take a month."

"We'd like to make the trip as soon as possible. When are you and your ship available?"

"How many will be in your party?"

"My father, Dr. Ralph Cowan and myself. As you guessed, we would like to see Mr. von Housen first. Then we'd like to visit the Islands of Guadalcanal, Bougainville and Saipan. My father was a medic with the Third Marine Division on those islands during WWII. He wants to visit there again, and to show me."

The more he listened to her the more interested he became. Thinking quickly about his action board and the ships, he realized that the schooner *Sea Hawk* would be in port in a week. It would provide more comfort than one of the cargo sloops. The ship *Adventurer*, which he had just come in on, was scheduled for Jakarta with a shipment of goods. Besides, it was too large for this venture.

He answered, "Our schooner *Sea Hawk* will be available in a week."

"What will it cost to charter it for a month?"

"Give me a moment to do some figures."

Jake quickly calculated crew members, himself included, the number needed and their wages, cost of a month's provisions, added on a good profit for the company, and gave the total costs to her.

She said, "Fair enough. I know my father would like to arrive early to formalize the trip and go over details. If we catch the next available flight to Manila, would that interfere with your plans?"

"That would be fine. Let me know your arrival time in Manila and I'll pick you up in my plane and fly you to Palawan."

Cynthia wasn't kidding when she said the next available flight. Next day Jake received a call from Cynthia. They were in Hawaii and she gave the arrival time in Manila as the next morning at 9 a.m.

Jake called the local airport and asked that his plane be fueled and ready for takeoff by 8 a.m. the next day. When he arrived at the airport, his plane, the albatross, was parked outside its hangar. Since it was such a short hop he didn't trouble bringing his crew along. Entering the plane he did a quick check, and cleared with the control tower for taxi and takeoff instructions.

Getting airborne he couldn't help but notice that Mother Nature was providing him with the full beauty of a beautiful sunrise. He thought of the old saying, "Red skies in the morning, sailors take warning. Red skies at night, sailor's delight." The ski was blue and clear. Was this a good omen?

Landing at Manila International Airport, he told the tower he would be picking up passengers. They directed him to a parking place next to the terminal. He picked up his sign COWAN and went to the unloading gate of the terminal. When the plane he was waiting for landed and passengers came streaming off, he stood off to one side and held up his sign for passengers to see. He was surprised to see a tall beautiful blonde and a distinguished older man approaching.

The blonde asked, "Are you Mr. Moore?"

Quickly mustering his wits, Jake replied, "Yes. People hereabout call me Jake. Mister makes me feel ancient."

Cynthia flashed a big smile, showing a cute dimple as she said, "Okay, I'll call you Jake, if you'll call me Cindy or CC."

All this bantering caused Cindy's father to smile and say, "When you two get your asides done, call me Ralph." Holding out his hand to shake Jake's, he continued. "It's good to meet you, Jake. Dirk spoke highly of you."

Jake escorted them to get their luggage and then out to his plane. Getting on board and shutting the door, he led them to the cockpit. Ralph decided his daughter would take the co-pilot's seat offered to him; that he would rather sit in the radio operator's seat.

Taxiing out for takeoff, Jake couldn't stifle the temptation to show off. He cocked the plane at a 45° angle and held the brakes while pushing his engine throttles to full. When he released the brakes the plane, turning due to torque, lined up with the runway. He did a short field takeoff.

He had his passengers put on their headsets so they could shut out engine noise and talk over the plane's intercom. It was a light conversation. All the way to Palawan, Jake was acutely aware of Cindy. Her long honey-gold hair hung down to her shoulder blades, and she had a nice figure. He enjoyed her sense of humor. She seemed ready to laugh at any given time. While heading to Palawan he asked if she would like to take over the controls, to get the feel of the plane.

An excited Cindy said, "I'd love to."

Turning over the controls to Cindy, Jake kept a close visual while carrying on light conversation with both her and her father. Approaching Puerto Princesa Airport, he took back the controls and made the landing. He parked his plane near his hangar, helped Cindy and her father take their luggage to his jeep, and told ramp personnel to take his plane inside its hangar.

With Cindy and her father in his jeep, he told them that he had two spare guest bedrooms in his house; that they were welcome to stay at his place. They accepted.

Cindy's father Ralph said, "We thank you for your invitation."

Cindy added, "And I think you for letting me take control of your plane. It gave me a strange feeling. Response from the controls was different from what I had imagined they would be."

Jake knew the drive to go around the bay to his compound would take half an hour, and he told them so. He asked, "I'd like to know about you, if you don't mind my asking."

"Not at all. What would you like to know?"

"Tell me about your company."

Ralph replied, "I think you know about my desire to show my daughter where I served in WWII. When I got out of the service, I went to Boise State to get a degree in medicine, with chemistry as a minor. I chose medical research and eventually started my own company to produce medicines helpful to fight various diseases. Cindy chose to get a degree at Boise State in botany. Both of us and our staff study medicinal plants, trying to find cures for various diseases. That quest has brought us to you."

Ralph had just finished when Jake pulled up to the gate of his compound. He used his gate device to open the gate and drive in, closing the gate. His two watchdogs, male peacocks, announced his arrival. Reaching into a paper sack on the jeep floor, he tossed out a handful of seeds to them as he drove by as thanks for their good vigilance.

Approaching his garage he used his remote control to open the door, then drove in and closed the door. With the time-controlled garage light on, he helped Ralph and Cindy take their luggage inside. The peacocks had alerted Frank and Evelyn, his caretakers. They greeted Jake and his guests, while Jake made the introductions. Evelyn quickly made some sandwiches for all, offering coffee, iced tea and milk or pop to drink, while her husband took the guests' luggage to their rooms.

During their snack and small conversations, Jake had the opportunity to size up his guests. He could hardly keep his eyes away from Cindy. The dining room lights accented her long golden blonde hair. He guessed that she was about 5'8" tall. Her face was well-shaped with high cheekbones. On each side of her mouth were lines that indicated she smiled a lot. Then there was the cute dimple. He guessed her to be in her mid-twenties. Jake's scrutiny must have triggered Cindy's senses. She turned her head and smiled at him. He smiled back and turned his attention on her father. He was tall and thin with dark hair that had tufts of grey hair around his temples. He had a commanding distinguished look about him. There was something about him that Jake sensed he liked. Jake felt that Ralph commanded respect while at the same time putting forth a friendly exterior.

After their snack, figuring they were tired after such a long trip, Jake asked if they would like to get some rest. Ralph and Cindy both indicated they were rather tired. Evelyn took them to their rooms and asked if they needed anything. They thanked her, saying they were fine.

Jake went to his office to read a bit. Maybe that would take his mind off Cindy. Jake had opened the sliding glass door to his atrium so that he could hear the tiny waterfall. Picking up his book, *The Count of Monte Cristo*, he put his feet up on his desk and began to read.

He was startled when Cindy, in sleepwear and robe, stepped into his office. She had a soft glowing expression on her face. Seeing what he was reading, she asked, "How do you like the story?"

"I'm really enjoying it. It's a rather sad story about an injustice done to the main character, Edmond Dante, and his seeking revenge, losing the love of his life."

"I know what you mean. I read the book awhile back." Changing the subject she said, "You have such a beautiful office. Your atrium is gorgeous. Whoever designed it is a genius. Those beautiful plants accent the area. I have a question before getting some rest: why were you studying me at the dining table?"

Jake, blushing, thought, "She saw me staring at her."

He clumsily replied, "Just trying to understand who I'm working with. How does your husband feel about your trip?"

"I'm not married." Turning, she said, "See you!"

With that she was gone and Jake spent a restless afternoon, unable to get her off his mind.

Ralph and Cindy rested until dinnertime. They talked briefly about the upcoming trip over dinner and retired early.

Next morning at breakfast Jake could tell their flight lag had dissipated and they were in high spirits. While making light conversation, Jake and Cindy would steal occasional glances at each other. This didn't go unnoticed by Ralph. Breakfast complete, the threesome adjourned to Jake's living room to discuss the proposed trip.

Jake said, "Dr. Cowan, it might speed things up a bit if you use my radio and contact Dirk. He could then organize whatever you want."

"Good idea. Where is your set?"

Taking Ralph and Cindy to the room that held his shortwave radio, Jake turned on the set and tuned in Dirk's frequency. Holding up his microphone he used Dirk's call sign. Dirk's voice came back loud and clear on the radio speaker.

"Hi, Jake. What's up?"

"Dirk, I have Dr. Cowan here. He wants to talk with you."

"I'm glad to hear that he's on his way to visit me. Put him on."

"Hi, Dirk. We've exchanged several letters in the past, but it's great to get to talk directly to you. I'm anxious to see those records you mentioned. If they are as good as you indicate I'd like to help you get them published."

"You can judge that when you arrive. When will that be?"

Ralph glanced at Jake. Jake held up seven fingers.

Ralph replied to Dirk, "Jake says it will be seven days."

"Fine. I might visit the Topaz Mine and make copies of my field notes for you."

"That would be great. Would it be possible to get samples of the plants you mention in your notes?"

"I think so. I'll ask the tribe I'm with. A Zippo lighter or a flashlight for the chief would be a good incentive to get his men to collect the samples before your arrival."

"Tell the chief I'll bring both."

"Will do. See you in a week."

With that, Dirk signed off. Jake then took Ralph and Cindy into the room where he had several nautical charts. Selecting one and spreading it out on a table, he charted a course to New Guinea, Guadalcanal, Bougainville, Saipan and back to home port. Ralph and Cindy nodded in agreement to the proposed course. Jake explained that the course could be modified, if so desired, while in route.

Jake, looking at Cindy, offered to take her father and her on a tour of his compound, and then a swim. Ralph, being an observant father, told Jake, "You two go ahead on the compound tour and I'll meet you by the pool."

Strolling around the compound, Cindy commented, "Jake, you have made your compound into a botanical paradise. There are so many different species of plants. Whoever designed and laid out your compound landscaping is a true professional, a master gardener."

"The credit goes to my architect, Daniel Lu."

"As a professional botanist, I can honestly say you have made your compound into a botanist's dream world."

Her saying that meant a lot to Jake. He could see she was speaking the truth, not just idle flattery. It was such a relaxing feeling, her being close by. Ending up by the pool, they joined Ralph. He was relaxing on a padded chaise lounge.

Ralph said, "Well, did you two enjoy your tour?"

Cindy answered, "Dad, you should see all the plants that Jake has in his compound. You'd really like them."

Ralph replied, "As for me, I like sitting around the pool. The water looks so inviting. Anyone interested in a swim?"

With that the threesome went to Jake's house to change into their swimsuits. Jake and Ralph arrived back at the pool before Cindy. They were spreading out towels on their chaise lounges when Cindy appeared, carrying her bathing cap in right hand and a towel in the other. She was wearing a sea-foam-blue one-piece swimsuit. It showed off her beautiful form. It was a stunning vision for Jake. She placed her towel on her chaise lounge and put her bathing cap on, tucking her long golden-blonde hair beneath the cap.

That done she said, "I'll race you two for two laps of the pool."

All three made a run for the pool and dove in. Cindy was like an Olympic swimmer. She quickly outdistanced Jake and her father. After the race Jake and her father sat on the edge of the pool and dangled their feet in the water while getting back their breath.

Cindy quickly exited the water and ran to the springboard diving plank, saying, "Sissies!" With that she bounced the board once and did a beautiful swan dive. Jake looked over at her father and asked, "Where does she get all that energy?"

Ralph smiled as he said, "Must be her mother. It certainly isn't from me."

Cindy joined Jake and her father. They retired to their chaise lounges and relaxed, enjoying the warm sun filtering through the tall palm tree leaves. A short time later they went inside, showered and changed.

In Jake's family room Ralph noticed Jake's record collection. He saw several WWII songs and asked if he could play them, that they brought back good memories. Jake and Cindy got comfortable in their overstuffed chairs, as Ralph put on various records.

Ralph would comment on the records as they were played. When "Coming in on a Wing and a Prayer" was played, he mention some of the B-17s that he saw that came in all shot up and the wounded to whom he gave first aid. The next record he played, "I'll Get By," bought forth heavy emotions. He told his daughter that this song was the song that helped him and her mother through those terrible war years. As it played, Cindy and Jake exchanged glances. Their soft emotions showed in those glances. They then heard "I'll Be Seeing You" and "It Had to Be You."

Cindy said, "Dad, put on some happier songs. I know they bring back memories of mom and you during that time, but they are making tears come to my eyes. I know of your deep love for mom. I greatly respect and love you for that."

Ralph replied, "You're right. I need to set nostalgia aside and not be such a bore. How about these?" He played "Ac-Cent-Tchu-Ate the Positive," "Boogie Woogie Bugle Boy," "Don't Get Around Much Anymore," "Amapola," "Maria Elena," "Ole Buttermilk Sky," "Straighten Up and Fly Right," which made them laugh, and several others.

Turning off the record player, Ralph said, "Jake, you have a great record collection. You must love good music. Some of your records go back to my generation, and further back. It's nice to meet someone that has that kind of taste."

Jake replied, "Yes, I love most anything from country to classics, except progressive jazz."

Cindy, with a mischievous smile quipped, "I love classical music, and you don't."

Jake fired back, "Maybe you'll teach me to enjoy classical music, and I'll teach you my songs."

Ralph was enjoying this light-hearted banter. It made for a relaxing and enjoyable evening. Jake felt it was nice having someone else changing the records. Having Cindy and Ralph nearby caused his feelings of loneliness to go away, and the record selections showed a gentle side of Cindy's father, a side that Jake admired. After the music the threesome went to their rooms for the night. Sleep was slow in coming for Jake. The song and words to "I'll Get By" and Cindy's reaction kept floating through his mind.

He realized that he was becoming attached to Cindy. The question that haunted him was, "Does she care for me?" They had known each other but a short time. How can such a feeling about someone happen so fast? Was this love or infatuation? He'd been away from the States for almost three years. Her being white and blonde really made her stand out in this part of the world. Was that what attracted him so much? Somewhere in all these thoughts he drifted off to sleep.

Next day Cindy and Jake took a stroll while Ralph selected a book from Jake's collection and began to read. As they strolled along, Cindy asked about his life as a youth, and things he had experienced in life.

Jake asked, "Are you sure you want to hear all that boring stuff?"

"Yes."

"I'll tell you on one condition."

"What's that?"

"That you tell me about yourself."

"Deal."

Strolling along the beach, they would pause occasionally, and talk about their past and present. Jake told of some mischievous pranks he was guilty of as a kid. This caused Cindy to laugh. He then told her about roaming the fields and mountain around his small town, swimming in an old strip coal mining operation that had filled in with water and swimming in a creek that had snakes. The snake statement caused Cindy to shutter.

After telling her all about him, Cindy told about herself. How from childhood she had this love of horses and riding. That she loved music, mostly classical, and played the piano. Also that she was a hopeless bookworm, and that her parents spoiled her when she was a preteen by giving her a pony and sleigh one Christmas. That her mother, Doris, was good in art. She became interested in botany while in high school, being influenced by her father's work. She received her bachelor's and master's degree from Boise State, and was now working on her doctorate. This was the reason she was accompanying her father on this trip.

Walking back to the house, Jake was pondering this when he felt a small hand slip into his. Looking at Cindy, warmth and affection shown in her eyes. He pulled her close and kissed her. Arm-in-arm the two walked back to the house. When they entered, Ralph lowered the book he was reading and looked at them. He was wise enough to understand his daughter had an interest in Jake.

Jake called his office and learned the schooner *Sea Hawk* was due in the next evening, and that it would be resupplied and ready to sail the following morning.

Jake gave the good news to Ralph and Cindy, and suggested they celebrate at the Blue Dahlia nightclub. He said the food was great, had South Sea island décor and a terrific small band, adding that American songs were popular in the Philippines.

His suggestion was quickly accepted. They went to their rooms and changed into formal wear. Jake and Ralph wore dark business suits. Cindy came out wearing a form-fitting black dress that came up over her bust line. From there up was a light see-through black material that covered the upper part of her body and her arms. Around her neck was a short pearl necklace. She had on black silk stockings and black high heels. Jake didn't miss anything. She was absolutely gorgeous.

Jake called a taxi to take them to the Blue Dahlia. After a leisurely dinner of Australian lobster, baked potato and salad, Jake and Ralph took turns dancing with Cindy. The music was furnished by a Filipino six-piece band. The band consisted of a sax player who also played the clarinet, a trumpet player, a trombone player, a piano player, drummer and bass fiddle player who also played the tuba. They also had a Filipina singer. Most of the songs played were American music.

When Ralph was dancing with Cindy it was plain to see that he was proud of his daughter, and that Ralph was a good dancer. They did the Magsaysay mambo, a cha-cha and a waltz called "Alice Blue Gown." Jake noticed that they frequently talked while dancing.

Mixed between those dances, Jake and Cindy did a rumba. In dancing to "The Waltz You Played for Me," Jake couldn't help but notice the lightness and gracefulness of Cindy's movements.

Dancing the slow dance to the words and music of "Little Things Mean a Lot," he kissed Cindy on her temple. She gave him a dreamy look and snuggled close. When "Harbor Lights" was played he told her the story about that night he flew back from the Farallon Islands to San Francisco.

While dancing to the tune "As Time Goes By," he whispered, "Your father and you seemed to have a serious talk while dancing."

"He was asking if I cared about you."

"What did you tell him?"

"I said yes."

Going back to their table, the threesome sipped on their cold drinks and chatted. The singer sung several songs made popular by Joni

James, a big favorite in the Philippines, and Jo Stafford's "You Belong to Me."

The band, showing their versatilities, played some boogie woogie music. Jake got a kick out of watching father and daughter really "cutting a rug." They were good. When the song ended Jake and a few other club attendees clapped their hands in approval.

While Cindy was getting seated, she said, "Whee! I'm exhausted after that dance."

Jake replied, "You two were really good. Others thought so too."

Sipping on their drinks, they watched an older couple do a Paso Dobra dance, a fast march-type Spanish tune with a mock bullfight in it.

Jake, happy over knowing that Cindy cared about him, motioned over a waiter, giving him a note. The waiter took it to the band leader, who talked to his singer.

He announced to the audience that there was a special song request for a Miss Cindy Cowan. The band struck up the tune and the singer sung the touching tune—"You're Always in My Heart." Cindy, with tears welling up in her eyes, reached over and took hold of Jake's hand. In silence she framed the words "I love you."

All too soon it became late and the threesome left for Jake's house. Cindy's father said, "I can see you two have an interest in each other. I can only suggest that you go slowly and be sure."

Arriving at Jake's place, he kissed Cindy goodnight at her door. Again he had trouble going to sleep. His mind was full of Cindy and the wonderful evening.

Next day the threesome began preparing for the trip. In the morning they would leave early. While getting out the nautical chart he had plotted the course on, a thought came to him. This being the dry season the Fly River, as far up as they were going, could pose a problem for the schooner. The main channel would be deep enough. The problem was near the banks. The water might be shallow, making turnaround tricky for the schooner.

Getting Ralph's attention, he explained his concern and suggested renting a smaller powered cabin cruiser at Port Moresby for three days. Ralph agreed and Jake used his radio to contact Island Ltd. field office in Port Moresby to make the arrangements. He let them know that they would be in Port Moresby in seven days.

With their things ready for the next day, the threesome strolled around the compound and relaxed around the pool. Ralph gave Jake an idea as to what he hoped to accomplish on the trip. He told of the many "miracle" drugs that had been found from plants in such places as the Amazon and Borneo. He was anxious to meet Dirk and go over his materials.

CHAPTER 14

Early next morning the three piled into Jake's jeep. Ralph sat in back with the luggage. Arriving at the dock where *Sea Hawk* was moored, they carried their luggage on board and to their individual cabins. By the time they were back on deck, the ship's crew was well along on getting underway. Jake told his helmsman to take the helm and told his crew to cast off. Using the power host, they raised the sails. A cool breeze caused the ship to slowly pull away from the dock. Jake, Ralph and Cindy stood by the railing, looking at the shoreline. Rounding a point, Jake pointed out his compound.

Ralph said, "I don't know about you two, but as for me I think I'll see if the cook has some herb tea, and retire to my cabin to read."

Jake and Cindy stayed on deck. Cindy asked, "That song you had played for me last night. Did you mean that?"

Slipping his arm around her waist, he said, "Yes."

Looking at Jake, she asked, "The words to that song are so touching. I've never heard that song before. Where did you hear it?"

"It's an old song that was played in a movie. It's about a musician sent to prison. He wrote the song for his wife."

"That's so sad. He must have loved her very much."

With that she snuggled closer to Jake. They remained silent for a time, looking out over the blue-green expanse of the Sulu Sea. Eventually tiring, they went to Jake's captain's quarters. Taking a seat at the only two chairs there, they had a lengthy conversation about life in general and some of their desires.

The days slowly passed. Jake would occasionally take over the helm. He'd let Cindy take the helm and stand closely behind her, putting his hands on hers. A fresh sea breeze blew her hair against his face. It had a fragrant smell. Whether at the helm or in his cabin, the two discussed many things. It was evident that two kindred spirits had come together. Cindy's father could tell that she really loved Jake.

Arriving at Port Moresby, Jake was told by his field office that a cabin cruiser was moored to the dock, ready to be boarded. Jake, Cindy and her father boarded the craft with their luggage. Jake's schooner crew would stand by for their return.

While stowing away their gear, Jake checked the small galley for food and water supplies. All three went up on deck. Jake got a schooner crew member to cast off the deck mooring lines. Jake took the helm, fired up the two powerful Detroit engines, made sure the craft had a full load of fuel, waved goodbye to his man on the dock and eased the two throttles forward. With Cindy and her father standing next to him, Jake moved the boat slowly out of port. Out in the bay he opened up the engines and headed for the mouth of the Fly River.

Entering the Fly River he used the radio to contact Dirk, to let him know they were on the way up. He also described their ship. He wanted to be sure that Dirk's cannibal tribe know they were friends.

Ralph asked, "How far up this river is Dirk's camp?"

"About 500 miles."

"How long will that take?"

"It's a good day's travel."

To Jake the massive world of green lining the riverbanks and everything in sight was familiar. Cindy and her father were in a botanist's dream world. They were constantly pointing out different vegetation species and naming them.

Jake nosed in the cabin cruiser at Dirk's dock at dusk. Dirk and several tribesmen were there to meet them. Jake had Ralph throw out an anchor line. This was quickly secured to the dock. Jake locked the cabin quarters and they followed Dirk to his place, escorted by a curious group of natives.

Jake, Ralph and Cindy visited with Dirk and his wife, making plans for tomorrow. Dirk escorted Jake, Ralph and Cindy back to their boat to spend the night. Jake gave his two mining friends a call on his radio. He told of his mission and a bit about his passengers. He asked how things were going with them and asked how Island Ltd. was performing for them. Cindy and Ralph listened in on the conversation. Shutting down the radio, the three had a quick sandwich and went to their beds for the night, sleeping in their clothes on makeshift beds.

Due to the hot sultry night, Jake left on the small oscillating fan, powered by the ship's battery.

After a quick breakfast, they joined Dirk. Permission was given by the chief for Ralph and Cindy to photograph their village. This done, the threesome joined Dirk in his study. He showed Ralph the copy he had made at Topaz Mining of his book of records—the plants and the recordings of how they helped the natives. He also showed several medium-sized bags that contained the plants used. Names of the plants were labeled on the outside. He went through each plant in the book with Ralph and Cindy, discussing in detail the results. This was way over Jake's head. He became a curious onlooker.

Jake was glad when Dirk's wife Anne-Marie interrupted them to let them know she had fixed some finger sandwiches for lunch. It was a welcomed break for Jake, since he had been fighting drowsiness for several minutes.

While having lunch, it was decided that the afternoon session would be a physical study of the plant samples Ralph had requested. Ralph let Dirk know that he had brought five Zippo lighters and five flashlights for the tribe. Dirk smiled and said, "They'll really like that. Such simple things like that are a mystery to them. They're like little children with a new toy."

In the afternoon session Jake learned that not only was Dirk a missionary, but he had been trained in the medical field.

Dirk began discussing and showing various plant samples he had collected for Ralph, and how they were used by the native tribe. In the discussion, Jake heard a word with which he wasn't familiar. He could tell it wasn't a botanical word, all of which were "Greek" to him.

He interrupted the conversation of Ralph, Dirk and Cindy, "Pardon me! I heard you mention ethnobotany. What's that?"

Cindy smiled and said, "Ethnology is a study of culture; botany is a study of plants. Ethnobotany means it's a scientific study of relationships that exist between people and plants. Mr. Von Housen is explaining that relationship."

Jake said, "Oh." Not having any idea what Cindy was talking about, he decided to be just a listener. Why show ignorance if you don't have to?

Close to evening, Dirk and a couple of natives helped carry the record book and the plant samples that Dirk had given to the Cowans to the cabin cruiser Jake had rented. Before night set in the natives wanted to show their skills at marksmanship with their bows to their new friends. When it became too dark to see, they showed off their new toys—the flashlights.

After the display, Jake and his party entered the cruiser's cabin, preparing for an early morning start. Cindy whipped up some food from the ship's stores. All turned in early. Next morning, after a quick breakfast of cereal, Jake fired up the ship's engines. Dirk and the natives were there to see them off. As Dirk cast off the anchor line, Ralph yelled to Dirk, "I'll see that your book of records are published and send you a copy!"

Dirk waved his reply as Jake advanced the ship's throttles and moved to midstream. Going downstream was quicker, the flow helping to propel the boat. They pulled into the dock at Port Moresby next to their schooner, *Sea Hawk,* in midafternoon. Jake hailed the watch on *Sea Hawk*, who sent some crew members to transfer items from the cabin cruiser to the schooner. He then locked the cabin cruiser door and joined Ralph and Cindy on the *Sea Hawk*.

He said, "I need to return the key to the cabin cruiser to our local field office. They'll return it to where they rented the cruiser. Would either or both of you like to visit our field office?"

The reply was, "Yes."

Jake hailed a taxi that drove them to the Island Ltd. field office at the airport, where Jake turned over the cabin cruiser key. He then gave Ralph and Cindy a tour of their facility, saying, "Bullion bars from the Topaz and Kiwi Mines are brought down the Fly River by a heavily armed gunboat. Shipments from Walkabout Mine have to be done by C-119. From the gunboat the bars are transferred by armored car to Island Security Bank, our bank. The bullion is then stored in below-ground vaults to await a monthly shipment by C-119 to Manila, Brisbane or Sydney."

Jake then took Ralph and Cindy to a hangar. Opening the door, the threesome stepped inside. The plane was being gone over by ground maintenance personnel to prepare the plane for its next flight.

Jake said, "This way."

Going to the port side of the plane, Jake opened the door located in front of the huge four-bladed prop, hauled out the plane's steel stepladder and helped them enter. In the cargo deck, he explained, "The plane can carry 34,000 pounds of cargo 2,280 miles. The back of the plane has clam-shelled doors that open wide for easy loading of cargo. Due to its shape its nickname is "Flying Boxcar." Continuing, he said, "Follow me to the flight deck."

Going up the attached steel stairs, he said, "As you can see, the command pilot's seat is on the left, or portside, and the co-pilot's seat is on the right, or starboard side. The rear facing seat on the starboard side belongs to the navigator and this side of him belongs to the radio operator. That's about it for the plane. Would you like to see our bank and vaults?"

Both Ralph and Cindy's voice sounded excited when they said, "Yes!"

Going back to the field office, Jake got someone to drive them to the bank. The bank looked like any other bank, the exception being heavy security and number of guards present. Going down to the vaults, the three had to sign a register to be cleared through two heavy steel reinforced doors. Ralph and Cindy gasped at the sight of so many gold bullion and platinum bars stashed in several rooms behind locked steel-bar doors.

Ralph said, "Jake, you've come a long way for someone so young."

"Thank you, sir."

The three got a ride back to the schooner in time for a late meal before going to bed.

Jake said, "We'll have an early cast-off time in the morning." Addressing Ralph, "Sir, we'll work on those places your want to see. Guadalcanal will be our first stop."

Turning to Cindy, he said, "Care to take a stroll on deck before turning in?"

"Sure."

Turning to her father, Ralph, he asked, "How about you, sir?"

"You two go ahead. I plan to look over Dirk's records in my cabin, and retire."

Up on deck a full moon lit up the night, almost like day. Jake and Cindy stood by the deck rail, looking out over the bay. Jake put his arms around Cindy's waist. She leaned back against Jake, saying, "It's so beautiful tonight. I'm so glad we met, aren't you?"

"Yes. I was lonely with no one to share life with. I became aware that success can't compensate for not having someone close to share life's adventures. Cold cash is a poor substitute for a warm, loving mate."

Escorting Cindy to her cabin, he kissed her goodnight and went to his cabin. Before retiring, he checked his nautical chart and his planned course for the next day, refreshing his memory in regard to compass headings.

Next morning, after a quick breakfast, the *Sea Hawk* put out to sea. Leaving Port Moresby they sailed southeast, following the coastline. Rounding the point at the southernmost part of New Guinea, the *Sea Hawk* sailed between some small islands, part of the Louisiade Archipelago.

The basic course from there was ENE to Guadalcanal. Jake estimated it would take about four days to Guadalcanal. Making frequent checks with his sextant, to check course and speed, he'd give course corrections that allowed for drift to his helmsman. Also, he tried to spend as much time as possible with Cindy and her father. They were using the open sea time to excitedly go over Dirk's record book.

While spelling his helmsman, Cindy came up on deck. She never ceased to amaze Jake. She seemed to have a new outfit daily. On breezy days, with a cool windy sea breeze, she wore slacks, short-sleeved cotton blouse and deck shoes. On hot sultry days she'd come on deck wearing walking shorts, short-sleeved blouse and deck shoes.

On cool days she wore her hair down; on the hot days she wore her hair up. For Jake, one thing didn't change. She looked good in whatever she wore. She was like models he'd seen in fashion magazines.

Midmorning on the fourth day they docked at Honiara, Guadalcanal. Jake assigned a watch to guard the ship while he and the Cowans went ashore. He told his first mate that crew members could also go ashore at staggering times; and that everyone was to be back aboard by nightfall. Jake used his radio to contact a local tour guide to take Ralph, Cindy and he to see historical sights.

When the guide arrived, Ralph took over. After talking to the guide, it was decided that first they would pay a short visit to the local historical museum to see photographs, some of the weapons used in the WWII battles, and uniforms of the opposing military. Pointing at some of the photos, Ralph would indicate that he had been there. In one photo he pointed at a young man in jungle fatigues and steel helmet, wearing a white Red Cross band around his left arm. The young man was giving plasma to a wounded marine. Pointing the young man out, he told his daughter and Jake, "That's me." They had a quick lunch in Honiara and headed for the airport.

Driving to what was Henderson Air Field, and was now an international air field, he told his daughter and Jake how his Marine unit fought their way to capture this Japanese airfield, which had been under construction. The airfield was captured and named Henderson

Field, the name of a pilot killed on Midway. He told about the airfield being quickly finished and nineteen Wildcats, twelve dauntless dive bombers and five Air Cobras being flown in. They were called the "Cactus Air Force." They were to protect the airfield from enemy air raids from the Japanese main base on Rabaul, New Britain. Those Japanese air raids happened on almost a daily basis.

Ralph told Jake and his daughter, "In the Japanese trying to retake Henderson Field in November 1942, there were three major land battles, seven large naval battles of which five were nighttime battles and two carrier battles."

Jake interrupted, "Why was Guadalcanal so important?"

"I learned later that Allied powers were concerned about the airbase the Japanese were building. The Japanese planned to station one hundred or more of their fighters and bombers here. It put Australia, Fiji and New Guinea, on which they had attacking forces, within range of their aircraft."

At the airport Ralph pointed out where a field hospital had been, where slip trenches had been dug and the many times he had to use them during air raids or naval bombardment. He pointed out where his Marine units had formed perimeters to protect the airfield. He told that enemy heavy cruisers, battleships and destroyers sometimes attacked the airstrip, while trying to land their troops from troop ships, to retake the airstrip.

Pointing out to sea, he said, "Out there is what's called "Iron Bottom Sound." So many ships on both sides were sunk there. Many planes were also shot down here and at Tulagi, where the Japanese had a seaplane base.

Visiting some of these sites he remembered, he would take pictures of the site first, and then ask the tour guide to take a picture of Cindy, Jake and himself standing together. Both Cindy and Jake could see the emotions on Ralph's face as he remembered those past events—events still vivid in his mind after over ten years.

On the way back to Honiara, from what was called Henderson Field in 1942, Ralph had their tour guide stop at the hill referred to as Bloody Ridge. He told about the battle there.

The tour guide dropped the three off at their ship. While having a late meal they talked about what they had seen that day. Both Cindy and Jake listened as Ralph talked of hardships, loss of friends and the carnage that took place on the island. They learned that 7,100 GIs lost their lives on the island, but the Japanese lost 31,000. Jake understood that the Japanese started the war, but was appalled by the number of lives lost.

Next morning they sailed for Bougainville. Ralph, knowing the widespread problems with malaria on Bougainville, brought along a generous supply of tablets from his company to ward off the disease. He recommended that all on board take the medication now to build up their immune system. This precaution was taken by Jake, Cindy, Ralph and the *Sea Hawk* crew.

Standing on deck and looking off the starboard side of the ship as the island of Isabel slowly passed by, Jake, with Cindy at his side, asked Ralph, "Do you remember this island? It's called Isabel."

"No. I just remember that we were preparing to make an assault on Bougainville the next morning. It was the first of November and I was attached to the Marine Third Division. We were making our landing at Cape Torokina, about the middle of the island and on the west side.

We were all too apprehensive to think about anything but tomorrow. We had been told there were about 65,000 Japanese on the island; that they had bases on Buin and Buka, located on the north and south end of the island. It was our task to establish a beachhead in the island's middle.

The code name for the operation was Cherry Blossom. The purpose of the landing was to construct an airfield for our Navy Corsair fighter planes. It would bring our fighters within range of the large Japanese base on Rabaul. The Japanese Navy tried to destroy our beachhead, but was repelled by our Navy. Navy Seabees built the airfield.

When our infantry tried to expand our beachhead, it led to protracted and often bitter jungle warfare. Many men on both sides came down with malaria and tropical diseases. I was hospitalized for a month with some sort of jungle fungus. It caused a tremendous need to scratch, which spread the infection. When I was released I rejoined my unit. In one of the battles a Fijian medical orderly and I administered plasma to a stricken marine. We tried to save him, but lost in our effort. That was in the area we called Pearl Ridge."

Cindy's face showed her shock, "Dad, this is the first I've heard about this. Does mom know?"

"No. I thought it best to not worry her. Being here brings back memories that I've tried to repress all these years. In a way it's good that they come out. Maybe I can put the past behind me and not be haunted by them. When I was on Bougainville I thought it was the worst. We then landed on Saipan. I realized that I was wrong about my assessment of Bougainville."

Changing the subject, Ralph said, "Jake, from what I've read Bougainville is still dangerous, many live ordnances lying around. It would be wise to see if we can get a local tour guide to show us around. Would you use your ship's radio and see if that can be arranged?"

"Sure."

Jake led the way to the ship's radio room. A station in Buin responded. Jake explained his need and was informed that his ship would be met at the Kangu Beach wharf.

Ralph said, "Ask him if that's where the old Japanese base was located in Tonolei Harbor."

Jake asked the question and was told that the Kangu Beach wharf was newer, in the same area and closer to Bruin.

It was late afternoon when *Sea Hawk* arrived and was moored to the Kangu Beach wharf. Seeing a man on the wharf, Jake hailed him, "Are you from Buin Travels?"

"Yes."

"Come aboard."

The guy hurried up the gangplank. On board, he said, "I'm Max Huber with Buin Tours."

Jake said, "I'm Jake Moore." Turning to indicate the Cowans, Jake continued, "This is Dr. Ralph Cowan and his daughter, Cynthia."

The introduction done, Jake said, "I think we'd be more comfortable in my cabin. We can discuss a tour itinerary there. Follow me."

Even though the sun had gone down, the air was still hot and muggy. Each of the cabins on the schooner, the crew quarters and the galley had oscillating fans, powered by the ship's small generator. Entering his cabin, Jake turned on the fan.

When everyone was seated, he explained, "Max, Dr. Cowan was a medic on Bougainville in 1943. His unit landed at Cape Torokina. Dr. Cowan, why don't you tell him what you'd like to see?"

"Thanks, Jake. Max, what's it like by our old base at Cape Torokina?"

"The airstrip is still there, but there're a lot of unexploded ordnances in the area. Local villagers are still getting hurt or killed. For those, like you, wishing to visit battle areas sometimes go over the central highland Numa- Numa trail from Wakunai to Cape Torokina. The trail itself has been cleared. You'd be safe as long as you stick to the trail. It's a 38.5-mile trek. How much time do you wish to take to look over the island?"

"I would think two to three days."

Max said, "Let me make a suggestion. Since your time is limited, I would suggest I fly you over the battle areas and land at the airstrip on Cape Torokina for you to look around on the old base. I wouldn't recommend leaving the immediate base area, due to so many live shells and bombs that might still be in the area. This will take a full day. Would you like to see the plane that Admiral Yamamoto was shot down in? It's a three-hour drive and a two-mile walk from the trailhead. Lots of tourists go there. I can take you there on your second day."

"That sounds like a good plan. Flying the island would cover a lot of ground in a relatively short time. It will give my daughter and Jake some idea of what we went through in 1943. I'm glad we can land at our airbase at Cape Torokina. We had a three-ward hospital there. And yes, I'd like to see the plane in which Yamamoto was killed. Wasn't he shot down by an American P-38?"

"Yes, sir. He was shot down by two American P-38s. Your American forces had intercepted a Japanese radio transmission that told of the admiral's flight plan. The P-38s laid in wait for him."

"I remember hearing something about that. He was the Japanese leader at Pearl Harbor, Midway and at Guadalcanal. Wasn't he on an inspection tour of the Japanese defenses on Bougainville when he was shot down?"

"Yes, sir."

"What is the charge for this tour?"

"2,500 Solomon dollars or $325 USD."

"That sounds reasonable to me." Continuing, he asked Jake, "Does this fit in with our charter time?"

Jake said "Yes." Continuing, he asked, "Max, you're not a native of Bougainville. Bougainville's are the blackest people in the world. If you don't mind my asking, what brought you to Bougainville?"

Max smiled and said, "I'm German. My father, Gustav, didn't like what was happening in Germany in 1932. He was a young mining engineer/geologist and took a job in the gold mining industry here. He moved my mother and I here when I was but two. When war came and the mines shut down, he decided to remain here and start our tour guide company, which has done well. My mother, Lucy, and I primarily run the business. My dad likes to take trips into the back country in search of mineral deposits. Since I've lived on Bougainville all these years, I consider myself a native."

Jake replied, "Sounds interesting. I also moved from my native country to the Philippines. When and where shall we meet tomorrow for that flight tour?"

Max answered, "Why not here at the wharf? I can pick you up at eight and drive you to our airport."

Jake glanced at Ralph and Cindy, and they nodded their approval. Jake said, "Sounds good. We'll see you tomorrow."

After Max left, Ralph asked, "Jake, do you have a map of Bougainville?"

"Yes."

"Can I use it?"

Jake went to the ship's map cupboard, found the map and gave it to Ralph. While Cindy and Jake looked on, Ralph spread it out and with a pencil made small marks by several places on the map.

Pointing to the different marks on his map, he said, "We're docked at Kangu in what's called Tonolei Harbor. Where the island makes this little hook, the Japanese had a naval base. It was protected by shore batteries and airbases located on these offshore islands, and in Buin, which is now their commercial airfield. Buin at that time was given the nickname of Little Tokyo."

Pointing to his mark on the east coast of Bougainville, he said, "The Japanese had a smaller naval base here at Kieta; then a larger one here at Buka with protecting airfields. As you can see, the Japanese strength was along the eastern coast."

Pointing to the western coast, he said, "We made our landing here at Empress Augusta Bay, near Cape Torokina. Our landing was supported by naval gunfire and aerial attacks on the Cape Torokina area for fifteen minutes. When our landing forces rounded Puruata Island, they came under attack by a number of Japanese machine guns and a 75 mm field piece.

"We positioned ourselves in the middle of the island with Japanese all around. The Japanese landed some reinforcements up the coast at Koromokina. Our marines set up a protective perimeter to protect us. Navy Seabees built the airfield in only forty days. They used Marston matting. With the airfield complete several Navy fighter aircraft were flown in. They kept the Japanese fighter and bomber attacks on us to a minimum. The beach we landed on was only about forty-five feet deep. Our supplies were stacked all along the beach. About five or six Japanese Zeros strafed our area during our landing.

"This offshore island is called Puruata. About three days after we landed, our Navy set up a PT boat base on that island. Any supplies our outfit needed was sent to Puruata Island and ferried in to us. The Japanese set up some field artillery on nearby hills to try and keep the base from being built.

"There was a bloody battle and the marines cleaned them out. Hill 260 was the scene of heavy fighting. Its height and a tall Banyan tree made it a good lookout post; the surrounding area could be seen from there.

"Sometimes in the swampy areas near the beach we had to walk through calf-deep mud. To take Bougainville took many men's lives."

When Ralph finished, both Jake and Cindy sat for a moment in stunned silence. While Ralph told about the various points he had marked on the map, Jake and Cindy, in their mind's eye, could visualize the horror Ralph had gone through.

Ralph broke the silence with, "Well, it's time for bed," and left. Cindy accompanied her father. Jake, still thinking about what Ralph had said, looked forward with interest on tomorrow's flight. He turned in for the night.

Next morning, as promised, Max was there to pick them up in an American WWII jeep. The early morning air and the open jeep made the nine-mile drive to the airport refreshing. Max stopped by his Cessna 170, a four-passenger "tail dragger," a bushmaster's dream. Ralph sat upfront with Max; Jake and Cindy in back. While Ralph, Cindy and Jake made sure their cameras were easily accessible, Max started the plane's engine.

They were quickly airborne and following the map Ralph had marked up. Aerial visibility of the war relic sites was limited. What they couldn't fully see from the air, Ralph's account last night and his account today presented a good idea of the war relic below. Each took aerial pictures of the sites. This was repeated again and again as they covered the island's east coast. Jake and Cindy were appalled at the ruggedness of the island, all covered in a massive coat of green vegetation. They could see it was a green hell and marveled how anyone could have survived the war in that type of setting.

Approaching the old airstrip and base at Torokina, Max made a low pass over the strip to ward off any wild animals that might be hiding in the patches of grass that had grown up on the field. Jake, from his flying experiences, could see that much of the runway wasn't useful. Max came around for the landing. He did a slip maneuver, correcting just before touchdown. Jake had to admire Max's skill at landing. The only thought that plagued him was, "He got in, but can he get out?"

Everyone exited the plane. For Ralph it as though he was in the past. He showed where the field hospital had been, where his canvas-covered quarters were located and told how everyone dug holes inside to give some protection from enemy mortar fire or bombing. Jake, Ralph and Cindy took several pictures of the area, alternating stand-ins with Ralph.

After photographing the area well, all returned to the plane. Max started the engine and taxied as close as he could to the jungle that was taking over the site. Turning the plane to face Empress Augusta Bay, Max held the plane's brakes and revved up the plane's engine. Jake crossed his fingers as Max let off the plane's brake. At the edge of the runway, Max pulled back on the plane's yoke and all went airborne. Once airborne, he banked the plane, making several passes, so that his passengers could get good pictures of the old base and Puruata Island. At Ralph's request, Max made several passes along Koromokina Lagoon area, where the Japanese had come ashore.

It was a good day's trip. They landed at Buin Airport just as the sun was sinking in the west, making the sky various shades of reds and gold. Max drove them back to the wharf and the *Sea Hawk*, promising to again pick them up in the morning for the trip to Yamamoto's plane crash site.

On board the ship the three discussed the day and had a nice meal prepared by the ship's cook. Ralph bid goodnight to Jake and Cindy, and went to his cabin. Jake and Cindy went up on deck.

Taking a stroll around the deck, holding hands, Cindy asked Jake a question. "Jake, why did you cross your fingers when we took off from Dad's old base?"

"You noticed! I wasn't sure that Max could take off from there."

She let out a small snicker, saying, "And you said nothing?"

"He's the pilot. I have to think he knows what he can do, and he did."

Jake escorted Cindy to her cabin door and kissed her goodnight, then went to his cabin.

Next morning Max was punctual. Knowing they would be spending most of the day in the sun, all wore pith helmets. Greeting Max, they got into his jeep. The cool morning air and riding in an open jeep made the morning pleasant. Reaching Buin, Max drove out the Panguna-Buin Road towards the small Aku village. In a world of seemingly unending green they drove. In several places the jeep forded small streams.

Max, being the good tour guide, would make remarks. While fording a stream, he said, "Our nation went through difficult times during WWII. Then to make matters worse we went through a bitter civil war and finally got our independence from Papua, New Guinea. Many of our small streams don't have bridges, making travel by jeep, Land Rover or tractor necessary."

The air was becoming hot and humid. After a short lull in conversation, while his passengers took in the mass of green vegetation—to Jake's mind "Green Hell"—Max commented, "I was fourteen when I heard that Yamamoto's plane, a Japanese Betty bomber, was shot down. The jungle in that area is so dense that it took months to locate the wreckage. His skeletal body, except for a few bones sent to his widow in Japan, is buried in a local cemetery. A trail to the site is kept clear for trekkers. The wreckage is guarded to keep anyone from taking a souvenir off the plane."

At Aku, Max parked the jeep near a sign that indicated it was the trailhead. Without the cooling effect of the drive, the air was hot, humid and oppressive. It being almost noon, Max carried a small cooler from his jeep to a shaded area, recommending that a light snack of finger sandwiches and cold water be taken before the trek.

While snacking Ralph said, "I had forgotten how hot it can get here. This brings back old memories, none good."

Cindy asked, "Dad, was there no relief from the heat?"

"At night it cooled a little, but then there were always mosquitoes to contend with, day or night. If I was lucky enough to pull some duty in our hospital it was a little cooler. They had large electric fans powered by a generator. To keep our wounded as comfortable as possible, their cots were covered with mosquito netting. Mosquitoes find it difficult to buck the winds created by the fans. Those that get through are then confronted by netting. All in all hospital duty wasn't all that bad."

Max said, "I brought along some salt tablets and this water pouch. Take a tablet and a drink." When this was done, he said, "We best get underway to the wreck."

Trekking the trail hacked out of the jungle in heat that felt like a blast furnace; Jake's mind conjured up what it felt like at his compound and the cooling sea breeze. He could see that Ralph and Cindy, who were in front of him, had sweat-stained clothes. Jake knew his must look the same.

Arriving at the site, the threesome took several pictures and returned to their parked jeep. Even though Max had parked under a large banyan tree the seats were uncomfortably hot. Starting up the jeep and heading back to Buin the flow of air, even though hot, gave some comfort.

At the wharf next to the *Sea Hawk*, the three got out, thanked Max and went aboard. Jake let the crew know they would be sailing with the evening tide.

Turning to Ralph and Cindy, Jake said, "I don't know about your plans, but I feel the need for a cool shower and a short nap before dinner."

Ralph replied, "That's the best idea I've heard today."

Cindy quipped, "Ladies first!"

After dinner and light conversation about Bougainville, the three went up on deck. The crew was busy getting the ship free from its mooring, bringing in the gangplank and securing it, and hoisting up the sails. Standing by the railing they watched as the ship slowly and quietly left the wharf. Holding onto the railing with his right hand, Jake slipped his arm around Cindy's waist. She gave him a loving look before retuning her sight on the receding harbor. The three silently reflected their thoughts on what they had seen and heard about Bougainville.

Jake excused himself and went to the bridge. Giving his helmsman the course to be steered to the Caroline Island chain and making sure he would be relieved by another helmsman, Jake rejoined Ralph and Cindy. It being late, all adjourned to their cabins.

By the time Ralph and Cindy joined Jake at the galley table for breakfast, he had taken his sextant reading and checked off their position on his chart.

Jake greeted them, "Good morning. Did you get a good night's rest?"

Ralph replied, "Being off Bougainville with a cool sea breeze blowing and the gentle rocking of the ship, I slept like a baby."

Cindy said, "Me too."

Ralph asked, "When will we reach the Caroline Islands?"

"If the winds hold, we should arrive there in seven days. Our course will take us between Satawal and Halik Atoll."

"Is that anywhere near Truk Island?"

"I'd need to check my charts, but I think Truk is about 200 miles east."

"Would it be too much out of our way to go close to Truk?"

"Not if I set a new course now. Why do you want to see Truk, if you don't mind my asking?"

"During the war, Truk Lagoon was often referred to as the Japanese Pearl Harbor. The lagoon was one of their strongest bases in the Pacific. Japanese engineers built strong fortifications and roads, bunkers and trenches. It had submarine repair facilities, five airstrips, seaplane bases and torpedo boat station. During the war the lagoon anchorage was home to Japanese giant battle ships, aircraft carriers, tankers, cargo ships, cruisers, destroyers, gunboats, minesweepers and a host of other ships. The lagoon had several coastal guns, mortar and machine gun emplacements.

"Our forces attacked in February 1944 in what was called Operation Hailstorm. The Japanese moved most of their heavy stuff, but our forces sank sixty of their ships and sent 275 of their airplanes to the lagoon bottom. I'm told that divers are allowed to go down in the crystal clear blue-green waters and view the wrecks and that in the massive ships' holds are row upon row of fighter aircraft, tanks, bulldozers, railroad cars, motorcycles, torpedoes, mines, bombs, boxes of munitions, radios and many other items. Many human remains are found in the wrecks."

Jake said, "I'd like to see that. I'll correct our course to Truk."

Going up on deck, Ralph and Cindy went to look over the ship's railing at a world of blue-green. Jake excused himself and went to the bridge, giving the helmsman a small degree starboard heading change from his original assigned course. Deviation at this time would not waste time. This done, he rejoined Ralph and Cindy.

Speaking to Ralph, he said, "Sir, our course has been changed for Truk. It will still take seven days."

"Thanks, Jake. My daughter and I were discussing the vastness of the sea and how it must have seemed to sailors in the early years of discovery. We're like a tiny pinhead in a vast sea of blue."

The three stood quietly looking out over a sea of blue, each with their own thoughts. Ralph broke the silence, "I think I'll go to my cabin and read."

Glancing at the sails, which were full, Jake told Cindy, "We've got a good wind behind us. If it holds out we might reach Truk sooner than I thought."

She nodded and then resumed her gaze at the sea, deep in thought.

Jake commented, "You seem to be deep in thought. Is something wrong?"

Turning to face him, she said, "I was thinking about us. Where do we stand?"

He considered the question. In his mind it was clear where they stood. He really loved her and enjoyed her presence. His experience with Rachel made him cautious.

He said, "You've known me a few weeks. How do you feel about me?"

"I think you know that I care about you. I think you've known that since you kissed me at your place. I just need to know where I stand with you."

"I think you know. I enjoy our talks about books, music, movies and places we've been and those we'd like to see. After two bad experiences I'm rather cautious. Then there's the situation of where we live and work. Do you think you would enjoy living in the Philippines?"

A big smile appeared on Cindy's face, "Is that a proposal?"

He smiled also and said, "Yes, it's a proposal."

"My answer is yes, with all my heart. I think I realized my feelings about you the night you had the band at the Blue Dahlia play that tender song. I was beginning to be concerned that you were only infatuated with me."

She put her arms around his neck and kissed him. A whistle call came from the bridge. They turned to see a smiling helmsman. Both returned the smile and waved.

Now that the big question had been resolved, both relaxed and talked about many things.

He asked, "How will your father take this? You seem to hold a pretty high position in his company."

"He'll be happy for us. He'll probably make some kind of remark about not losing a daughter but gaining a son.

"As for the job, I've been thinking about that. Living in the Philippines I would be closer to the source of plants that might have medicinal potentials. I could set up some type of lab here to study them, unless you object."

"I wouldn't object. I'm interested in plants, especially the floral kind. It'll be nice having my own special botanist around." Both laughed at that.

Cindy asked, "Do you think you'll ever return to the States?"

"Sure. I don't hate the States. Maybe, if business keeps going the way it has, we could have another home in the States."

"That would be really neat."

Time quickly passed as they stood discussing their potential future. That evening over dinner, Jake told Ralph about the engagement.

Ralph laughed and slapped Jake on the back. "Congratulations!" he said. "I hope you both will be happy. Let's face it, I'm not losing a daughter, I'm gaining a son!" Jake glanced at Cindy. She had a big smile and winked.

The next few days to Truk were spent in discussing ideas about the wedding. Cindy's father suggested that she use some of the sailing time to consider and make a tentative wedding invitation list; he suggested the same to Jake.

The *Sea Hawk* entered the Truk Lagoon and tied up at the wharf at Chuuk. Using the ship's radios they reached the Lagoon Dive Shop, telling them they would like to make arrangements for a dive to the sunken wrecks. The shop said they would send someone tomorrow morning at nine to pick them up and bring them to the shop to be fitted up with what they'd need for the dive.

Next morning they were picked up and taken to the shop. At the shop they were introduced to a guy named Rex, head diving tour leader.

Rex asked, "Have any of you done any scuba diving?"

Being told no, he said, "Then you'll need full-face diving masks, not having experience in using a mouthpiece. The full-face mask covers your eyes, nose and mouth. It allows us to talk to one another while below, and regulates our air breathing mixture according to our depth. The wrecks are fifty feet, some more, below the surface. We are to stay together and you follow me. Okay, you'll be escorted to your dressing rooms and helped with your dive equipment. Then meet me at the dock."

When they arrived at the dock, the three smiled at each other. They carried their full masks, dive tanks and huge swim fins. Getting in the waiting boat with Rex, they headed out into the lagoon. The water was crystal clear and calm, being protected by coral reefs from ocean swells. When they reached the dive spot, a sea anchor was dropped. Rex helped each into their adjusted dive equipment. Speaking into the full-face mask, he made sure that each could hear his voice and had them respond. With that they put on swim fins and rolled over and out of the boat.

Jake made sure he stayed close to Cindy as they descended into the clear water.

Rex called, "Can each of you hear me?"

The three replied, "Yes."

Rex replied, "Good. The most spectacular wreck we're now approaching is the San Francisco Maru. It's a Japanese cargo ship loaded with supplies. We divers refer to it as the Million Dollar Wreck. You'll see what I mean when you see its cargo holds."

Following Rex, they entered the hold of the ship. What they saw brought a gasp from Cindy. Here were row upon row of spherical sea mines with boxes that contained their detonators. Following Rex to the next hold they saw several trucks, fuel drums and aerial bombs. Swimming around they got a closer look at the trucks, giving the bombs plenty of room. Though the trucks were being taken over by coral and sponges, it was like seeing a parking lot of an automaker. The dashboard instruments and their markings were still visible.

After a few moments, Rex said, "Follow me to the Aikoku Maru. It's a Japanese troop carrier. There's a lot of silt and debris. It also contains the skeletal remains of an estimated 400 Japanese soldiers."

After viewing the Aikoku Maru, Rex showed the drivers the holds of several other ships. In the massive ships' holds they saw tanks, motorcycles, boxes of munitions, rows of fighter planes, some bulldozers, railroad cars, torpedoes, radios, weapons of all sorts and spare parts. Rex escorted them to the wreck of a Japanese submarine, telling them it was the Shinohara which was part of the attack force on Pearl Harbor. It was shocking to see all this display of military hardware scattered around on the lagoon seabed.

Rex looked at his diver's watch and motioned upward. All returned to the surface and the waiting boat. Once on board and with their diving gear off, they discussed what they had seen on their way to the dock. Jake, Cindy and Ralph all agreed that it was the most spectacular sight that they had ever seen.

Cindy said, "War is horrible. It makes me shiver to think about all those men down below that lost their lives, and the cost of all the military items lost down there. Why can't people live peacefully together?"

Ralph, who had been in deep thought at what he had seen below, answered Cindy, "As long as there are leaders who are greedy for power, covet what someone else has or want total control over their subjects, there will be wars. Wars happen when such leaders are either stopped or individuals lose their freedoms and become pawns to be sacrificed to the god of war."

Arriving at the Dive Shop dock, the three let Rex know they appreciated his services and went to their rooms to change into their regular clothes. After getting dressed they returned to the dive shop, paid for their services and again expressed their appreciation for being shown such an outstanding site. They were then taken to wharf where the *Sea Hawk* waited.

Going on board, Jake instructed the crew to make sail. Jake and Cindy went to the bridge deck, where he gave his helmsman a NW course towards Saipan. Ralph watched as the *Sea Hawk*'s busy crew members went about their tasks to get underway. As winds filled the ships' sails, the *Sea Hawk* began to move forward. Watching small islands and atolls slowly pass, Jake made sure they cleared north pass, a break in the coral reefs.

Once clear of the north pass, Jake went to his cabin to plot the new course. Cindy, who had accompanied him, watched as Jake did his calculations, determined the compass heading and, using his dividers, judged the distance and estimated time to cover the distance. This done, Jake and Cindy went back to the bridge and gave the new compass heading for Saipan.

Ralph joined them to watch the sun slip below the horizon to the west. The sky turned a vivid mixture of red and gold, an outstanding sunset.

Jake made reference to an old sailors saying, "Red skies at night, sailors delight." Continuing, he said, "Tomorrow should be a beautiful day." It being a rather full day, they had dinner and went to their cabins to read or relax before turning in.

Jake was up early next morning, had a quick breakfast and went to the bridge. It had the makings of a beautiful day. The sky was a deep blue with thin wisps of white clouds. The sun, beginning to add warmth, was tempered by a cooling sea breeze. The ship's sails billowed from a strong breeze from the south. He told his helmsman he'd spell him for awhile.

It was times like this that Jake understood the feeling that ancient sailors must have felt. Steering a huge power-driven boat of today doesn't have the same mystique as what is felt by steering a sleek schooner under full sail. It always reminded him of the old saying, "Master of my ship and captain of my soul." It gives off such a powerful positive feeling that he felt he could conquer any obstacle in life that came his way. At the wheel, Jake could feel the breeze ruffling his hair and cooling his face.

Cindy joined him. Snuggling close, she seemed to sense his feelings, and that she was a part of those feelings. It was like the movie *Flying Dutchman*, where the heroine chose to go with the Flying Dutchman to forever sail the seas together. And, like the Dutchman, Jake felt a closeness with Cindy that he had never felt before in life. They were two kindred spirits sharing an earthly paradise together.

Cindy broke the silence. "Are you thinking what I'm thinking?"

"What's that?"

Cindy almost phrased his very thoughts. They were two people in love and sharing this adventure in a form of tropical paradise.

Cindy's father joined them. "I was wondering what had happened to you two. Now I know. The expressions on your faces remind me of when I met my wife Doris, and we realized we were deeply in love. I wish you both all the happiness in the world. That reminds me that I must call her from Saipan and give her the good news."

The voyage to Saipan seemed like a dream. The weather was good, no problems with the ship, the love of his life nearby and a future father-in-law he liked and admired. Much time was spent going over ideas both in business and in future family matters. With Cindy setting up a lab in the Philippines, it would benefit her father's pharmaceutical company, and Jake would be a part of that operation, using his ships to sail to remote areas to collect plant samples to test their healing powers. It was a partnership made in heaven.

Jake calculated that his ship would arrive at Tanapag Harbor docks on Saipan just before ten in the evening. According to Jake's charts, Tanapag Harbor was the main port for Saipan. It formed the best break in the coral reefs that are prominent around the island. His *Harbors of Southeast Asia* book showed that the main wharf was Charlie Dock and clearance to that mooring had to be obtained by contacting the Port Captain on VHF Ch 16.

Going to his ship's radio room, he adjusted the frequency to channel 16 and called, "Port Captain, this is Jake Moore, captain of schooner *Sea Hawk*. Over."

"*Sea Hawk*, this is Port Captain. Go ahead."

"Port Captain, we will be arriving in Tanapag Harbor at ten o'clock this evening. We're a schooner and seek mooring instructions."

"Roger. Go to Charlie Dock wharf and moor behind the cargo ship Sumatsu Maru."

"Roger. Will do. Thank you. Out."

Looking through his charts of harbors he located the Charlie Dock wharfs, located near the City of Puerto Rico, and determined his approach to his assigned mooring spot.

Next he called Puerto Rico, requesting information.

A voice replied, "Puerto Rico Chamber of Commerce. How can I help you?"

"Chamber of Commerce, this is Jake Moore, captain of the *Sea Hawk*. I have a vet who was on Saipan in WWII. He, his daughter and I would like a tour guide. Who would you recommend?"

"The best is Mr. Yamasaki at Garapan. He lived on the island during the war."

"How can I reach him?"

"You can reach him on channel 26. His call sign is Shinto."

"Thanks, Chamber. Over and out."

Jake called Mr. Yamasaki, "Sir, I'm Captain Jake Moore of the schooner *Sea Hawk*. Dr. Cowan, his daughter and I would like a tour of Saipan WWII sites. Dr. Cowan was with a Marine Medical Corps. You were highly recommended. Can you help us?"

"Yes. Are you moored in Tanapag Harbor?"

"Yes. We're moored at the Charlie Dock wharf, behind the cargo ship Sumatsu Maru. What's your fee for an all day excursion?"

"$800 USD. That includes transportation expenses."

"Agreed. When would you pick us up?"

"Tomorrow morning at eight, on the dock. I'll be driving a light yellow 1953 Chevy Bel Air."

"We'll be ready. Thank you, Mr. Yamasaki. Over and out."

That done, Jake went up on deck. Ralph and Cindy were relaxing on top of a cargo hatch, enjoying the late afternoon sun. He joined them.

With a smile, Cindy said, "We were wondering where you were. We figured you might be having some ship duty work."

"That was what I was doing. I was setting up our mooring berth and making arrangements for a tour tomorrow." He then told what he had arranged.

Ralph commented, "It seems so strange being back to Saipan after ten years. Before our troops made their landings, fifteen of our heavy battleships fired, what I was told, 165,000 shells at the beachhead area at Susupe. Seven of our modern fast battleships poured in another 2,400 sixteen-inch shells. They were concerned about the landing area being mined and fired from about six miles offshore to clear our beachhead for us."

Jake commented, "That must have been scary."

"It was. We couldn't see how anyone could have survived such a pounding. Then the next day Admiral Oldendorf, with eight pre-Pearl Harbor battleships and eleven cruisers, replaced the seven modern fast battleships. It was a sight to behold.

"Due to the reefs, we were loaded onto LVT Amtraks, twenty-four combat-ready marines with two Amtrak drivers. To protect us from Japanese troops and their small arm fire, the LVT had one .50 and three .30 caliber machine guns. On June 15, 1944 approximately 300 LVTs, or more, landed 8,000 of us marines. Our landing was supported by eleven fire support ships. Our naval support was from battleships Tennessee and California, cruisers Birmingham and Indianapolis, and destroyers Norman Scott, Monssen, Colahan, Halsey Powell, Bailey, Robinson and Albert W. Grant.

"The invasion caught the Japanese by surprise. They had been expecting an attack further south. Admiral Soemu, Commander-in-Chief of the Japanese Navy, gave the order for his Operation A-Go force to attack the U.S. Navy forces. It was called the Battle of the Philippine Sea. It was a disaster for the Japanese Navy. They lost three aircraft carriers and hundreds of planes. Their garrison on shore was cut off from reinforcements or resupply."

Jake and Cindy were spellbound. Ralph's comments were given without passion, just a straightforward report of that day. Jake's mind made up a clear picture of that eventful day.

Ralph continued, "Careful placing of flags in the bay by the Japanese gave their artillery gunners the range. They destroyed about twenty of our amphibious tanks. On shore they had strategically placed barbed wire, machinegun emplacements and trenches to maximize causalities. It was like we were advancing into the hubs of hell. I and other medical corpsmen were kept busy. By nightfall the second and fourth Marine Divisions had established a beachhead six miles wide and a half mile deep. That night the Japanese counterattacked and we suffered heavy losses.

"Next day units of the U.S. Army's 27th Division landed and advanced on Aslito Airfield. Again the Japanese attacked at night and were repulsed. The Japanese commander, Lt. General Saito, had issued an order to his troops that whether they held their position or attacked, all would die. He said, "There are no distinctions between civilians and troops. Death will bring life in a peaceful hereafter with our ancestors."

"Many Japanese civilians—men, women and children—who had lived on the island since WWI, committed suicide by jumping off a tall cliff on the northern part of the island."

Cindy gasped and her hand went to her throat, saying, "How could mothers do such a thing, killing themselves and their children?"

"Their beliefs are very different from ours. To them the Emperor is a living God on earth. He had sent a message that all those who died for their nation would find happiness in the afterlife."

General Saito organized his troops on Mount Tapotchau, a mountainous terrain in central Saipan. They were in small caves, hard to find. They killed many of our troops. Some of these areas were called Hell's Pocket, Purple Heart Ridge and Death Valley. Our troops had to use flamethrowers and explosive charges to eliminate them."

Cindy said, "Oh! How awful! Were you part of that?"

"Yes. I think I helped save several of our men."

"Did that end the battle on Saipan?"

"No. At the last Saito ordered a banzai charge. About 3,000 Japanese troops followed by their wounded, some on crutches, charged our lines. Between our machine guns and small arms fire all the Japanese were killed. Saito himself committed suicide along with commanders Hirakushi and Igeta in one of the caves. Vice-Admiral Nagumo, who led the aircraft carriers at Pearl Harbor and Midway, was on Saipan to lead the ground forces. He also committed suicide."

Cindy said, "Horrible! Why would they do such a thing? Why not just surrender?"

"It's difficult to understand the Japanese military code of honor. They knew they were the last defense of their homeland; and believed that death was more honorable than surrender. Our Superfortress, the B-29, had just come out. With its range our country could now attack the Japanese home islands and the Philippines from Saipan, from bases our Army engineers built on Tinian Island next to Saipan. It was from Tinian that the Enola Gay took off to drop the first atomic bomb on Hiroshima."

"Why did we do such a thing, Dad?"

"From the way the Japanese civilians acted on Saipan, and how they responded to their Emperor, what would millions of their citizens in their home islands do?"

Cindy thought for awhile and said, "They'd probably fight and die to the very end."

Ralph replied, "How many of our troops would die, and how many civilians would be killed?"

Cindy replied, "I would guess that a great many of our troops would be killed, and a horrible number of civilians would lose their lives."

"That's the same conclusion that our nation's leaders came to. It's sad that over 70,000 people were killed in Hiroshima, more on Nagasaki, but many thousands more lives would be saved by their quick surrender."

"Dad, I've never heard you tell of this at home."

"It's something one doesn't like to talk about. I feel that mentioning this here I can get the horrors behind me. War is horrible. Many people die. It scars some for life. Freedom is dear. I hope and pray our nation doesn't ever have to fight another war."

Jake noticed it was getting dark. He suggested that they have dinner and get some rest. Tomorrow would be a busy day looking at war relics around the island. He followed his own suggestion, partly to go over in his mind what had happened here only ten short years ago.

Mr. Yamasaki was punctual. He drove up in his Chevy Bel Air. The three were waiting on the dock. Ralph sat up front with Mr. Yamasaki. Jake and Cindy sat in back. The thing that Jake noticed immediately, and was pleased about, was that the car was air-conditioned. Introductions were made and they were off.

Heading down Beach Road, Mr. Yamasaki talked a little about Saipan's history and the large sugar cane plantation. He said all the beach area on the west side had bunkers and fortifications placed in strategic places. Like children on a vacation trip, Jake and Cindy sat in the back seat, gawking out their windows at the sights. Going through Garapan, Yamasaki let them know that this was where he lived.

Ralph told of how different it looked from when he had gone through here. It now had stores and businesses similar to that in the U.S. in the '30s. Yamasaki said it would be a good place to stop for lunch after making the swing around the southern part of the island to visit Aslito Airfield.

At San Jose, they were driven to a Japanese bunker that had a Japanese tank on top. Yamasaki took a picture of the three with the bunker in back. While making the drive, Jake noticed some piled-up soils. He asked Yamasaki about them. He was shocked when Yamasaki said bodies of Japanese Army and Navy soldiers were said to be buried there, together. He went on to say that nearly all 30,000 Japanese defenders on the island were killed; and that thousands of Japanese civilians also died.

At Susupe they visited the sites where the 2nd and 4th Division made their landings. Ralph indicated the area where the amphibian tractor he had been in came ashore. He pointed out the edge of the coral reef, one mile offshore. He remarked that the Japanese had markers in the harbor so their guns knew the range, and that many were killed that day on both sides. He asked Jake and Cindy to pose with him on the beachhead, with the Philippine Sea as background. Yamasaki took their picture.

They visited a place where Ralph said Camp Susupe had once stood. He told of how it later became a refugee camp that housed over 18,000 civilians. He said that it seemed like a baby was born each day and that initially there was a lack of baby bottles, which had to be rushed in, keeping medical staff busy devising means to feed the babies until the bottles arrived.

When shown the Sherman tanks in the coral surf, Ralph explained that in preparation for the assault on Saipan those tanks were hermetically sealed and equipped with air intake snorkels so they could drive, partially submerged, over the coral seabed.

Arriving at Aslito Airfield, Ralph talked about its capture. The capture of Aslito paved the way for attacking the Japanese airfields on Tinian. There the Japanese had constructed four airstrips, two for bombers and two shorter runways for fighters. When Tinian fell to American forces, airfield engineers and Navy Seabees came in and extended the four runways to accommodate the new B-29 bombers, capable of making bomb runs on the Japanese main islands and the Philippines. They also added two additional shorter runways.

Heading back north on Saipan's Beach Road, Yamasaki stopped at a small café for lunch. Light conversation was carried on by all. After lunch, Ralph, with Cindy and Jake in tow, went in search of a public telephone, to call his wife.

Finding one, and getting his wife Doris on the line, he told her the good news about Cindy and Jake. Cindy and Jake took turns chatting with Doris. Jake liked Doris' cheery voice on the line. When Ralph hung up after the extended time on the phone, Jake could only imagine the cost of the call.

On the way back to a waiting Yamasaki, Jake noticed a sign that read, "Battlefield Map of Saipan—1944 Japanese Mandated Islands." He stopped and bought two, one for him and one for Ralph.

Getting into Yamasaki's car, they headed north to see Banzai Cliff and Suicide Cliff, where many civilians had committed suicide.

Cindy asked Yamasaki, "How could so many do such a thing, especially women, mothers and their children?"

Yamasaki calmly replied, "One needs to understand the Japanese culture of that time. Courage facing almost sure death was prized. It dates back to the ancient Shogun warriors. Japan in the late '30s and early '40s was ruled by the warrior clans. It was considered a great honor if one died protecting the Japanese homeland, and Saipan was considered the last protection to the homeland. Those that died were doing so for their ancestors; to not do so would bring shame and disgrace to their families."

Cindy sadly said, "All those poor babies."

"I know. Japan has become more Americanized and has changed many of their old ways."

It was a long and eventful day. They visited the area where so many Japanese soldiers had hidden in caves near Mount Tapotchau and had to be taken out one by one; the cave where Admiral Nagumo and Saipan commanders, Saito and Igeta, committed suicide. All in all that day, they had visited the landing beaches at Susupe and Chalan Kanoa, the beautiful Catholic Church at Mount Carmel, the Japanese Last Command Post at Mount Tapotchau, Memorial Park, Katori Shrine,

Shunji Matsue, Managaha Island (also known as Bird Island), the suicide cliffs and Aslito Airfield. They were a tired threesome when Yamasaki let them off on the wharf where *Sea Hawk* was moored. Going aboard, they had a light dinner and felt the need for some rest.

Before getting a little rest, Jake contacted the wharf supply store and gave a list of what *Sea Hawk* would need in the way of supplies before sailing. He told his helmsman to alert him when the supplies arrived, and then went to his cabin to rest. Ralph and Cindy were already resting. About three hours later, a knock on his door awakened him. It was his helmsman stating that the supplies had arrived and were being stowed in the ship's hold. Jake went up on deck and signed for the supplies. Going to the ship's hold, he made sure the supplies were secured.

He went up topside and instructed the crew to make ready the sails; they were heading for home port. He was joined by Cindy and Ralph while his helmsman was steering the ship, under auxiliary power, to clear the Tanapag Harbor. He went below to radio the port captain that *Sea Hawk* was departing. He then checked his charts to get his compass heading for home port. That done, he went topside and gave the heading to his helmsman.

Rejoining Cindy and Ralph at the ship's rail, he told them, "Well, that's done. We're heading back to the Philippines. It's been an interesting voyage." Addressing Ralph, he continued, "Thanks to you I've learned a lot." Looking at Cindy, he continued, "I not only gained a lot of information on WWII, I gained your promise to share life with me."

Ralph recognized the signals being transmitted between the two and said, "It's been a long and tiring day for me. I think I'll go below and leave you two alone."

Jake and Cindy stood quietly watching the harbor navigation lights slowly pass. Out in the open seas the ship's crew struck sails. A nice breeze caused the sails to bellow. The auxiliary motor was turned off. Thought of home and Cindy caused Jake to slip his arm around her waist. Never had he felt so much peace.

Cindy partially turned towards Jake and said, "Going over Dad's wartime experiences, I realize you have told me only a little about your Korean War service. Would you tell me about that?"

"There's not much for me to tell. The Marines and Army are the ones that had it really tough. They deserve the credit. They suffered a lot and lost many friends, like what your dad went through. To this day I can only imagine the intense cold and horror they went through in Korea. They are the true heroes, in my opinion."

"I seem to recall that you mentioned receiving the Air Medal. I don't think that was for doing nothing."

"You're right on that. My crew and I flew ten missions behind enemy lines. We took in and extracted agents and spies, to be more exact."

"That must have been dangerous."

"Yes. We were lucky. We were shot at only once by an enemy shore battery."

"Did that frighten you?"

"I was too busy getting airborne to be scared. That doesn't come close to the horror our Marines went through at Chosen Reservoir. It was so cold that they couldn't bury their dead. They had to look at those frozen faces of friends before finally breaking free of the enemy encirclement."

Cindy gasped, "How horrible!"

The two drew strength from each other, picturing such horror. They snuggled closer. It was now near midnight. Jake escorted Cindy to her cabin door and kissed her goodnight.

Next morning the three were up early, enjoyed a nice breakfast and went up on deck. The beauty of the Philippine Sea, with sun low on the eastern horizon, and overhead fleecy clouds amidst a deep blue sky was awesome. The three relaxed on the ship's cargo hatch, soaking in such beauty. They talked some about their trip. The morning sun giving out warmth and the sound of waves lapping against the bow was too much for them. Lying on their backs, soaking in the sun and feeling the cool sea breeze, they dozed off.

They were awakened by a crew member, as Jake had requested, for him to use the sextant to be sure they were on course and to pinpoint their location. Jake asked that the sextant be brought to him. A curious Cindy watched as Jake took his readings. She followed him to his cabin to see him pinpoint their location.

She asked, "Will you teach me how to do that?"

"Sure. I'll explain how it's done. When I take the next reading, you can see what you come up with. That's the way I learned from Captain Santos."

"That sounds exciting. I look forward to that."

Continuing, she asked, "What supplies did you take onboard in Saipan? It seemed interesting."

"I learned from the ship warehouse that coconuts, papayas and Thai hot peppers grow wild here. I had a generous supply of papayas and hot peppers taken on board. They will sell well in the Philippines, a good profit. I also had some mangos and taro root brought on board. The rest of the supplies are general items we've used up on our voyage."

Cindy replied, "I've been on powered cruise ships. I never realized how much pleasure can be had on a sailing vessel, and outfitting it for a voyage. When we're married, can I come along on some of your voyages?"

"For sure! I've already been toying with a honeymoon trip."

"What are you thinking about?"

"What would you think about a trip to Darwin, Australia, Bali, Sri Lanka, Bombay, Egypt, then Luxor and finally to England?"

Jake chuckled at the shocked look on Cindy's face.

She said, "We'd do all that? How long would such a trip take?"

"Probably two months, maybe more."

"What about your business?"

"Michael can run that while we're gone. We'd go on the *Sea Hawk*. Or would you prefer the larger schooner, *Adventurer*?"

"Oh my gosh! Only royalty go on such voyages."

"We're not royalty, but I do own the ship and crew."

Time and days slipped past. When they crossed the Mariana Trench, Jake let them know it was the deepest part of the ocean.

Cindy asked, "How deep is that?"

Jake said, "To keep everything in a recognizable scale, it's so deep here that if you put Mount Everest here it would still be about 7,000 feet below the surface."

"Oh my gosh! Just how deep is it to the ocean floor, here?"

"The charts say 35,997 feet deep."

Cindy just gasped. When her dad joined them, she was quick to relay the information she had just received from Jake. Ralph just smiled. Having been through such situations when he courted his wife to be, Doris, some twenty-seven years ago, he recognized the blending of two lives into one. He thought to himself, "They make a nice-looking couple, and will probably go far in life." The main thing that pleased him was that they were happy.

The thing that troubled Jake was the thought that Cindy would soon be leaving for Idaho. Sure, she was going there to make preparations for the wedding, and he would be joining her. It was just that she would be gone. He would really miss her presence. He had become accustomed to her daily lighthearted sense of humor, or the times she's very serious about something and can express her point of view so intelligently. He would certainly miss that. Besides, when she was around he felt a sense of peace that he had never felt before.

Sea Hawk's crew was also happy they were near home and family. They knew the Philippine Islands like Jake knew his compound. *Sea Hawk*'s helmsman steered the ship past Samar and Leyte. Jake and Ralph talked about the American forces who landed on Leyte. The three watched as Bohol slipped by on the ship's starboard side and the town of Cagayan de Oro, on the island of Mindanao, appeared on the portside. With the Island of Negros approaching on the starboard, *Sea*

Hawk entered the Sulu Sea and a quick run to home port at Puerto Princesa.

Once moored, *Sea Hawk*'s crew was relieved of duty and left ship. While passing Negros, Jake had radioed his office, stating they would need transportation to his home compound; that they would arrive at home port at 2 p.m. It was waiting for them when they arrived. The three loaded their luggage and the items from Dirk, the missionary in New Guinea, into Island Ltd.'s minibus jeepney.

Arriving at his home compound, Evelyn, his housekeeper and cook, and her husband Frank happily greeted their return. They were even happier to learn that Jake and Cindy were engaged to be married.

While Cindy and Ralph were putting their things away, Jake made a quick call to the office, catching up on the happenings while he was gone. He also told them he was engaged. They were quick to congratulate him. He let them know that he would be taking the Albatross to Manila to get the wedding ring set.

Next day, after arriving back from the voyage, the three spent a day of relaxing by the pool or roaming the compound grounds. Jake and Cindy spent some time discussing their wedding plans.

Cindy said, "Jake, you've not said anything about your parents. Will they be attending our wedding?"

Jake's facial features changed to one of sadness, "No. They were killed in an auto accident while I was in college."

"I'm so sorry. Please forgive me."

"There's nothing to forgive. Life goes on."

Next morning, Cindy and Jake drove to the airport and the hangar where the Albatross was parked. Knowing he was on his way, Jake's maintenance crew had the plane parked outside. They informed him the plane had been run up and everything checked out good.

Entering the plane, Jake took the pilot's seat and Cindy the co-pilot. Jake commented, "This is the way I like it, side by side. If you're interested in getting your pilot's license, I'll help you when we get back from Idaho."

Cindy smiled and said, "That would be great."

Arriving in Manila, Jake and Cindy caught a jeepney taxi to Joseph Nino's jewelry store on Calle Escolta. Joseph was happy to see Jake, and even happier when he learned the purpose of the visit. Of the many sets shown to them, Cindy chose the one with a plain gold wedding band and an engagement ring with a small diamond. Joseph managed to get Cindy to agree to a larger stone, saying it was his wedding present. Jake slipped the engagement ring on her finger. Cindy gave him a "peck" kiss of appreciation. Placing the ring box with the gold band in his pocket, they went outside.

Cindy said, "That's so sweet of you to buy me such a pretty ring."

Jake said, "Only the best for my girl." Changing the subject he asked, "Do you wish to head back to Puerto Princesa, or would you like to look around Manila?"

"Since I'm going to be making the Philippines my home I'd like to look around, if it's okay with you."

"Fine with me."

Shops on Calle Escolta Street between Jones and MacArthur Bridges, along the Pasig River, catered to well-to-do shoppers. There was a leather shop with women's handbags, gloves and shoes imported from Italy. There were clothing shops, a bookstore, medical supplies and about any item a discriminating buyer could want. At a small boutique shop Cindy bought her mother a pair of pearl-studded earbobs and a stylish evening handbag. After covering the shops, Cindy let Jake know she was through shopping.

Jake flagged down a taxi. He asked the driver the cost to hire him for the day; that they wanted to go sightseeing. Jake felt the fee reasonable, and they'd be guaranteed a ride at their leisure. He told Cindy that he visited several places in Manila while he was in the Air Force, and would like to show her these places. She agreed. He instructed the driver to take them to Intramuros, the "Walled City," and to let them out at Fort Santiago. On the way, he told Cindy about its dark past under Spanish rule in the 1600s.

Arriving at the entrance to Fort Santiago, they got out of the cab and told the driver to wait for them. Over an elaborate ornate entryway, common for the architecture of the 1600s, was a stone-sculptured Spanish coat of arms. Jake picked up a printed pamphlet that told the history of the fort and gave it to Cindy. Inside the fort walls was a large open courtyard. He took Cindy up on the fort's wall. She read that the walls were eight feet thick and stood twenty-two feet high.

From their vantage point they could see the Pasig River below, where it emptied into Manila Bay. When she read in the pamphlet about the underground dungeons and how they flooded at high tide drowning any prisoners in those cells, she said, "How could anyone do such a thing?"

Jake said, "You should read about the Spanish Inquisition and the horrors that they did to their own countrymen and foreign conquered nations. The Filipino fighters stood up to them. Many were executed within these walls. Their hero, Jose Rizal, was executed by a Spanish firing squad within these walls. He was only thirty-five."

Cindy said, "Let's go. This place is too depressing."

Walking back to their waiting taxi, Jake said, "I agree that this place is depressing. However history teaches us that if we don't learn from the past it can repeat itself. From such horrors perpetuated here, we learn to be ever vigilant and ready to protect our freedoms." Continuing, he said, "Do you know that American and the Philippines were once at war?"

"No! When was that?"

"From 1899 until July 4th, 1902. We had conquered Spain in the Spanish-American War. The Philippines were ceded to us by that war. Filipinos helped us in that war, thinking we would give them their freedom as an independent free nation. America didn't do that. Filipinos on Samar Island used the church bells in Balangiga to signal a surprise attack on a company of American soldiers eating breakfast, almost wiping out the entire company. That triggered an all-out war between America and the Philippines. The bells were taken as war booty. America put down the rebellion and eventually gave the Philippines their freedom at the close of WWII.

The captured bells are still in the possession of America. Personally I think at least one should be returned to the Philippines. They, like us, wanted their freedom. The bells were their liberty or freedom bells. We broke a promise to the Filipinos when we didn't give them their freedom for helping us defeat the Spanish. Returning them their liberty bell would be a gesture of good will, and greatly win their support, which we'll need one day."

Cindy said, "I never was told of this. My heart goes out to the Filipinos. Where did you hear about all this?"

"From history books."

Jake looked at his watch. It was lunchtime. He said, "I'll now take you to a more delightful setting for lunch."

He told the driver to take them to the Manila Polo Club. Cindy, from her field of botany, was a-gasp at the beautiful growing plants at the entrance gate and surrounding the main entry into the club. Going inside it had subdued lighting, dark hardwood floors and was air-conditioned. A waiter in a white jacket and black pants escorted them to a table next to a wall of glass and took their orders.

Cindy said, "This is really something. The dim lighting not only contributes to the feeling of coolness, but, makes observation of the polo field more pronounced. Have you attended any of the polo matches?"

"Only once. I was the guest of our banker. Since our business has been so successful we were offered membership, and we took it. We figured it good business to join. The Who's Who of Manila circulate here."

A smiling Cindy said, "Well, my husband-to-be, you certainly live an exciting and interesting life."

After lunch Jake asked their driver to take them to Malacanang Palace. He informed Cindy that it was the President of the Philippines' home, similar to the White House back in the States. They were allowed to see much of the ground level rooms. Cindy, like Jake, was taken by the beautiful chandeliers in the Conference Room. The huge crystal chandeliers, being reflected by large mirrors hung on the walls at each end, and the dark wood paneling were outstanding.

Next they went out onto the rear-covered patio. The grounds in back were beautifully landscaped, similar to the front. A short distance away was the boat dock for the president's yacht. Seeing it wasn't there, they could assume the president was on a voyage.

Leaving there, the driver drove them through the University of the Philippines campus. Jake let Cindy know that the University of the Philippines had a good medical school, and they had the Los Banos University of Agriculture at Laguna, Luzon.

Cindy became excited, saying, "That's great! Maybe I can finish my doctorate degree there."

Jake said, "I'm now going to take you to a place I think you'll find interesting. It's the Saint Joseph Parish Church at Las Pinas."

"You're acting mighty mysterious. What's there?"

"You'll see."

Arriving at the little chapel, they went inside. They were greeted by a priest.

Jake said, "Father, I've told my fiancée I would show her something remarkable. Would you let her see your bamboo organ?"

The Priest smiled and said, "This way." Continuing, he said, "The church and organ building were overseen by Father Diego Cera de la Virgin Del Carmen in the late 1700s. Father Carmen was a gifted man, a natural scientist, chemist, architect and community leader, as well as an organist and organ builder." Indicating the front wall of the chapel he pointed to the bamboo organ which had its own built-in loft next to the choir loft. He explained that it was the only one of its kind in the world, and was still being played.

Cindy said, "It's absolutely beautiful. It's amazing that he could build such an organ, and you say he used only bamboo?"

"All but the trumpet stops. They're metal."

"Amazing! I can appreciate the accomplishment. I sometimes fill in as organist at church back home."

The surprised Priest said, "You play the organ? Would you care to try this one?"

"May I? I'd love that."

The priest signaled some young boys to come and pump the organ's bellows, using a long bamboo pump handle. He then escorted Jake and Cindy to the organ loft. There she sat down at the bench, played and sang an emotional "Ava Maria."

The priest, Jake and some visitors who had entered were touched by the song so emotionally sung and played.

Jake and Cindy thanked the priest and left. It was the finish to a delightful day. On the way to the airport, Jake said, "You didn't tell me you play the organ and sing so well."

"I didn't think them important. It's something I frequently do. I'm in my church choir. Sometimes as organist and sometimes singing soprano."

"By the way, what church are you a member of?" asked Jake.

"We're members of the Church of Jesus Christ of Latter-day Saints, referred to many by the nickname Mormon. May ask what church you're a member of?"

"I've been both Baptist and Methodist at times. I've also attended Catholic and Assembly of God services."

"Why so many churches?"

Jake thought for a moment before replying. "Each church I found what I considered pieces of a giant puzzle that answers what I call the 'Purpose of Life' picture. So far I'm getting bits and pieces of the puzzle from churches I've attended, but no clear finished picture."

"Do you have any preference on where we're married?"

"I figure that's the bride's choice."

"Thank you. Can we be married by my Bishop?"

"Fine by me."

"Since you aren't a member of my church, ours will be a civil service. Hopefully in a year we can have a Temple Wedding, for time and eternity."

This was all strange to Jake, but nothing mattered as long as he had Cindy to be his partner in life.

Arriving at the airport and his parked plane, Jake paid the taxi driver and gave him a good tip. Jake and Cindy were quickly airborne. While making the short flight to Puerto Princesa they talked on the intercom of their big eventful day. Cindy held up her ring finger to display her beautiful engagement ring, and smiled at Jake. The two were as happy as a bug in a rug. Or, as Jake's Aussie friends would put it, "Happy as Larry."

At Jake's house she was eager to tell her father about her day with Jake. She showed her ring and went into the details of the day, of what she had seen and how much she liked the Philippines. He smiled and said, "I'm glad you had such an eventful day. I hate to throw cold water on your day. I talked to your mom and to my office while you were gone. We need to be heading home. Your mom and you have lots to do to get ready for your wedding day. Have you decided on the day?"

"Yes, November 20th."

"That's a little over a month away. Do you think you can get everything prepared by then? Why that date?"

"That's just before Thanksgiving. It's a fitting reminder of how thankful we are to have met."

Two days later Jake flew them to Manila and saw them off. He was saddened to see them go. Cindy tried to cheer him up by saying she'd see him in Boise on the 18th, gave him a goodbye kiss and boarded the plane with her father. Ralph had shaken Jake's hand and echoed Cindy's "see you on the 18th." Jake watched their plane lift off and disappear. With heavy heart he flew back to Puerto Princesa. He felt so lonely. He'd have to get heavily into his business until he rejoined Cindy in Boise.

--The End

11995952R00150

Made in the USA
Lexington, KY
15 November 2011